KISS OF THE VAMPIRE

BLOOD MOON
BOOK 1

TERRY SPEAR

PUBLISHED BY:

Terry Spear

The Kiss of the Vampire
(Blood Moon Series)
Book 1
Copyright © 2011 by Terry Spear
Cover by Am Design Studios

All rights reserved. No part of this book may be reproduced or transmitted in any form or by any means, electronic or mechanical, including photocopying, recording, or by any information storage and retrieval system, without written permission from the author, except for the inclusion of brief quotations in a review.

Discover more about Terry Spear at: http://www.terryspear.com/

SYNOPSIS

The motto of the vampires is that humans have to deal with problems on their own. But when Levka and his friends risk all to save human girls, he is injured and so the adventure begins. A cruise. A human girl who is terrified of water. And a vampire who has targeted her for his mate. But she has some secrets of her own. Forced to take a cruise ship to babysit her foster sister,

Caitlin has to face her own demons. But add to that her foster sister's and her friend's antics and Caitlin's inability to use her witch's magic over water and she has little hope to enjoy this trip.

Until she meets a wheelchair-bound teen and wants to make friends with him in the worst way. Levka and his friends make a hasty retreat from Dallas before the vampire elders stake them for getting involved in human affairs--again. But when he meets Caitlin on the cruise ship, hating that he's so weak after being injured so severely that he has to use a wheelchair, he finds their troubles have just begun.

To those who love sexy and hot blooded vampires like the one I saw on the Brevard Community College stage when I was a teen and fell in love with them forever.

1

Two horrified girls' screams penetrated the thick fog that cloaked Dallas early that spring morning, catching Levka's attention. His blood hot with anger, he wanted to right a wrong in the worst way. In the distance, the faint sound of beating drums resonated from one of the local bars in the otherwise deserted warehouse district.

In warning, Arman touched Levka's shoulder. "The elders forbid us to interfere in the mortals' affairs."

Levka glared at his lifelong friend. "Since when have we gone strictly by the league's rules?"

"The last time we got involved, they said they'd punish us severely—maybe even banish us from the city—despite our royal ties. There has even been talk of terminating those of us who cause any more trouble."

"Then we won't let them know, will we?"

Arman scanned the dimly lit brick factories shrouded in the ghostly wet mist like a fuzzy gray blanket. "Stasio says they're keeping a closer eye on us now."

"Let the league watch and do nothing to help these people

then. Punish me if they have to, but after my sister and parents were murdered, and I did nothing to prevent it—"

"You couldn't have prevented it, as young as you were. Besides, that was over nine-hundred years ago."

"I have a good memory."

"And *you* hassle Stasio for living in the past."

Levka ignored his friend's jibe. He knew the girls had gotten themselves into the predicament all on their own without any help from anyone else. Like the league said, mortals had to deal with their own difficulties if they were to grow and flourish. Still, the girls' sobs tore at his soul, the same mournful wailing he couldn't vanquish from his mind when his mother and older sister had pleaded for their lives so many centuries ago. Yet the girls screaming made it seem like yesterday.

The league be damned.

Levka vanished and reappeared in the vicinity of the screams, where more factory warehouses stood idle at two in the morning, except for a dingy club hidden from sight, two blocks away.

Four male teens dressed in jeans and grungy jackets—all appearing about the same age as Levka—threatened two girls with knives. "Take off your clothes or we'll cut them off," the heaviest-set of the boys growled, his fat cheeks flaming red, and his beady eyes narrowed.

Teary-eyed, one of the girls unzipped her jacket while the other unbuttoned her coat, their fingers shaking.

"Please...," the girl in the zippered jacket said, her mascara dripping down her face in black rivulets, her gaudy crimson lips quivering.

Levka stepped out of the fog, appearing just a few feet away from the thugs. "Can I join the party?"

Instantly, all eyes were upon him.

"Where did you come from?" a lanky kid with curly black hair asked, waving a ten-inch blade in Levka's direction.

"It's a private party," the biggest guy said, threatening Levka with his knife. "Get lost unless you want us to carve you a new face."

"Such bravado from ones so young." Levka clapped his hands together slowly in mock appreciation.

The big guy's face turned redder. "Let's teach this bastard a lesson."

Levka gave him a small smile and a slight bow of his head. "Teach me all you know."

Before anyone moved, Levka's three friends strolled out of the mist like Gothic specters, all dressed in black jeans, all wearing black ankle-length coats, and demonic smiles. Ruric, the curly redhead of the bunch, who Levka swore looked like a Viking warrior, waved his arms in a martial arts-like dance, pretending to yield two light sabers and said, "Let the force be with you, my friends."

Arman shook his head, his dark brown hair sweeping across his shoulders, his brown eyes nearly black. "We really shouldn't get involved, Levka. I feel it in my blood. We'll be in the worst kind of trouble this time."

Stasio pulled his long sandy blond hair into a tail. "I don't like the odds. Fighting the Marcher Barons along our borders in Wales was much more to my liking."

Levka gave him a warning look, not that it ever did any good. Stasio never seemed able to keep up with the changing centuries.

"How scary. A bunch of long-haired Goths, who don't know when to mind their own business!" the leader of the bullies shouted. "Let me add a little blood to your costumes to make you really look creepy."

"Certainly," Stasio said, his voice dark and menacing, his

stockier build readied for a fight. "We could always use a little extra blood."

The girls trembled in their heels, and they looked as scared of Levka and his friends as they were of the thugs. Levka tried to diffuse the situation without bloodshed because he knew if it came to that, the league would come down harder on them. "Go. Leave. There are four of us now, and you're well out-matched."

"Ha! Well, you won't be any match for this!" The big guy yanked out a gun hidden in his denim jacket.

"That's the way to show him, Joey!" the lanky boy said, and lunged at Ruric with his knife.

Ruric smiled, the look pure evil, and swung his ghostly light sabers at the guy. He moved quicker than the mortal's eye could see, grabbed the boy's arm, and twisted hard. *Snap.*

Screaming in pain, the teen dropped the knife. He grabbed his arm and ran several paces backward. "He...he broke my damned arm!"

"Better that than your scrawny neck, eh, cockroach?" Ruric asked, the humor sparkling in his green eyes.

One of the other thugs stalked toward Arman, probably figuring he was a wimp because he didn't want to fight.

Stasio slipped in closer to the blond. "Hey, he looks kinda like Johanne Von Kruger, eh? German Nazi, killer extraordinaire? Even has the butch that looks like his, only the blue streak down the middle kinda destroys the tough guy image."

Levka rolled his eyes. Everywhere he went, Stasio had to give a living history lesson.

Ignoring Stasio and concentrating on Arman, the Nazi-looking kid waved a blade inches from his face.

Arman straightened his back and towered over all of them by a couple of inches, his willowy appearance deceiving others into believing he had little strength. "No good will come of this, I say."

"Afraid?" the boy asked, baring his yellowed teeth.

"Yes, of what I might do to you."

The guy leapt at Arman, thrusting with his knife into the misty gloom. From behind the creep with the curly black hair, Arman said, "What about you? Want to fight?" The guy let out a frightened cry and bolted down the deserted street.

"Don't run with a knife," Arman said under his breath. "My mother always told me that."

The boy tripped on his own two feet. He fell to the asphalt, jabbing the knife into his chest.

"Guess my mother was right."

The big teen shoved the gun in one of the girl's faces. "I'm going to kill her, if you don't leave, now!"

With his finger squeezing the trigger, he was shaking so hard, it was only a matter of seconds before he fired the bullet. At this close range, he couldn't miss, and the girl could very well die.

Without hesitation, Levka faded into nothingness, then reappeared between the gun and the girl. The bulky guy fired the gun, though whether it was because he wanted to or because Levka's sudden action scared him, Levka would never know. The bullet ripped into Levka's chest, tearing a hole through his shirt, skin, and blood vessels. The pain traveled through his nerve endings, clouding his mind, blurring his vision. Even the girls' screams behind him quickly faded.

His movement sluggish, Levka leapt toward the gun-toting teen. A second bullet shattered one of Levka's ribs, and a third lodged in his liver, or at least he thought it had. The fourth and fifth went heavenward when Stasio grabbed the guy's neck and yanked his gun arm upward.

The gloom closed in on Levka. The pain filled his entire chest, burning, sharp, excruciating. For a second, he wondered why he had taken another bullet for a mortal. Every time hurt as much as the first.

The gray mist faded to black, and he was semi-aware of falling hard on his knees.

"Get the girls to somewhere safe, Arman," Ruric ordered.

"What about Levka?"

"Levka? He'll live, if the league members don't have us staked. And remember to wipe the mortals' minds."

Stasio snorted. "It would serve them right to remember."

Levka felt his body lift off the ground. Opening his eyes, he saw Stasio holding him and tried to give an order.

Arman did instead. "Wipe only enough of the experience to make them remember what is safe for us. Maybe they'll learn."

Ruric bowed his head. "Done." He ran toward the kid with the knife wound, passed out in the street.

"Meet you at our club house," Stasio told them.

"Club house," Levka moaned.

"Yeah, buddy. I'm afraid the league will want our heads for this. The club house is the only safe place for us until you get strong enough, and we can figure out where to go until things cool down."

"The girls—"

"Safe. Arman will get them to someone safe."

"Their memories—"

Stasio shook his head. "You know, even when you're half dead, you are so bossy just like General Patton was on the battlefield. Let me be in charge for the moment, all right?" Levka attempted a smile, but the pain in his chest intensified.

"We'll get you better in no time, Levka. Just keep giving me those evil smirks of yours, and I'll know you're going to live."

"Someone's coming! And he's not mortal!" Arman warned.

ALICIA HOWARD STALKED into Caitlin MacEvin's bedroom, folded her arms, and glowered at her. "I can't believe my parents would send you along with me on the cruise."

Stunned, Caitlin stared at Alicia. Caitlin's foster parents had no clue she was a witch, although Alicia suspected she could do things she shouldn't be able to.

But Caitlin couldn't conjure up her magic over a great body of water. Not that that was the reason she abhorred the notion of going with Alicia on the cruise. She glanced at the new short story she was penning for *Teen Writer's Magazine*, that she'd hoped to get done during spring break while her foster sister was away on her cruise.

Alicia's scowl turned into a mean-hearted smile. "They know how much you're afraid of the water." Her smile faded, and she motioned to the door. "Go on. My parents want to give you the good news." She turned so hard on her stilettos, Caitlin was surprised she didn't twist them right off.

Then, though she knew she shouldn't, but once she was on the water, she would have no powers whatsoever, Caitlin silently spoke an incantation, the carpet rippled, and Alicia tripped. A heel snapped off and she went down, landing hard on her hands and knees and cursed a blue streak.

Alicia glanced over her shoulder, glowering, knowing in some deeper way that Caitlin was different, that she'd made her fall, but she could never prove it.

Caitlin frowned with feigned concern. "Oh my. Those were your favorite shoes, weren't they?"

Then with every intention of swaying her foster parents to allow her to stay home instead, Caitlin hurried past her and headed downstairs, her heart pounding with pent-up worry. They couldn't mean to make her take a trip on the ocean. Not after what had happened to her and her family.

Smiling at her as if he knew she was thrilled to have the

opportunity to go on a cruise, her foster dad, Thomas, motioned for her to take a seat on the sofa in the living room with a wave of his hand, her foster mother, Mildred sitting on a chair, all smiles also.

"Listen," he said, in his most convincing fatherly voice, the one he always used on Caitlin when he wanted her to see something his way. "You've been a good influence on Alicia for the past year, and I know you didn't want to go on the cruise. But because she stayed out until four in the morning with that Daryl kid last night, I don't want her going on the cruise unless you keep an eye on her."

Alicia despised having a foster sister on the best of days, but this would definitely be the worst. Why didn't they just ground the brat and say she couldn't go? But no, that would be too much punishment for the princess.

Caitlin was sure Alicia was the reason both Alicia's parents had turned prematurely gray.

"She doesn't listen to me, really," Caitlin tried to explain for the hundredth time. What did they think she could do about a girl who would do whatever she wanted no matter what they said? How did they think Caitlin could get her to mind when she wouldn't even mind her own parents? Especially when Alicia acted like she hated Caitlin.

"We want you to give us progress reports. We've told her that you'll be with her at all times, so to behave herself. No sex with boys, no drinking, and no using drugs. If she doesn't agree, she can't go."

"What if she doesn't listen to me?"

"I want you to inform me, and when you reach the first of the Caribbean Islands, I'll meet you there and take you both home. If she doesn't behave, she won't be going on her trip to Hawaii this summer," Thomas said.

Like that would happen. Another horrible thought occurred

to her. Inwardly, she groaned.

Please don't make me chaperone her this summer, too.

"Caitlin," Mildred said, "you are so responsible and well-mannered. She'll listen to you. Besides, dear, you need to have some fun. You shouldn't be sitting around this big old house with nowhere to go. It's your vacation time, too."

Right, which was why Caitlin wanted to do what she wanted to do with her free time. "But I—"

"I insist," Thomas said. "Alicia has a suite, so the two of you girls should have plenty of room. It has a balcony, too."

"But—"

"We know you're not fond of water, honey, but we talked to your psychiatrist, and he says this is an excellent way for you to overcome your anxiety about it. You know, he says facing your fear is the only way for you to get rid of it," Mildred said.

And that was settled, as far as they were concerned.

Caitlin stared out at the palm fronds blowing in the hot Florida breeze. Two days to prepare for the worst spring break ever, a tiny ship traversing miles of open sea, and one stuck-up foster sister who was sure to make her life miserable, along with dozens of others, just like her.

And no way to even cast a spell on any of them to improve the trip one bit.

∽

ARMAN PASSED another stolen bottle of hospital blood to Levka, while they watched the latest news on television.

The reporter stood in the Dallas factory district in an area cordoned off by police. Dozens of vehicles sat nearby, their lights swirling blue and red like a disco club.

"In the latest rash of gang-related incidents, four seventeen-year-old males from one gang fought four from another, an altercation that apparently started when two girls were attacked after leaving a club in the area. Police report that one male was stabbed in the lung and is currently in serious condition at Mercy Hospital. Another fell and broke his arm and is being held for further questioning. A third hasn't been located. Police are holding the fourth gang member after he allegedly shot one of the opposing gang members three times at point blank range. Blood was found at the scene, but the teen who was shot and his friends disappeared. The gunshot victim has not been seen at any local hospitals or clinics and is feared dead. If anyone has news of the teens' whereabouts, please call—"

Arman clicked to another channel. "No news is good news, my mother always said." He leaned back in an old plush fur chair. "In other news though, the league has men looking for us as we speak. They've never found our club house before, but I'm afraid this time they're really pissed." He shook his head. "I knew we shouldn't have gotten involved. We need to leave the city for a while as soon as Levka's feeling up to it. I don't think he's ever looked this bad."

"Hmpf, what about the Battle at Gettysburg? He'd been skewered six or seven times before we could come to his rescue. He looked pretty bad that time, too," Stasio said.

"Yeah, there was that time," Arman said. "But getting blood to him was a little more difficult."

The door opened and Ruric stood in the entryway, blending in with the black night, though with his night vision, Levka could see him perfectly, and the look on his face, one of pleasure, made him close his eyes. When Ruric had a plan, it was always far out.

Ruric closed the door behind him. "He doesn't look a whole lot better," Ruric said frowning. "Are you giving him the best blood you can?"

"Yeah, what's up, Ruric? Did you locate somewhere else we can hide away for the time being?" Arman asked.

Ruric pulled a brochure out of his back pocket and handed it to Arman. "Spring break starts day after tomorrow. We're going on the cruise ship, the Sea Wanderer. This one caters especially to teens. Until Levka gets back to his ornery self, we'll have a safe place to stay that no league member will ever think of. Best of all, we can have plenty of fun."

Arman shook his head and handed the brochure to Stasio. "Looks too risky to me. We're able to keep our identities secret in the city, but we would be surrounded by ocean for miles around. Nowhere to go if anything goes wrong."

"What will go wrong? We'll dance, kiss the girls, take a little blood, wipe their minds. We have nothing to lose." Ruric turned to Levka. "What do you say, old man?"

Thinking his friend with his wild, curly red hair and affinity for exploration was indeed a descendent of the Viking explorer, Eric the Red—as Levka had always alleged—he flipped through the cruise brochure.

"We have to go." Ruric folded his arms. "I ran into one of our snitches, and he warned me that the league has people watching for us at the hospitals and clinics, Red Cross, anywhere we might go to get blood. We have to leave. They're sure to catch up to us before long. Until you're well enough, we'll bring the cutest girls to your room every night."

Levka made a face.

"Jeez, Levka, you've been moping about Cassandra for a hundred years. And you say Stasio lives in the past. It's time for you to have some fun before you become an even older man and make us the same way."

"All right," Levka said, his voice weary. "But no girls."

"Boys then," Ruric teased.

Levka made a face. "Bring bottled blood."

Ruric pulled tickets out of his other back pocket. "Good, we're all set to go. I just had to make some changes in the room arrangements. Some of those rich kids had their own staterooms. Now they have to buddy up a bit so we can have one of the rooms. Otherwise, the cruise was booked. Lots of mortals to feed off."

"Reminds me of the time we traveled with the shipload of passengers colonizing America." Stasio shrugged when Arman shook his head at him.

"Hey, maybe if you're feeling well enough later, Levka, you can go on a nighttime snorkeling trip," Ruric joked.

Someone banged on the door.

Arman glanced out the window. "It's the police, five cruisers, and a ton of guys."

Stasio lifted Levka from the worn couch and the pain nearly made Levka pass out.

"It's now or never," Ruric warned.

Something slammed into the door.

"Now!" Levka commanded.

2

The door to the club house banged open and police shouted warnings.

Arman carried Levka out the back-office window and into the night sky, flying, invisible to the world. Levka chastised himself for not reacting quickly enough when the burly gang leader had fired the gun, but stopping the quick succession of bullets was all he had really had time for. Sure, he told himself, he could have dodged them, but the bullets would have hit the girl, and she could have died.

Taking a ragged and painful breath, he realized he and his friends could have traveled the distance to Fort Lauderdale in half the time, invisible to vampires and mortals alike, if it wasn't for his blood loss. Telepathically communicating their plans to each other, they agreed to stay overnight at a bed and breakfast in Atlanta, Georgia, while Stasio raided the nearest blood bank.

Hours later, Levka sat on the mattress of their new accommodations, a canopy bed that looked similar to one he'd had in the fifteenth century, robin's egg blue curtains draped around the frame to keep out the bitter cold on winter nights.

Arman unwrapped the bandages around Levka's chest. "You're healing nicely, though it might be a couple of days or so before you're fully healed."

Ruric leaned over and looked at the wounds. "Good thing we mend so quickly. If you'd been mortal, you would never have made it. But I would say it'll take another four days at least. Now if we had a portable, laser surgery tool like Dr. Leonard McCoy did, we could just mend the broken rib and seal those pesky wounds right up."

"*Star Trek*," Arman said, shaking his head. "Could you live in the here and now?"

"Don't laugh. Just think of what the future could hold. Laser surgery wasn't even heard of when *Star Trek* was aired on T.V. in the 1960's. And weapons..." Ruric swung his phantom light sabers over Levka's head. "They'll be better than anything they have today."

"But will we survive them?" Arman asked. "Blades and bullets have little effect on us. They hurt and cause damage that will take a short time to heal—depending on how bad the wounds are—but what about laser weapons? I would think that could be the death of us. So watch what you wish for." Arman replaced Levka's soiled bandages with clean ones.

Levka gritted his teeth. The wounds still pained him, and he wondered again why he'd protected the girls. Because their screams called out to him, beseeching him to save them. That's why.

"You don't like the idea of the future because you're not adventurous like Levka and me," Ruric said to Arman. "A stick-in-the-mud."

Ignoring the taunt, Arman didn't respond.

If it wasn't Arman arguing with Levka about the future, Stasio was. Levka tried to distance himself from the discussions, though on occasion the others tried to drag an opinion from him.

Like now.

"What do you think, Levka?" Ruric asked.

"He doesn't like to get into this debate." Arman raised his dark brows. "You look like you're still hurting, Levka."

"Some."

"We shouldn't have interfered at the warehouse district," Arman scolded again.

"What happened to the girls?" Levka's breathing was still labored and even speaking hurt.

Ruric smiled. "He refutes the idea he cares for girls. For a hundred years, he has denied this, since Cassandra died. Are you now interested in the fairer sex, Levka?"

"Why is it," Levka bit out, wincing, "I can't ask a simple question of you and get a simple answer?"

"The girls are fine," Arman assured him, casting Ruric a sour look. "They are fine. They're sticking close to home for now. No more partying at that raunchy club near the warehouse district, and in fact, the police are investigating the place. The public is incensed, and most want it closed down for catering to underage teens."

"Good. And the boys?"

"One's arm is in a cast." Ruric eyed his faux light sabers as if inspecting them for damage. "The other is still hospitalized from his self-inflicted knife wound. The one who shot you has been charged with attempted murder for starters. Even if they don't find your body, the girls have sworn out statements that the boy shot you four or five times. They said you collapsed, appeared dead, and blood soaked your shirt. Of course, the police figure we're from an opposing gang and are just as rotten as those guys or we wouldn't have gone into hiding."

"Any more news concerning the league?" Levka hated how strained his voice sounded.

"They're pissed off. Luckily, they've kept a lid on the rumors among our people that vampires attacked the teens. Only a few of our kind in the city seem to know about it. So we should be safe at other places as long as they don't connect you with being the wounded teen in the Dallas shooting," Arman said.

Levka gave a start when Stasio walked into the bedroom.

Stasio pulled a backpack off his shoulder and deposited it on the bed. "I got the blood, but I set off some alarms."

"Were you seen?" Ruric asked, his voice terse.

"I don't think so. I'm not sure though. I sensed someone following me." Stasio unzipped the bag and handed a bottle of blood to Levka.

"One of our kind?" Ruric asked.

"Yeah. One of our kind. He may be one of the local enforcers, wondering why four male teens suddenly appeared in their territory. Maybe he's afraid we'll stir up trouble." Levka gave a strangled laugh.

"What?" Arman asked.

After drinking the rest of the bottle of blood, Levka leaned back against the bed. "We *are* trouble. Didn't Stasio just rob a blood bank?"

Ruric sat on the edge of the bed. "Can you move in a couple of hours?"

"An hour," Levka said, not intending to put his friends at any more risk than they already were.

"I stole enough blood to last us the trip, Levka. Sorry about setting off the alarm."

Levka wanted to ask Ruric why he hadn't gone instead. Arman wouldn't have, as much as he didn't like breaking rules. But poor Stasio. He was always making some kind of mistake, despite having the best intentions. Ruric should have gone.

"We'll leave soon," Levka reiterated, intending to rest until they had to move again.

But then he and the others sensed a vampire near the Applewood Bed and Breakfast Inn, attempting to scan for vampiric telepathic communications.

For a moment, no one said a word. Still feeling like he'd been run over by an eighteen-wheeler, Levka swung his legs over the edge of the bed and closed his eyes against a wave of dizziness. Hating his inability to do anything for himself, Levka said, "We leave now."

Arman carried him again. "Next stop, Fort Lauderdale and the Sea Wanderer Cruise."

Ruric opened the bedroom's back window and raised his specter light saber to the star-filled sky. "To sailing in the wide-open galaxy."

The four vanished and flew under the cloak of blackness. Neither vampires nor mortals could see them, invisible until they chose to become visible again. They communicated telepathically the entire time to keep their bearing and stick together. Masking their communication, they ensured other vampires in the vicinity couldn't hear their thoughts.

At one point while they were flying, Levka and Arman lost the others, but they soon saw a landmark, a white steeple on a church and headed in its direction, directing the others to do the same. Twice more, they lost each other, but by nightfall they reached the port of Fort Lauderdale, and Arman set Levka down on a bench resting under palm trees in front of a hotel.

"What do we do until the ship leaves tomorrow?" Ruric asked.

"We'll get a suite at the Holiday Excursions Hotel." Stasio waved his hand at the five-star hotel behind them, brightly lit on the dark night.

"All right. I'll check us in, then bring a wheelchair out for

Levka. It'll look a little odd if any of us carry him into the hotel," Arman said.

Everyone else stayed behind and kept their senses on high alert, scanning the area for any of their kind that might suddenly appear who may be trouble. Levka couldn't shake the feeling the vampire looking for them in Atlanta hadn't remained there.

HALF AN HOUR LATER, Levka was resting in a bed in the hotel suite, glad they'd had no more difficulties. Though he'd insisted on sitting on the sofa in the living area instead, his friends outvoted him.

"We'll get our gear," Ruric said, motioning to Stasio.

"Maybe Stasio should stay with me." Levka tried not to show his distress, but he was a much better actor when he wasn't suffering so much.

"No, I'll stay with you," Arman said quickly.

They didn't need any more mistakes, and Stasio might very well make some, but Levka kept his concern to himself.

Arman shook his head again as if reading Levka's mind. "I'm the most able doctor we have. You need me to look after your wounds."

Levka's wounds were healing just fine without Arman's pampering. But he couldn't fight Arman's stubbornness when it came to him helping them out if he felt it was wrong.

"I'll be super careful," Stasio said, apology lacing his words. Then he grumbled under his breath, "I didn't make any mistakes when I had to raid the Fort Worth clinic after Ruric was injured by that knife-wielding mugger last year."

"I'll watch him," Ruric assured Levka.

Despite feeling bad that he might have hurt Stasio's feelings, Levka couldn't totally conceal his worry something more might go wrong. "Be careful, both of you."

When they left the hotel suite, Levka scowled at Arman. "You know Stasio tends to make mistakes."

"I know, but I can't do it. Wiping store clerks' minds and taking the clothes and other items we need without paying for them is just plain wrong."

"We can't use our credit cards or the league members can trace them. And none of us came away with enough cash. We just don't have any choice. We couldn't get back to our place to grab extra clothes." Levka tugged at his bloodied, bullet-ridden T-shirt. "I don't think I'll be too presentable when we board the ship."

"Sorry. I guess I could have washed it for you."

Levka poked his finger through one of the holes. "And the holes?"

Arman looked apologetic. "I can't sew. Although the way some of the kids dress nowadays..." He shrugged. "Could be a new fashion statement."

"We need more clothes." Levka sighed deeply, unable to stop worrying that Stasio would create a scene, and the Dallas league would learn they were in Fort Lauderdale before they could safely get away on the cruise ship tomorrow morning.

Two hours later, Levka woke to hear his friends talking in the living room of the hotel suite, their voices lowered, but with his acute hearing, he still made out what they were saying.

"Yeah we're all set to board tomorrow morning. Do you think Levka will be able to walk on his own?" Arman asked.

"I've reserved a wheelchair," Ruric said.

Levka called out, "Any word about anything?"

The guys walked into the bedroom, their faces grim.

"What's the matter? You didn't set off the alarms in any of the stores, did you?"

"No," Stasio said. "But we sensed the same aura of whoever it was outside of the Applewood Bed and Breakfast Inn in Atlanta. We're afraid he followed us here."

"He's got to be a tracker then." Levka ran his hands through his unbound hair. "Great." "Do you want us to kill him?" Stasio asked.

"Kill him?" Levka shook his head. "Of course not."

Stasio looked disappointed.

Levka settled back on the pillows. "If he learns we're getting on the ship, and he tries to stop us, we'll knock him out. Under no circumstances are we to kill him. Understood?"

"Yes, we'll knock him out," Arman heartily agreed.

"Good. But only if he comes after us. Once we're on the water, no one can follow us." Levka pulled the cover up to his chin, hating feeling so weak and useless. "Let's get some sleep. Ruric, you have first watch."

"I'll go after you," Arman said to Ruric.

Stasio untied the leather strap from his blond hair. "I've got last watch."

A tracker, Levka thought. Why would the Dallas league send a tracker after them? Or was he an assassin? The league hired assassins to eliminate vampires who were deemed unstable, uncontrollable, any who might give their kind away. A tracker was one thing, and he could cause problems enough. All he would have to do was alert a local vampire squad to grab them and turn them over to the Dallas league.

If he were an assassin, he wouldn't need to call anyone at all.

Dread wormed its way into the marrow of Levka's bones. His

mind told him they should move again. His body revolted and won out as he succumbed to another fitful sleep.

CAITLIN TUGGED her bags through the security check point at the Fort Lauderdale cruise ship terminal, but a teen sitting quietly in a wheelchair caught her eye. The longer she watched him, the more she realized he wasn't as calm as he first appeared. His dark brown eyes watched nearly everyone and everything. Was he looking for someone? It appeared no one was with him. Maybe his parents were checking in their luggage, and he was worried about their departure.

Her foster sister, Alicia, snorted behind her. "Why would anyone bring an invalid on a cruise? What a waste of money."

"Maybe he's dying, and this is his last chance to take his first cruise or something, Alicia. You know, you could be nicer sometimes."

"What's not nice? How can he enjoy a cruise when he can't do anything? Seems stupid to me. Haven't you finished checking in your luggage yet?"

Caitlin could hardly take her eyes off the teen. He wasn't the kind of guy she was usually interested in, long dark hair pulled back into a tail, dark eyes, more of a sleek panther look. She liked the kind of guys who were fairer and more muscular. Yet she couldn't help worrying about him being all alone, unable to fend for himself.

"Hurry it up, will you?" Alicia said. "I want to get on the stupid ship and get with my friends."

A redheaded guy joined the teen in the wheelchair and glanced her way. His wild, curly hair hung way down past his shoulders, making him look like one of the guys she had seen at a Celtic festival, though this guy didn't have a beard. Still, it was the other boy who totally intrigued her. The redhead smiled at her, then said something to the dark-haired boy. He looked her way, his penetrating dark eyes capturing her, holding her hostage.

Alicia shoved Caitlin. "Go, will ya?"

She gave Alicia an annoyed look and glanced back at the teens. The redhead was pushing the wheelchair toward another security checkpoint. Satisfied he was taking care of the guy in the wheelchair, Caitlin hurried through the rest of the security checkpoint.

When Caitlin climbed the boarding walkway, Alicia walked beside her, repeating most of what she'd said to her on the short flight from Orlando to here. "I can't imagine why my mom and dad wanted you to come with us, you *poor* thing. I think it's totally cruel of them to force you to travel across miles and miles of open water when you're so afraid of it." She gave Caitlin a snide smile. "But don't worry. If you feel uncomfortable, you can stay in our suite and sleep. That's what I would do if I were you. Me, as soon as they open the pool, I'm going swimming. So, if you want to find me, that's where I'll be, either beside the pool tanning, or in it."

"Pools don't bother me," Caitlin lied, determined to stick by Alicia's side like she'd promised Mildred and Thomas. "And I'm not afraid of the ocean anymore."

Alicia gave a short bark of laughter. "Yeah, right. Oh, and it'll be a while before we get our luggage so maybe you can find an inside lounge to sit in so you don't have to see the water."

"Thanks, I might do that." *Not.*

"Good. We'll get along fine if you do."

Caitlin wasn't interested in getting along with Alicia. She had a job to do, despicable as it was.

Alicia headed for some of her high school girlfriends gathered next to the railing on the upper deck. "Hey, anyone see Dylan yet?"

Unwelcome among Alicia's clique of girlfriends, Caitlin chose to watch the people down below, loading food and drinks onto the ship, and the antlike parade of passengers walking up the ramp. The teen in the wheelchair caught her eye again. The redhead was still with him, and a blond and another brown-haired guy appeared to be friends of his, the way they stuck close and spoke to him. All wore ponytails, which seemed a little odd. Which school were they from? Which state?

An announcement on the public-address system stated that a snowstorm had held up a flight of passengers from Chicago and would further delay the ship's sailing. Not believing a cruise ship would delay departure for a few people, she shook her head. Though if she was lucky, it would be delayed for a week, and the ship would never leave the dock.

A deep voice penetrated her space. "You're not really planning on chaperoning Alicia and me the whole trip, are you, Caitlin?"

She turned around and found Alicia's latest boyfriend, Dylan, standing behind her. His spiked blond hair made his angular features and blue eyes seem harsher than normal. He lived on the edge, just avoiding getting into trouble with the police, but barely.

"Yep, I am. So be forewarned." Caitlin knew there was little she could do about Alicia's actions, but she had no intention of letting either of them know how she truly felt about her impossible mission.

Once they disembarked at the islands, beware. She'd be itching to use her powers, and anyone who gave her grief would quickly cease and desist.

Towering over her at six feet tall, Dylan gave her a smirk.

"Really. See ya around then." He stalked off toward Alicia and her girlfriends.

Someone stumbled behind Caitlin and bumped into her, dropping his backpack on her sandaled feet. "I'm sorry," the blond-haired guy said, grabbing his bag.

She recognized him as one of the guys with the wheelchair-bound teen. "It's okay," she tried reassuring the poor guy as he nearly dropped his bag again.

Then she noticed the redhead, the brunette, and the boy in the wheelchair behind him. All smiled at her except for the one sitting in the wheelchair. Did he feel bad that he was confined?

He quickly looked away from her. Did he think she pitied him? Taking a deep breath, she realized at once that she did.

"Hi," she said, not usually that outgoing with people she didn't know. But there was something about them that made her feel more welcome than the group she came with from her own high school. *Snobs, all of them.* She was an outsider. A foster teen. Someone who didn't belong. "You must all be from the same school."

"They said they would let us into our room early," the one in the wheelchair said to his friends, ignoring her.

His voice was brusque, and again she sensed he felt embarrassed for being different. Disregarding his rudeness, she stuck her hand out to him, determined to offer her friendship.

"I'm Caitlin MacEvin from Orlando, Florida."

The boy ignored her. She took his hand and shook it anyway. But he didn't shake her hand back, and she noted then he didn't seem to have any strength. Horrified that he might be dying and wished to be left alone, she felt a twinge of remorse.

His brown eyes darkened to midnight when he looked up at her, then he turned to the redhead and said with an authoritative voice, "To my room."

She stepped aside, and the boys continued on their way.

Each of them glanced back at her, warmly smiling, except for the one in the wheelchair. Apparently, at least as far as they were concerned, they liked her and maybe hoped she could bring their friend out of his shell. Caitlin loved dealing with lost causes, except when it came to Alicia. But this guy, she was going to befriend. At least she hoped.

Maybe this trip wouldn't be so bad after all.

3

Levka shook his head as Ruric helped him onto the gaudy pink and orange floral couch sitting beside the suite's large balcony window. The black, orange, and gray zigzag carpeting was enough to make him dizzy again. Two queen-sized beds covered in the same wild flamingo pinks, orange, and black, with touches of turquoise hurt his eyes. What was worse, black mirror tiles covered the walls and reflected the bright colors, making it appear there were double the number of brightly-colored couches and beds in the surprisingly spacious stateroom. The robin's egg blue of the Applewood Bed & Breakfast Inn looked good about now.

Turning his attention to Stasio, Levka said, "I swear you dropped your backpack on that girl's feet on purpose."

"Not I." Stasio grinned, opened the class door to the balcony, and looked out. "She's pretty and she likes you. Good start, I should think."

The sea breeze blew a tangy fishy smell into the air-conditioned room.

"She pities me." Levka held his chest to quiet the discomfort.

"She likes you." Ruric unpacked a bag. "Do you want me to bring her to you so you can...feed later?"

Levka growled. "I told you already, I only want bottles of blood. And if I ever finish healing, I won't even need that for a few days."

"I'm going to check out the facilities and the girls." Stasio waggled his blond brows.

Levka glanced at Arman.

"I'll go with him." Arman opened the door to the room. "After a while, they'll be calling the lifeboat drill."

"I'm not going."

"Everyone has to go, Levka. Maybe Caitlin MacEvin will be assigned to the same boat." Stasio shut the door behind Arman and himself.

Ruric turned on the T.V. "She *was* cute, you know. You haven't shown any interest in a girl in eons, Levka. Maybe she would be good for you."

"Go, Ruric. Keep the others out of trouble. I don't want to hear this nonsense from you or any of the others about this girl."

"Do you realize whenever you begin to get better after you're injured this badly, you're an ogre?" Ruric grinned, then left Levka alone, like he wanted.

Levka had seen Caitlin MacEvin speaking to the blond with the spiked hair and hard blue eyes. What bothered him most was her words to him, *"So be forewarned."* And the guy's cavalier response, *"Really. See ya around then."*

At first, he thought the guy was her boyfriend, but not after he heard the tone of their voices, or the words they spoke. Was he stalking her?

Levka stared at the T.V. but didn't see the screen, his mind studying the memory of her, the way her blue eyes and lips smiled at him, the way the ocean breeze caught her black hair and caressed her cheeks, the warmth of her hand in his.

He snorted. She pitied him. *Him*, a prince of darkness and former prince of Wales. He who could barely stand—but had the strength of several grown men when he was uninjured—would not be pitied by a mere mortal girl.

The public-address system crackled in his room: "The lifeboat drill requires all passengers to secure their lifejackets and go immediately to your lifeboat station. You must use the diagram in your cabin, and you must use the stairs as all elevators will be shut down during the lifeboat drill. The lifeboat drill is required of all passengers, and crewmembers will be inspecting passengers' rooms, so no one can remain behind."

Levka closed his eyes and rested his head against the sofa cushion. If any of the crew bothered him, he would just wipe their minds, and they would forget he was even here.

The ship's staff repeated the lifeboat announcement over and over again, and Levka clenched his fists. "Enough already. Get it over with, all right?"

He glanced at his watch and wondered where his friends were. A knock sounded on the door, then a key twisted in the lock. The door squeaked opened, and three men came into the room, wearing the ship's uniforms.

"Your friends," the one said, "asked us to come get you because you were in a wheelchair. We're here to take you up to your assigned lifeboat."

They hustled him out of the room so quickly, he couldn't focus on any one of them to control their minds. He would kill his friends as soon as he had the strength.

When he reached the deck crowded with passengers wearing their orange lifejackets, he saw no sign of his friends. Hiding somewhere else, no doubt, so they didn't have to bother with this nonsense, or face his irritation.

A blond-haired girl stood in front of him in extremely short shorts and said, "See, I told Mom and Dad how stupid it was for them to send you with me. You're shaking so hard you're about to come unglued."

"I'm fine, Alicia."

He recognized the second girl's voice at once. *Caitlin MacEvin.*

"You can lie all you want to me, but you're going to be in a psychiatrist's care before this cruise is ended. Oh, oh, Dylan!" Alicia moved away and headed for the guy with the spiked hair, the one Levka had thought was Caitlin's boyfriend, or stalker.

Caitlin clutched her lifejacket with a death grip, her eyes round with terror. When she had said she was fine, she sounded so. But he could see now she wasn't.

"Levka." He stretched his hand out to her. Every effort, no matter how little, pained him. He tried not to reveal the agony he felt, but she turned and studied his face for a minute, her own terror forgotten, and she took his hand and squeezed.

"I'm sorry if I was so pushy earlier. I don't have any friends on this trip and—" Levka looked in Alicia's direction.

Caitlin shrugged and wrapped her arms around her lifejacket; her eyes narrowing. "My foster sister."

He looked at the guy with the spiked hair.

Caitlin turned to see who he was observing. "Her boyfriend. Her parents want me to keep her away from him as much as possible on the trip."

Levka couldn't believe the pretty girl didn't have any friends on the cruise and was being made to baby-sit her foster sister.

"Are you from Florida?" she asked. "A lot of the kids are."

"From...Texas." He'd thought about naming some other place, but sticking closer to the truth often avoided problems later.

"Oh." She offered the most charming smile. "A Texan. That's cool."

He wondered if she would think he was even cooler if she

knew he'd run cattle on Goodnight's ranch for a spell, fought Apaches, and cattle thieves, but worse, had to deal with stampeding longhorns during a thunderstorm? Being a real cowboy wasn't as romantic a life as it was made out to be, but he and his friends were always first to try out new experiences.

The lifeboat drill ended, bringing him back to his current set of circumstances. Except for Caitlin and Levka, everyone moved en mass and returned to their rooms to ditch their lifejackets before first dinner.

"Where are your friends? Did you want me to take you back to your room?" Caitlin asked.

"No, thank you. You must look after your foster sister."

Rolling her eyes, she said, "I'm afraid that's my *mission impossible*. Are you sure you don't want me to help you?"

"I'm sure." He folded his arms across his chest and winced with pain.

"But I don't see your friends." She looked around the empty deck.

He would kill them. "Please, go. I'll be fine."

"I don't want to leave you alone."

He wondered why she seemed so bothered that he would be left alone. Defenseless? Helpless? Well, he was kind of that for the moment. But it didn't bother him, too much, except for the part of being weak.

"What's wrong, Caitlin?" With his vampiric gaze, he caught her gaze and held her captive. For a moment, he wanted to control her, to will her to take him back to his cabin, and offer her blood to him. Not in a hundred years had he felt the urge so strong to have a female companion.

"I..." She turned away from him, breaking the connection.

Not since Cassandra had been in his life had he ever met a girl who could break the bond he made between them. He seized Caitlin's wrist, wondering if in his weakness, he'd lost the ability to control a mortal's mind now, too. "Caitlin, what scares you about my being alone?" He forged the connection with her mind again, but once more she resisted and pulled away. Again, he lost the ability to find out what troubled her, distressing him even more than being confined to the wheelchair.

"I'll send a porter to help you. You're right. I have to keep an eye on Alicia." Caitlin hurried off, spoke to a man dressed in a white crew uniform, then dashed down a spiral staircase.

He felt he was seeing dear Cassandra all over again, except not light-haired and dark-eyed like her, but raven-haired and blue-eyed. The memory of Cassandra's life slipping away as he cradled her head in his lap filled his vision. He wanted to cry out like he did then, kill the bastards who had murdered her, satisfy his need for revenge, but nothing would bring her back to him.

The porter headed in his direction, breaking into his morbid thoughts, but Ruric's voice behind Levka heated his blood. "I'll take him, thanks."

Levka jerked his head around, sending another shard of pain through his chest. He glared at Ruric, who grinned back at him. "I knew you liked the girl."

"Where were you guys?"

"Around and about. You know if this had been a real drill, we would have had you in the lifeboat already."

"Where are the others?"

"Getting to know a couple of the girls. We're supposed to be on a vacation, too. As soon as you're feeling better—"

"What about Stasio? Is Arman keeping an eye on him?"

"They're double-dating, sort of." Ruric took Levka back down the elevator to their room.

"I'll baby-sit Caitlin's foster sister so you can spend time with Caitlin."

"Forget it."

"She has got the hots for you. I wouldn't let her slip away."

When Levka gave Ruric another glare meant to make his friend quit this nonsense, Ruric smiled and unlocked the door. "Did you want to change for dinner? First night, we have arranged seating and—"

"We're sitting together, right?"

Ruric wheeled him into their room. "Yes. We're seated together. But there's room for four others, eight to a table. A few small tables are reserved for couples. If you want me to make different arrangements for you and Caitlin..."

"I'll get room service."

"They don't offer room service on this cruise." Ruric flipped through the shirts hanging in the closet. "It's a dress-up night. Which shirt do you want to wear?" He held out a white one and a pin-striped shirt.

"Got anything black?"

Ruric gave an exaggerated sigh. "Whatever His Majesty desires. She'll think you're in mourning. Or a Goth."

"Quit it, Ruric. No more about the girl."

Ruric handed him the shirt. "She's like Cassandra, isn't she?"

Levka glowered at him.

"Isn't she?"

Levka tried to jerk off his shirt, but shrill stabs of pain streaked through every nerve.

Ruric helped him to change. "I couldn't read her mind. She's like Cassandra. She must be telepathic, I think, but very controlled. And despite what you say, I know you want her."

WITH THE CURLING IRON, Caitlin curled her hair again. For the first time on the cruise, she was really interested in how she looked. Before, she didn't care. None of the spoiled rich guys on the cruise had interested her. But Levka, jeez, she didn't even get his last name, there was just something about him that drew her attention. She couldn't put her finger on why she was so intrigued by him. For a moment, she forgot how much she hated being on the ship, sharing a room with Alicia—who was hogging the bathroom again—and dreading being around the other high school kids. Now she was hoping she would catch a glimpse of Levka at dinner. Maybe he would even go to the comedy show afterward, and she would see him there.

She let out her breath in exasperation. She had to keep an eye on Alicia.

Unfortunately, the ship's staff hadn't filled the pool with water earlier, so Alicia was acting like a grizzly. Caitlin glanced at her watch. They had two minutes to get to dinner.

"Alicia, it's time to go."

"Go without me. I'll be right up."

Caitlin leaned against the wall. "I'll wait." She could imagine Dylan and her foster sister slipping off to his room, or even their own, while she went to dinner, and they never showed up.

Alicia threw the bathroom door open and stormed past her. "My parents were not serious about you watching every move I make. They only pulled this so you would go on the cruise. You are such an idiot, you know? And I mean that in a nice way." She shoved the door open and stepped into the hall. "They wanted their privacy and with you hanging about, they weren't going to get it. That's why they send me on all these trips; don't you get it?" She stalked up the stairs.

Caitlin hurried after her, half wondering if what she said was true. But then knowing Alicia, she often twisted things to suit her own purposes. Yet the idea her foster parents felt Caitlin was a nuisance nagged at her. Her parents had always taken family vacations with her and her sister. The idea that parents would send their kids off for separate vacations seemed foreign to her, and it made her wish again that she was with her own family.

She couldn't dwell on that now, yet the sound of the ship splashing through the waves, the smell of the fishy water, and the stiff, salty breeze tugging at her hair, all reminded her of their final days together.

She blinked the tears away and caught up to her foster sister.

When they reached the formal dining area, a man dressed in a tux led them past tables covered in white table cloths. Mirrors lined the walls, making the large dining room appear even more expansive. A few small tables were situated opposite the eight-person tables, she figured for honeymooning couples.

Alicia pointed at a two-seater table. "That's what I want to sit at with Dylan tomorrow night."

As long as Caitlin could still watch her, it didn't matter to her. "Sure."

The man motioned to a table where Levka sat in his wheelchair, and his three friends were seated around him.

"Oh, *no*," Alicia said. "I specifically asked to be seated with seven of my friends."

"This is the arrangement, miss, and it cannot be changed tonight," the man said, with a thick Serbian accent and an edge to his voice.

Levka looked up from his menu, and his eyes widened when he saw Caitlin. She wanted to smile at him, but he didn't seem pleased to see her. He quickly looked at his friends, all who were smiling like she was the best thing they'd seen in years. The redheaded guy jumped up from his chair and offered it to Caitlin so she could sit between Levka and him, while Alicia continued to argue with the guy in the tux.

"Excuse me," the blond said, taking hold of Alicia's hand. "Have we met?" His blue eyes captured hers, held them.

She stuttered something unintelligible, then he led her to a seat across the table from Caitlin and sat next to her.

"Hey," Dylan said, rushing to join her, "I thought we had a table of our own. Who are all these guys?"

The blond motioned for him to take a seat on the other side of Alicia. "Sit, please."

Caitlin couldn't believe Alicia would shut up and behave for once like an adult. Dylan hesitated, giving all the guys the evil eye, then sat next to Alicia and jerked his napkin into his lap.

One more girl joined them, Lynne Raven, the one that goaded Alicia—more than any of her friends—to give Caitlin a hard time. She sat in the only open seat between the redhead and Dylan.

"I thought we had our *own* table." Lynne gave Caitlin a disparaging look. "I thought we made sure only the *right* people sat with us."

So, Alicia and her friends had planned to exclude her from their table at dinner. Caitlin gave Lynne a small smile, glad they hadn't gotten their way.

"I'm Ruric." The redheaded guy bowed his head to Caitlin.

"Stasio," the blond guy said. "Who apologizes most profusely for dropping his backpack on your feet earlier today."

Caitlin smiled at him. "It was no big deal."

"Arman," the brown-haired guy offered and bowed his head slightly.

They all seemed genuinely pleased she'd joined them, and it couldn't have made her feel any more welcome. Since no one else introduced themselves, she said, "That's my foster sister, Alicia, her boyfriend, Dylan, and her friend, Lynne." She didn't bother with last names because the guys from Texas didn't either. "And this is Levka," she said, touching his arm.

Lynne snarled her lip. "Sweet." She turned to Alicia. "So, are we swimming later?"

Alicia stared blankly at her.

Caitlin frowned, not sure she could handle sitting poolside. She'd so hoped to go to the comedy entertainment.

"What do you want to do tonight, Caitlin?" Ruric asked.

Everyone looked at her, waiting for her to speak.

"I thought the comedy show would be fun."

Dylan smiled.

"But I'll watch Alicia swim."

Instantly, Dylan's expression turned sour.

Lynne tilted her cosmetically-reduced nose up. "You're scared of the water."

Caitlin couldn't help that she was terrified of the water, but she didn't want her new friends to know she was seeing a psychiatrist for it. Squaring her shoulders, she said, "That's old news, Lynne." She felt Levka and his friends still watching her and felt totally naked, like she could have no deep, dark secrets around them.

Alicia didn't say anything, which wasn't like her at all. What was wrong with her? Normally, she would have agreed with Lynne and made a sarcastic comment to back her up.

The waiter came to the table, explained the special for the evening, and everyone ordered their dinners.

When he left, Stasio turned to Alicia. "Wouldn't you rather see the comedy show following the meal?"

Alicia stared at his entrancing blue eyes, and Caitlin held her breath.

Stasio asked Alicia again, "Wouldn't you?"

4

When Stasio asked Alicia again if she wanted to go to the show, Caitlin was sure she would say no. Instead, Alicia nodded.

Dylan blew out his breath. "You hate those comedy shows." Putting his arm around her shoulders, he pulled her closer. "We'll go swimming together."

Stasio's blond brows rose. "She wants to go to the show. But why don't you go swimming with..." He looked over at Lynne. "...her."

"All right with me." Lynne raked her fork through her mashed potatoes. "But Alicia's his girlfriend. So, if you think you're going to make the moves on her..." She shook her head.

"She's going swimming with me, and that's final." Dylan slugged his soda down.

Stasio smiled, the look handsomely arrogant and decidedly menacing. Yet, Caitlin couldn't help worrying that Stasio was getting way over his head on this. Dylan had tons of mean-hearted friends on the ship, any of whom wouldn't have any regret about throwing Stasio overboard if Dylan asked them to.

She suspected Stasio was trying to get Alicia to go along with seeing the show so that Caitlin could see it, and not because he was interested in Alicia. There was no way Caitlin wanted him hurt over her. Was he still feeling guilty over dropping the bag on her feet?

"It's okay, Stasio. I'll go another night." Caitlin tried to give him her most convincing smile.

Levka leaned back in his wheelchair and stared at Alicia. "The comedy show sounds good." He wore a stern face and didn't seem pleased, more forced into the situation than anything. And he didn't look Caitlin's way, just watched Alicia.

Arman shook his head.

Ruric grinned and raised his water glass in a salute. "To stellar performances."

"Right," Stasio said. "You know the jesters always performed at medieval castles to entertain, and they've found laughter aids the digestion. So, after we eat, the comedy show will be perfect."

Arman set his napkin on the table. "You can drown if you swim right after you eat." He gave Dylan a pointed look.

"We're going swimming," Dylan growled.

Wait-staff brought the first course of the meal to the table, and everyone grew quiet while they ate their salads or soup. All but Levka, who drank only water.

Caitlin was dying to know what was wrong with him, but as much as she wanted to know, she felt it rude to ask. Then she had a brilliant idea. She would ask either Ruric or Stasio, maybe later tonight, *if* they managed to get Alicia to the comedy show without Dylan sending a hit squad to change their minds.

She shook her head. Anytime during the long voyage, Stasio and his friends could be at risk. It wasn't worth it so that she could watch the show to get her mind off the volumes of water surrounding her.

Reaching for her drink, she nearly had a heart attack when Levka shoved it into Dylan's lap.

"Sorry," Levka said, though Caitlin didn't think he was at all.

"You freak!" Dylan hastily wiped the ice and soda off his lap.

Levka's action could only escalate the problem with Dylan, though part of her wanted to cheer Levka on.

She planned to tell everyone, convince everyone, she wanted to watch her foster sister swim once they finished their meal. But after Dylan wolfed down the dinner special, some kind of fish, he clutched his stomach and ran out of the dining hall.

Lynne, who had the same meal, pushed her plate away and didn't eat any more of the fish. Levka and his friends had eaten the beef, and she and Alicia had the chicken, but none of them had gotten sick on their meals. Thank God for small miracles.

Once they finished eating, Stasio asked, "Ready to enjoy the entertainment?"

Lynne threw her napkin on the table. "I guess since you're not swimming, I'll go with you, Alicia." She didn't seem thrilled about the prospect.

Neither did Alicia. She just went along with it like she was Stasio's puppet girlfriend. Caitlin had never seen her so quiet and manageable. She loved it.

Levka was back to his brooding self.

She prayed the comedy show would be truly funny and worth the trouble it might cause.

LEVKA HOPED his friends were enjoying their matchmaking efforts for the time-being because once he was well enough, it would be his turn to get back at them.

Ruric communicated with him telepathically in private, *"She's terrified of water, Levka. We're doing her a big favor."*

All right, Levka couldn't argue that. He recalled the way she'd trembled when she'd worn the lifejacket during the lifeboat drill and the comment her foster sister made to her about needing a psychiatrist once the cruise was done. Had Alicia wanted to swim because she knew how much the water frightened Caitlin? How could her foster parents be so cruel as to send her on a cruise?

"*What was up with her soda?*" Arman asked.

Levka watched as Caitlin took her seat at the end of the row so he could sit next to her in his wheelchair. "*Her drink was drugged. Dylan slipped something into it when he thought none of us were looking.*"

"Bastard," Stasio said.

Levka glanced at Caitlin. Seemingly forgetting for the moment, they were at sea, she smiled and laughed at the comedian's jokes. Ruric seemed more amused that she was having a good time than anything. Alicia stared blankly at the show. Lynne folded her arms and scowled. Levka imagined she didn't get half of the jokes. Stasio seemed to enjoy the show as much as Caitlin. Watching behind them, Arman appeared to be looking for Dylan or some of his buddies to arrive.

"Can I get three volunteers from the audience?" the comedian asked, with a distinctive Irish accent.

Six female teens jumped up from their seats and waved their hands.

Stasio twisted his blond hair into a ponytail, then made his way down the stairs to the stage to join in on the fun.

Levka gave Ruric a warning look. He shrugged when the comedian chose two girls and motioned for Stasio to come up on stage, though he hadn't needed the invite.

Ruric said privately to Levka, "*I cannot always keep Stasio under control. You know that.*"

Levka frowned. "*Convince the comedian you want to join them.*"

"*It's too late for that.*"

The comedian had Stasio and the two girls sit and face the

audience, then said, "With your permission, I will hypnotize the three of you and have you do something that isn't too terribly embarrassing."

The audience whooped and cheered.

"What's your name, miss?" the comedian asked.

"Marissa."

"Marissa, I want you to watch this crystal sphere, relax, breathe deeply, allow your eyelids to grow heavy, and close."

After learning the other girl's name was Chelsea, he had her do the same. Then he walked over to Stasio and said the same.

All three volunteers sat with their eyes closed while the comedian asked the audience,

"What should we have them do?"

"Take off their clothes!" a teen guy yelled. The theater exploded with cheers.

"We have to keep it G-rated, folks." The comedian grinned, then walked over to Marissa. "Isn't the gentleman seated over there cute? Wouldn't you like to kiss him? Why don't you walk over and kiss him?"

The audience sat in silence.

Marissa didn't move.

The comedian cleared his throat. "Despite what some people would have you believe, you can't hypnotize someone to do what they don't want to. Is Marissa's boyfriend in the audience?" A guy stood up and whooped.

"See," the comedian said, pointing at the guy. "That's what's causing Marissa's reluctance. You'll have to leave the theater." Everyone laughed.

The boyfriend smiled, shook his head, and sat back down.

"Okay, well, Marissa will dance with Stasio and, Stasio, you will dance with Marissa. You both may open your eyes and join each other." The comedian motioned with his hand and a waltz began to play.

Stasio rose from the chair, as wooden as Marissa did.

Levka would have to put a tighter leash on him.

Stasio took Marissa into his arms and danced across the stage, one of the best dancers Levka knew of any time period. But before the music ended, Stasio led her back to her seat and held his hand out to the comedian.

The comedian frowned. "You haven't finished the dance."

"Dance with me."

The audience roared. Levka propped his elbow on the arm of his wheelchair and rested his head in his hand. Arman folded his arms. Ruric grinned.

For a minute, the comedian seemed to resist, then he accepted Stasio's hand and waltzed around the floor with Stasio for several minutes as graceful as he'd danced two-hundred years earlier. When the music ended, Stasio said, "Now you will dance with the other young lady."

The comedian did as he was told and once the dance ended, Stasio said, "You may take my chair and continue with your show." After bowing to the audience, Stasio walked off the stage, while the crowd went wild with cheering.

"Showoff," Ruric said. "Wish I'd thought of it."

Stasio retook his seat while Caitlin smiled at him. "You did a great job."

He gave her a satisfied smile and bowed his head to her, but Levka couldn't help feeling perturbed. Caitlin would surely assume Stasio was using hypnosis on her foster sister now that she saw his act.

When the show ended, Stasio asked Alicia, "Do you want to take a walk on deck or return to your room?"

Alicia just stared at him.

Stasio tried again. "You're tired and want to return to your room?"

Alicia nodded.

Caitlin took a deep breath. "We've had a long day."

Lynne shook her head. "I'm going to find some friends who aren't going to bed before it's even midnight." She stormed off.

"There's a band playing in the lounge downstairs. Do you want to listen to them?" Ruric asked Caitlin and Levka.

"I better go back to the room if Alicia's going," Caitlin said.

"Alicia," Stasio said, "you would like to see the band, wouldn't you?"

Levka rolled his eyes. Caitlin was no dummy and would soon, if she hadn't already, realize what Stasio was doing.

Alicia nodded.

"We'll go down for about a half hour," Levka said, "but then I need to get some rest."

Arman's eyes widened. "Are you all right, Levka?"

"Yes, quit worrying about me." Arman's fussing over Levka was bad enough when they were alone but in front of Caitlin it made him feel more than inadequate.

"Are you sure you're okay?" Caitlin asked, her voice concerned. "You do look tired."

"He's fine." Ruric wheeled Levka the rest of the way into the dimly-lit lounge.

A band played a medley of instruments including pipe whistles and stringed instruments in one corner, and passengers seated on the low-backed cushiony chairs sipped drinks. Behind the band, colorful fish swam in a tank of saltwater.

"New Age music." Ruric smiled. "The stuff of the future."

They sat down on big zebra-striped lounge chairs and ordered sodas. Caitlin watched the fish in the tank, and Levka wondered what she was thinking. Everyone remained quiet as they listened to the musicians for a quarter of an hour, until Alicia began to snore.

Caitlin laughed. "I guess she was really tired."

"We'll walk you to your room," Stasio offered.

"Maybe you should take Levka back to his room first."

"No," Levka said. "We'll take you back to yours." He couldn't help but worry Dylan or some of his friends might try to bother the girls. Even if Levka felt he was mostly useless, he wanted to be there to see them tucked safely inside.

After Stasio guided Alicia into their room, he said, "Sleep well and pleasant dreams."

"We'll have breakfast together in the morning," Ruric said to Caitlin.

Looking at Levka, she waited for his approval. He bowed his head. "Tomorrow."

She gave him one of her radiant smiles. "All right. Yes. All right. In the morning. Good night." She shut the door.

Levka scowled at Ruric, who grinned back at him.

When they were safely back in their suite, Levka asked Stasio, "What was with you using mind control so much on Alicia? The others were too self-absorbed to notice, but Caitlin's very observant."

"Sorry. Caitlin seemed scared of the water. I wanted to help her out."

Levka couldn't deny he felt the same way, only they had to be careful how they dealt with Alicia and the rest of her friends. "How did Dylan end up getting sick on the fish?"

His friends all smiled, but no one said a word.

Levka shook his head. "I thought I could get by without more blood tonight, but I'm not quite there. Can someone get me a bottle?"

Stasio looked at Ruric, then back at Levka.

"What?" Levka asked, unable to curb the irritation edging his word.

"I dropped them."

Levka held his tongue, waiting for the rest of the story, but when it wasn't forthcoming, he said, "And?"

"Sorry, Levka, truly I am. A porter bumped into me, and I dropped the bag. I'm afraid all the bottles broke."

Levka couldn't believe it. He looked at Ruric, who nodded.

Arman sat on the sofa. "We normally can go without blood for several days and just eat human food. But your body is still healing so you'll need to feed."

Levka groaned. "I don't want to feed off a mortal."

"How about Lynne?" Ruric asked. "I wouldn't mind draining her enough so she would have to sleep the rest of the cruise as mean as she was toward Caitlin."

"Someone we don't know," Levka finally said. "I have to get out of this blasted wheelchair."

"I'll get someone since it was my mistake." Stasio hurried out of the room.

"Watch him," Levka growled at Ruric.

"Aye, aye, Captain." Ruric saluted, then hastened after Stasio.

Arman fussed with making down the queen-sized beds, while Levka wondered what else could go wrong.

Twenty minutes later, Stasio and Ruric returned to the room with a guy in tow, his thick cologne preceding him. When they moved out of his way, Levka stared at him, then looked at Stasio.

His friend shrugged. "He was the only one who hadn't been drinking. I know you don't like alcohol mixed with your blood."

Levka considered the grinning comedian standing before him. "An Irishman who doesn't drink? Isn't that an oxymoron?"

5

Caitlin yanked the curtains closed to hide the glass door to the balcony in her stateroom. She couldn't see anything in the dark, but it was enough to hear the waves pounding the ship, beating it to death. Just like the water had bashed her parents' sailing yacht, hammering it until it sank beneath the black waters a year ago today.

Spring break, family vacation, their last.

Clenching her teeth against the memories, she sat on her bed and stared at sleeping beauty, Alicia, still fully dressed, lying on top of her made bed. Caitlin had only seen one hypnotist act before, and she figured the whole thing was staged. But not this time. Not when Stasio seemed to control Alicia's mind before the meal and afterward. And she didn't figure the entertainer would have planned to have someone from the audience steal his show. Thinking of Stasio's actions made her smile. She just wished she could use her own magic on board the ship so that she didn't feel so helpless.

Taking a deep breath, she weighed her options. She could try to sleep, or she could go up on deck and take a look at the pool. Maybe she could get her fear under control before Alicia forced the issue.

Certain Prince Charming Stasio had put Alicia under his spell for the night, Caitlin vowed to fight her own demons without Alicia's goading. Grabbing her sweater, Caitlin left the room, her shoulders straight, her chin up. She could do this. She might not be able to look over the railing at the ocean just yet, but she could look at the stupid pool.

~

Levka had fought with his friends ever since they'd brought him the Irish comedian for a nighttime snack. Finally, winning the argument after feeding, he had them wheel him up to the railing of the upper deck. "Just leave me here," Levka ordered. "I want to sit here for a while. Alone."

"All right," Ruric said. "But call us when you want us to come get you."

Levka motioned for them to leave. He was tired of being coddled. Tired of them hanging around the invalid. And he wasn't ready to retire for the evening.

The three hesitated, then wandered off.

Levka listened to the ship cutting through the waves, glanced up at the dark sky, not a star in sight, no glimpse of the moon behind a bank of thunderclouds. He tried to get out of the wheelchair.

"Concentrate," he commanded himself, trying to obliterate the pain in his chest. He grabbed the railing, his fingers gripping the metal rod, the ocean spray slapping his face. Triumphant, he stood.

"Well, well," a familiar voice said behind him.

Dylan.

"Need some help climbing over the railing?" Some other guys laughed.

Levka didn't turn away from the railing, couldn't let go for fear he would collapse in front of them. He couldn't gauge how many there were behind him, but as weak as he felt, even two husky male teens would be enough to overpower him.

Dylan shoved Levka's shoulder hard. "You and your buddies better leave my girl alone, or else—"

"Too insecure to take on my friends? Have to go after the guy in the wheelchair?"

"Why, you—" Dylan said, his voice dangerously dark.

"Levka!" Caitlin called out from farther back on the deck.

Gripping the railing for dear life, Levka looked over his shoulder and saw Caitlin running across the deck, her dark hair flying, her lips parted, her eyes worried.

Four boys were backing up Dylan's threats.

"Stop her," Dylan ordered, motioning to her.

Two of the guys went after Caitlin. She backed away from them, her hands clenched. "Dylan, leave him alone!"

One of the guys grabbed for her arm, and she swung her fist at his cheek. The other seized her wrist.

Instantly, Levka released the railing, twisted around, and grabbed Dylan's throat with one hand. "Have your thugs release Caitlin, now," he growled low, his vampiric gaze locking with the mortal's.

Dylan's blue eyes bulged. Clawing at Levka's hand on his throat, he couldn't speak, but finally waved for the others to let her go.

"Levka!" Caitlin screamed and flew across the deck toward him.

"Leave us," Levka said to Dylan.

Dylan nodded, his fingers still grappling with Levka's hand at his throat, his eyes watering.

Levka released him and reached for the railing, but found Caitlin's arms wrapped around him instead.

"Let me help you," she said, embracing him hard.

She felt warm, soft, and huggable. Her jasmine perfume teased his nose, and he nuzzled his face against her neck, listened to the blood pulsing through her veins, heard her heart pounding, felt her warm breath rapid against his ear.

"Are you all right?" she asked, still hugging him with a death grip.

Cassandra came to mind and all the anguish he'd felt in losing her washed over him like a cold blue norther.

"Help me into the wheelchair," he said, his voice rough, unfeeling, ill-tempered. He couldn't, wouldn't fall for another mortal girl. He wouldn't drag another into his dark world.

Caitlin stumbled when she tried to help him into the chair. She was only about five feet-four inches tall and he, a little over six feet. She couldn't manage, and the two of them fell to the deck. He groaned.

"Ohmigod. I'm so, so sorry, Levka." Her small hands were all over his arms, his shoulders, his hands, trying to console him for her mistake. "I'm such an idiot. Here, let me try again."

"No!" he snapped, unable to control his anger that he was so inept, that he'd made her feel so inadequate. "Leave me."

She stared at him. "But what if they come back? Dylan and those creeps? What if—"

"Go!" he said, giving her a devil of a glare.

"You...you weren't trying to jump, were you? You wouldn't do that, would you? Please tell me you wouldn't." Her lip quivered.

He couldn't bear to see her like this. "You can't know how I feel. I was just trying to stand on my own two feet. Just leave me."

"But what if Dylan and the others come back?"

"I can take care of myself. Just go!"

She brushed away tears dribbling down her cheeks. "You've got to fight for life, Levka. You can't let anything..." She sniffled. "...anything stand in the way." She stalked off.

All at once he felt crueler than her foster sister, Alicia, had been with her. Yet, if he let things go the way his dark heart wanted, he would make Caitlin his, and that would be even crueler. Struggling with dwindling strength, he tried several times to get back into his wheelchair to no avail. He swore he sensed his friends nearby, but none of them came to assist him, and he was not going to call on them either.

DETERMINED to practice what she preached, Caitlin headed back to the pool. She had been shocked to see Levka standing, but she could tell he was too weak to do much else. Though when he grabbed Dylan by the throat, he'd totally stunned her. But it seemed it was only a bit of reserve strength, because when she held him, he was as weak as a new sapling trembling in the breeze.

She couldn't quit belittling herself for being unable to help him into his wheelchair. She'd humiliated him, and she hated herself for it. God, how she wished she was home. *Home*, she snorted. She didn't have a home any longer. Not a home to share with her own loving family.

When she reached the swimming pool, goose bumps trailed down her arms. No one swam because it was closed for the night at this late hour. Overhead lights didn't penetrate the dark waters of the pool that she envisioned connected in some bizarre way with the black ocean beneath the ship. The rolling of the vessel created waves in the pool as if it were a miniature sea on deck. Thunder cracked nearby, sending a shiver down her spine.

She clutched a lamppost and stared at the water. A shower of cold rainwater wetted her hair and clothes. Staring into the pool, she envisioned herself floating in her lifejacket, seat cushion flotation devices drifting around her, all that was left of the yacht. The rain poured down on her from above. The waves pulled her up one swell and down into a trough. Sharks circled underneath her, around her, playing with her until they took a bite.

"Caitlin?" Ruric asked, his voice concerned.

Turning, she saw him standing there, his face dripping with water like hers was.

He tilted his head to the side. "Are you all right?"

She broke free of her memories. "Is Levka still out in this weather?" She started back to the railing, but Ruric caught her arm.

"We've taken him back to his room. *But,* are you all right?"

Caitlin clenched her teeth against the tears. "I was such an idiot. I tried to help him into his wheelchair, and I didn't have the strength."

Ruric took her hand and led her back inside the building. "Levka's angry about his injuries, but he'll get over them. It's not your fault."

"How...how was he hurt?"

Ruric didn't say anything for a moment, then he looked at Caitlin and raised his red brows. "He tried to save a girl's life. The guy shot Levka instead. He should be better in a day or so, but he has been sick for months. That has made him pretty grouchy at times. We're used to it, but anyone who doesn't know him, wouldn't know how to take him."

Ruric smiled in the most devilish way. "You're the first girl he has been interested in, in a long time. So, if you want to be his friend, don't give up."

She shook her head. "It wasn't his fault. I...I just didn't realize I couldn't—"

Ruric lifted her chin. "You're stronger than most girls we know. I'll take you back to your room. We have an early breakfast call."

"If he still even wants me to come."

"Hmpf. We do. If he doesn't, that's his problem. He can return to his room and sulk."

Envisioning Levka doing just that, she smiled. "Does Stasio do his hypnotism act a lot? I mean, like for money? Entertainment?"

Ruric smiled again. "He's pretty good at it. Don't you think?"

"Yeah. I've seen a show like that before, but I was sure it was faked." She looked up at Ruric. "Thanks, for making me feel better."

"I want to take all the credit, but I have to admit Levka sent me to check on you."

Taking a deep breath, she said, "Thank you."

"You're welcome. I would give you the goodnight kiss he should be giving you, but he would be pissed off. Night, Caitlin. Pleasant dreams."

"Night, Ruric, and thanks."

She shut the door, wondering if everything Ruric said was true, that Levka was really interested in her but couldn't show it, maybe until he felt better about himself. The ship rolled partially on its side, and she grabbed the doorframe to the bathroom. Terror filled every inch of her, the memory of her family's yacht rolling on its side, the way the ship lifted and fell in the rising waves, rising and crashing with a thunderous boom.

Lightning flashed outside even through the lightweight curtains. She pulled them aside, but couldn't see the water for the dark, except for the rain streaking against the glass.

Her stomach roiled when the ship lifted again and dropped

with a bang. She bit her lip, causing it to bleed. Sitting down on the mattress, she clutched at the bed frame and closed her eyes. She didn't need her lifejacket yet. She didn't need to panic. It wasn't like before. Not like before.

You'll be lower in the ship, more in the middle where you won't feel the waves as much, her foster mother had assured her. *The people who really have the ride are the ones in the bow of the ship.*

Deeper in the ship. Safer.

Caitlin changed into dry clothes, then walked back to the balcony door and peered out. If the ship went under, she and Alicia could get off by way of the balcony. Unless the ship's vacuum or whatever it was, sucked them under when it went down. She swallowed hard. The ship's engines roared, the ship rolled, rose, and crashed.

For an hour, she tried to sleep in her jeans and T-shirt on top of her pink bedspread, but the storm grew worse. "Alicia," she whispered.

"Hmmm."

"Alicia, let's get our lifejackets on."

"Hmmm."

She tugged at Alicia. "Come on. We're already dressed. Let's go up to our lifeboat deck and…" Alicia didn't stir.

Caitlin grabbed their lifejackets and said, "Alicia, sit up." Alicia sat up on the mattress.

Caitlin shoved the lifejacket at her. "Put the lifejacket on." Alicia slipped her arms into the lifejacket.

Taking a deep breath, Caitlin grabbed her hand. "Come on. We're going somewhere safe." Leading Alicia, Caitlin made her way to the deck where they'd conducted the lifeboat drills and found Levka sitting on a sofa playing a game of cards with his friends, his wheelchair nearby. All at once, she felt like an imbecile, wearing a lifejacket, holding Alicia's hand and a pole to keep her footing as the ship rolled again.

Levka looked up at her, his face nearly expressionless, though she thought she saw a hint of surprise. His friends turned around to see what caught his eye, and all of them smiled. Her skin heated with chagrin.

In a flash, Ruric rose out of his cushiony chair and took Alicia's arm. Stasio did the same for Caitlin.

"Kind of rough weather we're having, eh?" Stasio guided Caitlin to sit beside Levka.

"I couldn't sleep." Caitlin clutched her lifejacket.

Alicia passed out as soon as Ruric sat her down on a sofa nearby.

"Hot chocolate?" Levka asked.

Caitlin nodded. "That would be nice."

Arman got up to get her some.

"We couldn't sleep either," Ruric said. "After we got some dry clothes on, we came up here, but we didn't think to bring our lifejackets. Smart move."

"Paranoid is more like it," Caitlin said, but no matter what, she couldn't take it off.

The ship continued to rise and fall, and she wondered how high the seas were and how much pounding a ship this size could take before it succumbed like her parents' yacht had.

"Was the...was the storm really bothering you, too?" she asked.

Levka patted her shoulder. "Too rough. Decided to try and play a card game until the seas quieted."

"Too bad you couldn't use your hypnosis on storms, Stasio." Caitlin tried to smile, but another bone-jarring jolt to the ship, stole her thoughts. Under her breath, she added, "Too bad you couldn't convince me to go to sleep."

"You're not easily hypnotized?" Stasio discarded another card on the coffee table between them.

"No, no one can hypnotize me."

Stasio glanced at Levka, and she noticed Ruric watching her with a curious look, too.

She shrugged, realizing how bulky and uncomfortable the lifejacket was, but she still couldn't take it off.

"Do you want me to try?" Stasio asked.

"It won't work." Not with being a witch. She just couldn't give up control to another in that manner. "It's been tried on me before," she said honestly, "and it won't work."

"You don't want it to." Stasio picked up a card.

"Oh, yes I do if it can help me sleep through this."

He looked up at her, his blue eyes fathomless. "If I tell you that you are getting sleepy, you will resist me."

"I want to sleep."

He smiled. "Yes, but not here, not in the ship's lounge. You find the idea disagreeable because you would feel vulnerable, and you wouldn't go along with it. If I took you back to your cabin, you would resist me because you would fear the unknown."

Her whole body grew hot. She glanced at Levka, whose lips were smiling slightly.

Ruric had the same bemused expression.

"You would fight me, because you wouldn't entirely trust me," Stasio added.

Arman came back with her hot chocolate topped with whipped cream. "Cheers. Maybe this will help you to relax."

She took a deep breath and thanked Arman. The guys continued to play cards while she drank the hot chocolate. Not once did they flinch when the ship shook or rolled or felt as though it was going to sink. She didn't think the storm bothered them at all. She stared into her dwindling drink.

"You are getting sleepy."

She looked up at Stasio, but she didn't think he'd said anything. Not with his voice, anyhow. But he couldn't have reached her telepathically. She kept her abilities locked up, not allowing anyone in, or letting her own thoughts out. Besides, she'd only known one person who could telepathically communicate with her besides her parents, and he was also dead.

Stasio continued to play his cards without looking at her.

Levka glanced at her nearly empty mug and looked at Arman, which seemed to prompt him to ask, "Want another cocoa?"

"Sure, thanks so much, Arman. I'll return the favor tomorrow." She took another deep breath and finished off the drink. "Okay, Stasio, go ahead. Try hypnotizing me. I promise I'll try and accept it."

He continued to discard a card, then picked up another. "I don't like anyone to think I'm a fraud."

She smiled. "I know you're not a fraud. You're very good at what you do."

Looking up at her, he said, "But you would be more of a challenge than I'm willing to risk."

"I give myself into your care." She yawned. "Well, after I drink my second cup of chocolate or Arman will be disappointed."

After Arman returned with her cocoa, she began to sip it, hating that the waves weren't quieting. Several times she nearly spilled her cocoa until she drank enough of it.

Though the others continued to play cards, she could tell from their shared looks, they thought she was nuts. "Okay, tell me to go back to my room and sleep." She set her mug on the coffee table. She knew it wouldn't work, but she didn't want to look any more stupid than she already did. Maybe Alicia had some of that seasickness medicine that might make her drowsy.

"Okay?"

Stasio looked up at her. "Go back to your room and go to sleep."

Caitlin stood. The ship rolled and she instinctively grabbed Levka's shoulder. He winced and she quickly released him. "Sorry."

She shook Alicia. When she didn't respond, she said, "Alicia, come with me back to our room." Alicia stood. Caitlin took her hand and grabbed a nearby pole, then without a backward look made her way down the hall to the stairs that would lead to their deck. She knew the guys were watching them, knew they were laughing to themselves. The lounge was supposed to be empty. They shouldn't have been there. She had wanted to hide there from the storm, from the crew, from the passengers, not show her insecurities to the world.

Minutes later, she unlocked the door to their room. "Go to bed, Alicia."

When Alicia settled back on her bed, Caitlin stared at the balcony door where the rain pounded the glass. It might have been waves and not rain as high as she imagined the crests were.

Searching through Alicia's bags, she couldn't find any seasickness medicine. She grabbed her pillow, walked into the hall, and shut the door to her room. With her back to the wall, she sat and laid her head on her pillow on top of her knees. She would not get near the balcony or the ocean. Here in the narrow hall away from the prying eyes of others and the wickedness of the cruel waters, she would be safe.

Sometime later, she dreamed Levka called to her, "Invite me in, Caitlin. Invite me into your room."

She felt she'd slurred the words, "Come in," but she couldn't have sworn to it. In the hazy fog of her mind, she further fantasized he carried her to her bed, pulled off her lifejacket, and covered her with her blanket. Leaning over, he kissed her forehead with a gentle caress. "Sleep," he said, his dark eyes overpowering her. "Sleep, and join us in the morning."

She studied his semi-sweet dark chocolate eyes, amusement

and intrigue sparkling in their depths. She wanted to reach out to him, to touch his pale cheek, and thought she had. But he captured her hand and kissed it. His lips curved up, and he leaned over and kissed her mouth this time. His tongue licked her lips, then he pulled away, seemingly startled, his eyes turning to midnight. Then he withdrew into the shadows. She wanted to follow, tried to, but he repeated his words to her, "Sleep, sweet angel."

It seemed that no sooner had the vision faded from her sight, that an annoying knocking on her door woke her. She stared at the door, but the knocking had stopped. Maybe it was next door.

She glanced at Alicia, still sleeping in her lifejacket. Caitlin was still dressed, too, only her lifejacket was sitting on the desk chair. Levka couldn't have brought her into her room. He was too weak. Still not completely awake, Caitlin sighed. She must have walked into the room half asleep without even realizing it.

The knocking began again, and this time Caitlin realized it *was* her door.

Alicia bolted from her bed, stared at her lifejacket, then jerked it off. Before Caitlin could say a word, Alicia grabbed her pillow and slugged Caitlin in the head with it. "You're a moron, you know!" Alicia shrieked.

Caitlin grabbed at the pillow before Alicia slugged her with it again when the knocking at the door grew louder and more frenzied.

6

Levka shook his head at Arman as they stood outside Caitlin's stateroom door. "It sounds as though Alicia needs to be under our control again." He stared at the door. "I can't believe as much sleeping medicine as you'd put in Caitlin's two mugs of cocoa last night, she ended up trying to stay awake in the hallway."

Arman shrugged. "Stasio says she's resistant to mind and drug control. But then, you already found that out, I suspect."

Yeah, Levka had when he'd tried to get her to tell him what had upset her so much during the lifeboat drill. "You amended the records at the doctor's station so no one would know you broke in and stole some of the sleeping medicine?"

"Yep, I don't make mistakes like Stasio."

Glad Arman had finally stepped in to help their cause despite breaking rules, Levka nodded.

"I'm the best trained to serve as the doctor, and she needed to sleep," Arman said, crossing his arms, defending himself.

"She did, and I thank you for helping her." Staring at the door, Levka said, "Knock again. I'm afraid she'll miss breakfast."

Arman pounded on the door again. "Caitlin, are you up? Levka's worried you're going to miss breakfast with him."

Levka scowled at him.

Arman shrugged. "Your words, Levka. You cannot fault me for being honest."

Caitlin yanked the door open, a hairbrush in one hand, a smile stretching across her face. "I'll be just a few minutes." She looked down at Levka and gave him a lopsided grin. "Sorry, I guess I finally fell asleep sometime this morning."

He looked at the cut on her lip where she must have bitten it earlier and even now could taste her blood on his tongue, sweet and spicy. Forever, her blood would be imprinted on his mind. He bowed his head to her. His friends were right. He wanted her in the worst way, and resisting her would take all his strength. "The seas have settled down."

"Yes, thank God. Did you want to wait for us upstairs? There's no reason for us to hold you up." The bathroom door slammed behind her, and Caitlin rolled her eyes. "Sleeping Beauty will take forever."

"Do you still need to use the bathroom?" Levka asked.

"I wanted to freshen up my makeup."

"No need," he said.

Her eyes sparkled. "Well, maybe you don't mind, but I would scare the rest of the passengers into jumping ship."

The bathroom door opened, and Alicia said, "It's free."

Caitlin glanced back at her. "Oh, okay, thanks, Alicia." Turning to Levka, she said, "We'll be right up."

Leaning back in his wheelchair, Levka folded his arms. "We'll wait."

Caitlin smiled, then shut the door.

Arman cleared his throat. "I can't believe you wouldn't let us take her into her room last night."

"I felt better."

Shaking his head, Arman said, "Today, you're so much better, Levka, despite not minding me. Maybe by tonight you'll be able to ditch the wheelchair."

"That is my profoundest desire."

"What about the seating arrangements for breakfast?"

Levka looked up at him. "Ruric said he would take care of it."

"That should be interesting."

Watching the door, Levka listened to Caitlin showering and Alicia swearing about something as she banged through drawers. The hair dryer came on, turned off, more drawers slid open and closed, then a several minutes later, Caitlin opened the door to their suite. "We're ready. Sorry we took so long."

She reminded him of a sunshiny day, warm and vibrant.

Brushing Caitlin aside, Alicia headed for the stairs. *She* was more like an annoying storm cloud, chilly, and moody.

Caitlin sighed. "I'd better go after her."

Levka grabbed her hand. "Ride with me in the elevator?"

She watched Alicia's retreating backside. "Yes, of course. You were nice enough to wait for me."

"I'll see that Alicia gets to our table." Stalking after her foster sister, Arman closed the gap between them, caught up to her, and escorted her up the stairs.

Caitlin raised her dark brows. "Don't tell me he's a hypnotist, too."

"We all play around with it," Levka admitted, easing Caitlin into their world, though he had no intention of bringing her into the darkest part of their existence.

Caitlin wheeled Levka to the elevator and punched the button. "We really shouldn't do this to Alicia the whole trip."

"You deserve to have some fun, Caitlin. Your foster parents shouldn't have made you take this trip, knowing how fearful you are of the water."

"They're right. I have to get over it somehow."

He breathed a heavy sigh. "It's one thing to have you work on your fear, but sticking you out here in the middle of the ocean is overdoing it. And the other thing is they shouldn't have made you babysit your foster sister. In dealing with your anxiety, you should be able to enjoy what you like doing. Like watching the comedy show last night."

She gave him a small smile but said nothing.

The elevator arrived, but was packed with teens.

"Sorry, no room," one of the guys said and gave Levka an ugly smirk.

"Why don't you take the stairs?" Caitlin asked, her voice harsh. "Looks like all of you could do a little climbing."

Someone hit a button, and the doors began to close. But then another guy punched the button to open them. Two teens got off. Then another two.

"Losers," the first guy said.

Caitlin pushed Levka's wheelchair into the elevator and ran the wheel over the boy's foot.

He swore at her and stalked out of the elevator.

Several chuckled.

"The guy's a jerk," one of the girls said. "Good move."

When they got off the elevator, two of the girls were talking to Levka like he was their long-lost friend. Caitlin pushed his wheelchair to the dining room, quiet the whole time.

They soon reached their reserved table and found the same seating arrangements. Red-faced Dylan glared at an unresponsive Alicia. Ripping apart a roll, Lynne scowled. Levka's friends raised their brows at him as they looked at the girls that had Super Glued themselves to him.

The girls seemed disappointed to see the seats at the table already filled. "Maybe we can get together with you later, Levka," one of the girls said, then patted him on the shoulder.

"See ya around," the other girl said and squeezed his hand in parting.

He swore Caitlin humpfed under her breath. A girl had never been envious over him before, not even Cassandra, which couldn't help but inflate his ego.

"What's up?" Ruric asked, moving into his chair with a backward glance at the other girls.

"A little trouble getting room on the elevator," Caitlin said. "Doesn't anyone teach their kids to be nice?" She gave Alicia a sarcastic look.

Dylan snorted. "Looks like all you're left with is the reject. What does nice get you?"

"It's a good thing not all guys are like you," Caitlin responded, her cheeks hot with annoyance.

"Well, seems you're finally speaking your mind." Lynne buttered a roll. "I've never known you to say more than a word or two and nothing nasty since you moved in on Alicia and her parents. Wheelchair guy got you all worked up?" She gave her a snide smile.

Caitlin ignored Lynne and looked over at Alicia. "You need to eat your eggs."

"We went ahead and ordered already," Stasio said. "Alicia told us what you like for breakfast."

Caitlin gave a short laugh. "I didn't think she knew."

Stasio sipped his coffee, then set his cup down. "Cinnamon roll, iced tea, and one egg-over easy."

The waitstaff brought Caitlin's breakfast, and she smiled. "Thanks so much." She glanced at Levka's empty place setting. "What do you like to eat?"

Everyone watched him, and Levka unfolded his napkin on his lap. "Steak, rare."

Lynne wrinkled her nose. "For breakfast?"

"And eggs, runny."

Caitlin grinned. "Like mine."

The Irish comedian's blood the night before had satisfied Levka, and he hadn't needed any other nourishment this soon, but the look of worry on Caitlin's face convinced him to share a meal. He knew his friends would rib him about it later. But he worried that with the other mortals taking notice, he had to make a good show of it. None of his friends were eating anything, and he assumed they'd found early morning snacks to satisfy themselves. They all drank cups of coffee, though, to fit in.

"That was some storm last night," Lynne said. "But now that the seas are calm, I'm going swimming right after breakfast. What about you, Alicia?"

"She's swimming." Dylan gave Stasio a look like he'd better not contradict him this time.

Alicia looked at Stasio as if she were waiting for him to tell her what to do.

Caitlin cut into her egg. "It's all right if she wants to go swimming."

Dylan glared at her. "Like *you* have any say in it."

She smiled at him and the look was pure pixie-like, mischievous and full of the devil.

"Are you going to watch Alicia swim?" Levka asked, figuring she would still take her babysitting job to heart.

"Sure." She sounded resigned to it.

"Do you mind some company? I would want to sit in the deck's shade. I burn easily in the full sun. Fair skin."

She nodded. "Me, too. That would be nice. I would like that."

Dylan said something under his breath, then tugged at Alicia. "You finished with your breakfast? Let's go."

"She'll go when I do." Caitlin said.

He turned and glowered at her.

"Well," Lynne said, "this is a first. I've never seen Caitlin decide things for you, Alicia. Hope you snap out of it soon. Come on, Dylan." She tossed her napkin at the table and it missed it and fell on the floor. "We'll get ready and meet Alicia later."

When they left, Caitlin said to Stasio, "Alicia's not a very nice person, but I think maybe we ought to let her be herself for a while. Don't you?"

Stasio's blue eyes studied her. "If it pleases you."

"No, but she's too weird like this."

Stasio bowed his head. "Finish your breakfast, and she'll be back to her own spiteful self."

Caitlin ate the last bite of her cinnamon roll and licked her fingers. "Okay, turn her loose."

Alicia slammed her fork on the table and jumped up from her seat. "I heard you call me spiteful, you, you, jerk," she said to Stasio.

Caitlin hurried to get out of her seat to keep up with her foster sister.

"As for you, Caitlin, what were you doing dragging me out of my bed last night to sit in the lounge in a lifejacket? Were you nuts?"

Caitlin glanced back at Stasio. He smiled and shrugged.

"You should have wiped Alicia's mind," Levka communicated to Stasio.

"Those under hypnosis remember what has gone on, though using our vampiric charm is not quite the same since we can convince people to do what they would not normally do. But if Caitlin knew that under hypnosis people remember what happens to them, I didn't want her wondering why Alicia had lost her memory. Caitlin might have worried."

Ruric shook his head. "Her foster sister is a terror."

"Take me down to the pool," Levka said. "I want the best seats out of the sun and with a view of the pool so she can keep an eye on her foster sister, but not too close that it will bother Caitlin."

"Got it," Ruric said. "I'll oust a few people right now."

Arman wheeled Levka to the elevator, and they heard Alicia down the stairs, her voice high pitched and whining. "I don't know how you ever talked me into going to see that comedy show. Stupid thing wasn't even funny. And from now on you won't be making my decisions for me about swimming or anything else. What will Dylan think?"

Stasio shook his head. "I liked her better when she didn't speak."

Arman chuckled. "Caitlin may decide she wants her back the way she was."

"There's something wrong with the ship," Levka said.

His friends turned their full attention to him.

"I heard one of the crew speaking to another about it this morning when Caitlin and I were waiting for the elevator. They were out of sight, but they were speaking Greek. Something about a stabilizer being out. Because the storm was so bad last night, they had to deter from our original course. When they put into our first port, they'll have the stabilizer repaired. But there's something else."

"What?" Arman asked as they loaded into the elevator.

Levka told them privately, *"I'm not sure. There's some concern about the passenger list. I wonder if they've found out we've moved some of the passengers together so we can have the stateroom big enough for the four of us. Or it may be that the Dallas league is having the ship's passenger manifest looked into. It may be nothing related to us, but I don't know for certain."*

In an exasperated manner, Arman threw his hands up in the air. *"I should have figured Ruric couldn't pull this off."*

"No sense in panicking yet," Stasio said. *"It reminds me of the*

time we got in the middle of those blokes storming the Bastille. We got out of that okay. We'll figure out something here, too."

Shaking his head, Arman wheeled Levka onto the pool deck.

Ruric rocked back and forth in a cozy covered swing for two, situated underneath the deck to ensure the sun never hit them. Swimmers filled the pool, and all of the lounge chairs were either occupied, or someone had spread towels over them, reserving them for future use.

Ruric stood and motioned to the chair. "My prince."

"You could have saved us a couple of lounge chairs. What if Caitlin had wanted to stretch out?"

"Your gratitude is underwhelming, Levka. You do realize the swings are the most sought after resting place? There's only ten on the whole ship, and some try to hang on to them day and night, leaving their belongings on them while they eat or sleep. Really quite rude."

"So you just moved their belongings to a chair?" Levka asked.

Ruric smiled.

"Ruric?"

"The couple charted a starship for unknown territories, beamed right up in the transporter, and whoosh, they were gone."

Levka glanced at a man and a woman lying on a towel in the hot sun a few feet away.

"Is that them?"

"Yeah, they probably didn't get enough sleep last night because of the storm."

"They'll get sunburned."

"They've been hogging this same swinging chair since the cruise began. It's time they gave it up to someone more worthy." Ruric bowed his head.

"Wake them and make them move to the shade."

Ruric took a deep breath. "They weren't cooperative before."

"I'll help," Stasio said. "You take the guy. I'll deal with the woman."

They walked over to the man and woman while Arman helped Levka to the swing. But as soon as he sat down, one of the girls who had spoken to him on the elevator headed in his direction. No way did he want anyone but Caitlin to sit with him. Then he spied them. Caitlin and Alicia were almost to the pool, though Caitlin was giving it a wide berth as she looked for him.

Arman waved at her and hurried to intercept the other teen before she took Caitlin's seat.

"Wow," Caitlin said, standing before Levka in short shorts and a T-shirt. "How did you ever manage to get one of these to sit in? They're always full." She glanced at Stasio and Ruric who were talking to a man and woman. "Don't tell me. They made them move."

Levka couldn't help but smile. "They wanted only the best for us."

She took a seat next to him. "I noticed everything else was reserved or being used." She sighed. "It must be nice to have such really good friends."

"You don't? It seems to me you would have lots."

She rubbed her arms as he rocked the swing gently. "I used to. When I had to...to move, I lost the friends I had. It's not the same where I live now. They are all really rich doctor's and lawyer's kids. Everyone has their own cliques. No one's interested in the new kid in town."

"Your foster father works as...?"

"A heart surgeon. Even Mildred is a pediatric nurse. They're loaded."

"And your parents?"

She stared across the deck. "My parents and sister drowned last spring break." Her words sounded hollow.

"Drowned?" he prompted.

Facing him, she said, "I...I don't want to talk about it."

She wrung her hands in her lap, and he took her hand and held it. "I know how that feels." Her eyes filled with tears, as she looked at him.

"My father was killed in the war," he said, purposefully leaving out the era or location, "and my mother and sister died, too. I was only six when an uncle took me in."

"I'm so sorry."

"He died later." Levka took a deep breath. "When I turned eighteen, I was on my own." He motioned to his friends. "All of us were. We became best of friends, watched out for each other, stuck together through all the good times and bad."

"You don't go to school?"

How could he tell her he'd been to schools for hundreds of years just to find out what other teens his age were studying, but that he'd already lived through so many of the events they were learning as *history*?

"Sure, we go to school," he said.

"But what about money? How do you live?"

"We all have inheritances, work side jobs, and are careful how we spend our money." He didn't want to tell her most of their money came down through the ages, that they were all Welsh princes with Russian family roots before this. No matter how enlightened she might be, she would never believe it.

She motioned to the ship. "But you're spending a small fortune on a cruise."

"Sometimes, you have to spend a little money and enjoy life." Although they hadn't had to spend a dime on it, just moved some rich kids out of their suite whose parents had paid for it.

Leaning against the seat, she seemed to relax. "I've never known anyone quite like you and your friends. I used to have a couple of close girlfriends, but after..."

When she didn't say anything further, Levka wrapped his

arm around her shoulder and pulled her close. "After what, Caitlin?" He was the dark prince who should have ensnared her with his powers, yet she was the one who drew him in, captured him with her impish, but beguiling smiles, her fragility, her strength.

She nestled her head against his shoulder and for the first time, he felt no pain in his chest.

When she didn't speak any further, he listened to her breathing, shallower, her heart rate slowed. She'd fallen asleep in his arms. Already, he felt himself slipping into the dark bottomless pit like he had when he'd met Cassandra. Like before, he couldn't seem to disentangle himself from Caitlin. Damn his friends for encouraging their relationship. Nothing but tragedy could ever come of it.

He wanted to run away as far as he could get from her, flee to the other side of the world, never see her bright blue eyes or her sunshiny, Florida smile again. She snuggled closer to him, and he tightened his hold, never wanting to let go.

Glancing at the pool, he saw Dylan and Alicia speaking. They looked in his and Caitlin's direction. They both grabbed their towels and headed inside.

Torn between waking Caitlin so she could continue to act as her foster sister's chaperone, or keeping her in his embrace, he saw a ship's crewmember speaking to Ruric, which brought the earlier worry to mind. Had discrepancies in the passenger manifest been discovered?

7

Stasio joined Levka at the swing and smiled. "Like old times, eh?"

"You know this is folly." Yet Levka couldn't fight the feeling Caitlin filled some need, an emptiness he'd felt for too long. With her snuggled against his chest, he felt whole again.

"*We have known you for so long, Levka. We know she's the one for you.*"

Levka ignored Arman's comment and motioned with his head toward Ruric, still speaking to one of the ship's crew. "*Do you know what's going on? Has it to do with irregularities in the ship's manifest?*"

"*I have no idea. Ruric is too busy conversing with the crew member to let us know privately. Did you see Caitlin's foster sister and Dylan slip away from the pool and go inside?*"

What was Levka to say? No, he didn't see them leave because he was too busy enjoying his time with Caitlin? Yes, he saw them slip away, but he was too busy taking pleasure in Caitlin's company and didn't want to let her go?

"I didn't wish to disturb her after the bad night she had and because we woke her so early."

Stasio gave him one of his all-knowing looks. "*Did you want me to check on them?*"

"*No. If Alicia wants to mess up her life, she'll do it no matter what Caitlin's foster parents said. Caitlin isn't responsible for her foster sister's actions.*"

Ruric finished his conversation with the crewman, then walked under the archway and headed toward Levka and Stasio. He masked his expression so well that Levka hadn't a clue what he was thinking. In fact, all of them could master that ability which made it impossible for any of them to know who had the best hand of cards during one of their games. Good news? Indifferent? Bad?

Ruric soon joined him, glanced at Caitlin sleeping in Levka's arms, and smiled. Tying his wild red hair into a tail, he scoffed at the wind. "The constant breeze on this ship makes me wish I'd cut my hair short. In a spaceship, we would have no annoying wind under perfectly controlled conditions that the most illustrious scientists could create."

"I remember a time when we were becalmed on a schooner and prayed for a good stiff wind. Now, we are on a ship that has no need of wind, and you're fussing." Stasio glanced up at the ship's Dutch flag, whipped around by the turbulent air.

Ruric smiled. "Everything's relative. Back then, we were running out of food and water. And, as I recall, the captain was trying to outmaneuver Jean Lafitte, the gentleman pirate."

"Gentleman, right," Stasio said. "He was as violent and bloodthirsty as all the rest."

"But eloquent in his speech," Ruric said, bowing.

"And the young women liked him."

"But not the men who he stole from," Arman argued.

"What news have you?" Levka asked, interrupting the history lesson.

Again, Ruric made a non-too subtle observation of Caitlin in

Levka's arms. *"I have no worry now that you have found the one for you. 'Tis good when it has been so long."*

Grinding his teeth, Levka said, "Enough!"

Caitlin stirred. Levka tightened his hold on her. His friends smiled.

"What news from the ship's crew?" Levka asked privately again, attempting to mask his annoyance.

"Good news. We dine with the ship's captain this evening."

Levka stared at him. "You cannot be serious."

"He was most generous. Though it will be nothing like dining with the captain of a star cruiser in deep space." Ruric switched to telepathic communication. *"Bad news is the ship's crew is verifying the passenger list, room by room. Initially, I had convinced the teens, now buddying up together with others, that that's the way their parents had arranged it. Since then, others on the cruise who knew it was not so, began asking questions. Worse, two of the guys do not get along. The other teens know this as well and are insisting the two would never have shared rooms with the kids from our suite. Someone—maybe one of the teens affected—contacted a parent. Now, the crew is trying to determine how we ended up with the larger stateroom and the other boys ended up sharing rooms with someone else from their high school."*

"And you said?"

"It's easy for me to handle one crewmember at a time. It's the unraveling of the fragile web of lies we have woven that is causing problems. Too many people to control. Oh, and by the way, Dylan is one of the guys who gave up his room to us." Ruric gave a sardonic smile.

"So, he figured he could get Alicia to his room privately, but now he's got a roommate?" Levka asked.

"Yep. And his roommate is a guy who could snore a wine cork off its bottle, according to talk I overheard. Not only that, but the guy's sneakers smell like something that had been dead for several days."

"I wouldn't wish Dylan a better roommate," Levka said. "So what about the room arrangements?"

"They're leaving them the way it is for now. Unless someone discovers we hadn't paid for the room."

"How did you manage to get us into the room?"

Ruric wiggled his fingers. *"Computers. I tapped into their billing and room reservations. The only thing I would like better is if I could just tell the computers verbally what to do and didn't have to waste my time typing in all the commands. 'Computer, report on status of room reservation.' Within seconds the computer would respond favorably. 'Prince Ruric, your room is now available.' Typing is not my forte."*

The others groaned.

"Ruric, just tell us what is important," Levka said.

"I overheard a conversation a deck above us earlier this morning that concerned me. A couple of guys were talking of pulling a prank on other passengers. They didn't say what or who they wished to cause trouble for, but I wanted to make you aware of it."

"Would you recognize them if you heard them speaking again?"

Ruric bowed his head, his green eyes ominous. "If I *see* who they are, I will make them think twice about doing anything aboard ship that is not...proper."

NOT WANTING TO EAVESDROP, Caitlin stirred against Levka's chest to let him and his friends know she was awake. But then she sat up abruptly, worried she might hurt Levka's wound. "I'm so sorry, Levka. You should have pushed me away."

His brown eyes darkened. "My chest no longer hurts. I'm

sure by tonight, maybe sooner, I'll be able to walk and will no longer have to use the wheelchair."

"Are you sure?" She couldn't believe he would truly recover that quickly when he'd been so weak earlier.

"I'm pretty sure."

"Maybe you can lend him a shoulder if he gets dizzy." Ruric smiled.

"Ha! Like I helped poor Levka the last time. I'm so sorry about that." She felt as if she'd been lying in the sun as hot as her skin grew just thinking about him sitting on the deck next to his wheelchair when he'd fallen.

She suddenly realized she hadn't been watching her foster sister and jerked her head around to look at the pool. Staring at the pool, then at the bodies soaking up the sun's rays nearby, she immediately saw both Alicia and Dylan were gone. "I've got to go."

"But—" Levka didn't get to say anything more, or if he did, she didn't hear him as fast as she proceeded in the direction of the stairs to her deck.

She would prove to Mildred and Thomas their faith in her was justified. But what nagged at her most were bits and pieces of the conversation Levka and his friends had been sharing. There was some problem with the passenger manifest. Some trouble with Dylan having a roommate when he shouldn't have. Some reason Levka and his friends ended up with the stateroom instead.

She'd just been waking from a warm, lazy sleep, snuggled next to a Phat guy, dark-haired and eyed, and totally mysterious and intriguing. His large hand had caressed her arm in a soothing, tender way. He'd only stopped to squeeze her more tightly against his warm, hard body when she'd stirred the first time.

But something had awakened her fully this time. A kid's shrill cry in the pool that seemed miles away. The splashing of water, too? Something had brought her out of her comfortable nap, and in her groggy state, she'd heard their strange conversation—words spoken, but not. Concerns shared, but hidden. Someone was planning on pulling a prank on passengers. But who and on whom?

Ruric was the one who had heard the *someone* talking. Ruric would take care of whoever it was.

She hurried down the stairs. Why was Levka reluctant to let her go? Worried what she would find? What *would* she find? Alicia fooling around with Dylan?

Clenching her teeth, Caitlin hurried inside, then down the stairs to her deck and to Dylan's room. Her stomach tumbled a million times before she reached his door. Then she remembered what Ruric had said—but hadn't exactly said. Dylan was sharing a room with another boy. She pressed her ear to his door and listened. No sounds. If they were in there, wouldn't they be talking or something?

She looked in the direction of her room. If they were in *her* room...

Stalking down the carpeted floor, Caitlin shortened the distance to her room. Her hands shaking, she pulled her key out of her pocket and jammed it into the lock.

When Caitlin stepped into the room, she found the beds made and the sunlight streaming in through the open window. The shower was running in the bathroom. Caitlin put her ear to the door and heard giggling, then Dylan's voice.

Caitlin's heart sank. If Alicia was going to do it with Dylan fine, but *not* in their suite. She banged on the door. "Alicia, tell Dylan to get his butt out of there." The shower shut off and whispered voices followed.

Her blood heating, Caitlin paced across the suite. How could her foster parents have expected her to chaperone the princess?

The bathroom door jerked open, then Dylan stormed out of

the steamed-up room, slamming the closed door behind him. All he wore were shorts. His hair, chest, and arms were dripping wet, his eyes as hard and cold as icicles. He stalked toward Caitlin, and she stood her ground, though her heart rate increased tenfold, while he looked bent on murdering her.

Had she interrupted their fun? *Good.*

She only wished she could use her abilities now and put him in his place herself.

He grabbed her arm and jerked her toward the balcony. She couldn't shake loose of the huskily-built creep no matter how hard she tried. Grabbing the door, he yanked it open and tossed her onto the narrow patio that accommodated two plastic chairs and a table.

She cried out, but her scream was caught by the breeze and drowned out by the ship splashing through the ocean, its engines thrumming at a dull roar. She hadn't ventured out here before, not this close to the water. A cold sweat erupted on her skin.

For a moment, Dylan glared at her, murder in his eyes. Then he smiled the most satanic look. "You didn't die the last time you were on a boat. But you know, if you fall from this height, you wouldn't have to worry about floundering in the water with the sharks. The fall would kill you."

She tried to look tough, unafraid, but her knees shook.

He took a step toward her. Grabbing up one of the patio chairs, she used it as a shield. Just as quickly, he tore it from her grasp and threw it aside. She bumped into the balcony's wall, and her heart skipped a beat. Seizing her wrist, Dylan jerked her to the railing.

Twisting, she tried to pull free and screamed again. But he secured her by the waist, lifted her, and slammed her stomach against the railing.

"Look good, Caitlin," he snarled, his voice as black as the

water several stories below them, where white foam capped the miniature waves like whipped cream. "You tell anyone I was with Alicia and you'll go missing." He shoved her head down, forcing her to see her family's watery grave. Threatening to push her over the top, his body wedged against hers so she couldn't kick him, couldn't move. "A poor mixed up girl who missed her mommy and daddy and little sister so much, she jumped. Didn't you tell the doctor that you wanted to die?"

"Alicia." How did she know? Unless…unless Caitlin's psychiatrist had told her foster parents and Alicia weaseled it out of them. But wasn't that privileged information?

"You wished you'd died with your family? Here's your chance."

The railing dug into Caitlin's stomach. She gripped the rod with all her strength. *"Please, dear God, don't let him push me over."*

"You won't tell anyone. Understand?"

The ship carved through the waves, sending the water flying in a fishy spray.

"Understand?"

She would not be cowed. She would not!

He released her, and she stumbled back to the deck, her arms and legs shaking as she collapsed on the patio. Stalking off, he slammed the patio door shut. She couldn't move, couldn't stand, couldn't cry, just sat on the deck, feeling numb all over.

Alicia stared at her through the glass, then said something to Dylan. He shook his head, brushed her aside, and left. Alicia opened the patio door. "Are you all right, Caitlin?" This time there was no sarcastic edge to her voice.

Alicia's hair was wet, but she was fully dressed, a bright red hickey on her throat. It clashed with her peach shirt. Odd how something like that would catch Caitlin's eye, when the ocean was so close by. When the black water threatened to swallow her whole. Just a few inches farther over the railing and Dylan could have thrown her overboard. Would the fall have killed her?

Divers off cliffs in Acapulco, Mexico, could dive over a hundred-and-thirty feet, couldn't they? And survive?

She was a good swimmer. She could swim for a while. Without a life jacket? Forever in the black waters? Until the sharks came to feed.

"Caitlin." Alicia touched her shoulder. "You're scaring me. Why don't you come inside?"

Why? Caitlin had finally gotten this close to the ocean. Why ruin a good thing? If she returned to the room, maybe she would never be able to get this close again.

"All right. If you don't want to come in right now, just stay out here. Uhm, you come in when you want." Alicia walked inside and shut the door, but she stood staring out the glass at Caitlin.

Caitlin wanted to stand, to look over the railing, to see the ocean and not be afraid, but she sat frozen to the patio unable to move an inch in any direction.

⁓

Swearing he heard Caitlin's silent plea for help, Levka rubbed his temple and concentrated. Determined not to return to the wheelchair, he stiffly walked alongside Ruric, attempting to help him locate whoever intended to pull a prank on a passenger or passengers. But he couldn't help worrying about Caitlin.

Finally, Ruric grabbed his shoulder. "I'm listening for the teens who were planning some mischief. What are you listening for?"

Levka stood taller. "We have the same mission in mind. Arman and Stasio, as well, as they eavesdrop on people's conversations."

Ruric began walking again. "It isn't so, Levka. You're trying to hear Caitlin's thoughts. Unless you wish to reveal who and what we are, I suggest you don't tell her we can converse telepathically."

"I fear she may already know this on some level."

Stopping, Ruric faced him. "How?"

"Stasio tested her last night. Told her telepathically that she was getting sleepy, though I would not have suggested it. But you know how he is."

"Yes, out of control."

"Caitlin looked in Stasio's direction, but seemed confused. I think she didn't believe others could have her ability. She probably has met only maybe one or two in her lifetime, if that."

"We shouldn't pursue this. Unless you're willing to make her yours." Ruric raised his brows and smiled.

"I worry about her. That's all."

Ruric turned down a connecting hall. "You kissed her last night."

Levka said nothing, realizing no matter what he said, Ruric would know the truth.

Ruric looked over at him. "You did not drink her blood." Glowering at Ruric, Levka did not respond.

Disbelief filled Ruric's face. "Did you?"

Quickening his pace, Levka scowled. "No, I did not. Not in the way you mean."

"What other way is there?"

Levka wouldn't say.

Forcing him to stop, Ruric stepped in front of him. "What other way?"

Levka narrowed his eyes, but Ruric wouldn't back off. "She'd bitten her lip earlier, and the blood had dried." He pushed Ruric aside and continued down the hall.

Ruric didn't follow at first, then he ran to catch up. "You tasted her blood. She is in your system forever."

"How can we discover the pranksters if you're going to question me to death?" For several minutes, they walked in silence, then Levka said, "Now *you* are not listening for the prankster's conversation."

"If you make her yours—"

"I have no intention of doing so."

"If you do, Levka, you'll have to get the league's approval. You know how they are about turning a mortal."

"I have no intention of doing that."

"You have already kissed her *and* tasted her blood. We never get emotionally involved with someone we drink from, unless we want to turn that individual, to make them our lifemate. Despite denying it to me and to yourself, you have already claimed her. But you must get the league's permission before you make her yours all the way. You cannot break the rule. Those who go against it, earn the death penalty, along with the one they have chosen. That's one rule we just cannot break."

Levka stopped in his footsteps. "You're not listening, Ruric! I didn't drink from her, exactly. And I will not—"

Ruric held up his hand for silence, and they both listened.

Directly above them on the next deck, they heard Alicia's tearful voice, "I'm...I'm worried about Caitlin. She...she's acting like she did before...when she first came to live with my parents and me. Can...can one of you guys talk to her?"

8

Levka turned so quickly, only another vampire could see his action.

Ruric grabbed his arm and warned him, "We *walk* there like the mortals would do."

Glowering at him, Levka stalked off in the direction of Caitlin's stateroom.

"What if she isn't there? Shouldn't we speak to Alicia first? Find out what's going on?" Ruric asked.

Levka telepathically communicated to Arman, *"Where's Caitlin?"*

"Her stateroom. We're on our way there now," Arman responded.

"What's happened?" Levka asked.

"Alicia said that Caitlin's on the balcony but too scared to leave it now."

"We're nearly to her room. Don't bring Alicia."

"But, Levka—"

"Don't bring her, Arman."

Ruric shook his head. "How can you deny you want Caitlin? It's written all over your face, in your actions, your thoughts."

Ignoring his friend, Levka knocked on Caitlin's door.

"Wait until Arman brings Alicia's key," Ruric said.

"Caitlin, open your door for me."

Ruric let out his breath. "You're getting deeper in this with no way out."

"Caitlin." When she didn't respond, Levka swore under his breath. "Forget it."

"Wait!" Ruric said, but Levka vanished and reappeared inside the stateroom.

Seeing the balcony door open, Levka moved with vampiric speed and reached the narrow patio in a fraction of a second. Caitlin was sitting cross-legged on the deck, her arms hugging her body. One chair sat half on the table and half on the other chair. He didn't think the wind had caused it.

He was crouching before Caitlin and resting his hands on her shoulders when Ruric said, *"Invite me in, Levka!"*

Levka communicated privately to Caitlin, *"It is me, Levka. Look into my eyes."*

When she didn't respond, he lifted her chin. *"Caitlin, look at me. You tried to be my friend when I didn't wish one. Let me be your friend and help you now."*

Her eyes lost their faraway look and rested on his gaze. "I...I —" Her eyes implored him to help her. "I can't get up."

"I'll assist you, Caitlin. Lean on me. It's okay to be afraid. Just use my strength now, and you'll overcome your fear."

He helped her to stand, her eyes never leaving his gaze, but when he took her wrists, her mouth dropped open, and she winced. Fighting the compulsion to look down, to see what was wrong, he kept his eyes focused on hers, willing her to come with him, to feel safe with him. He shifted his hands to her waist. "Come with me, and we'll play some cards?" He was not sure how else to handle someone he had so little control over.

She didn't say anything, just inched her way back into the stateroom with his guidance.

A key twisted in the lock. Then the door to the room opened. Arman called out from the hallway, "Invite us in, Levka!"

"We're coming to you." Levka sensed his friends' annoyance with him, but they had no need to enter her room.

Once he'd shut the balcony door, he asked, "Why were you on the patio, Caitlin?"

Her eyes watered, but she didn't answer him.

"Were you trying to force yourself to face your fear of the water?"

She broke eye contact with him, and instantly his blood chilled. It reminded him of Cassandra. When she didn't want to reveal her darkest secrets, she would break the connection between them. He glanced down at Caitlin's wrists. Finger marks had bruised her slender wrist. Looking back at the balcony and the mess that the furniture was in, he realized Caitlin must have struggled with someone.

"Caitlin, tell me what happened to you on the balcony." He tried to keep his voice calm, but he was losing the battle.

When she wouldn't speak, he sat her down on one of the beds. *"Arman, Ruric, Stasio, you may come in."*

"About time," Ruric grumbled.

"Do I always have to be last?" Stasio asked.

"He always goes in alphabetical order," Arman said in a teasing manner.

"Arman, find Alicia and question her about Caitlin being on the balcony." Levka pointed to her bruised wrist. "She didn't go to the balcony on her own, and she won't tell me what happened."

Arman's face darkened. *"At once, Levka."*

"Gently."

Arman bowed his head, but Levka didn't believe he was in the mood to be gentle.

Despite Arman always wanting to stay out of mortals' affairs, it appeared Caitlin had gotten under his skin, too. She was like a siren of the sea, calling to Levka and his friends, and if they weren't careful, she would pull them all under.

"What can I—?" Stasio started to ask.

"Stay with her. Come with me, Ruric." Levka led him onto the balcony.

"What are we looking for, Levka?"

"The fishy sea breeze is so strong it nearly masks any other smell. But I can still catch a subtle whiff of Caitlin's jasmine perfume if I concentrate hard enough."

"Yes, I smell it."

"Is there any other scent that you can make out?" Levka walked toward the chair stacked on the other furniture.

"Like?"

"Someone's cologne?"

"You don't think Alicia made Caitlin come out here?"

Levka took a deep breath and analyzed the air. "Her flowery perfume, different, more rose like, is here, too. Probably because Alicia tried to get Caitlin to return to their stateroom."

"I smell nothing else but the pungent fishy sea breeze. You suspect Dylan was here?"

"I smelled his cologne in the stateroom, the same as when he sat at our table."

"Yes," Ruric said. "The odor is as obnoxious as him."

Levka and Ruric returned to the room, rejoining Caitlin and Stasio. "Would you like to play a game of cards with us?" Levka asked her again.

Her eyes gazed into his. They were full of questions for which he didn't want to answer, not now, not in front of his friends.

"You...you talked to me like this."

He took a deep breath. "*And you responded in the same manner.*"

She stared at him, and he could tell she didn't trust her instinct to know it was really so.

"Caitlin, do you want to go to one of the lounges and get a soda? We could listen to a band, or play cards, or something."

"You...you're telepathic."

He looked at his friends. They both gave him their best card faces, no emotion whatsoever.

Though he knew behind those masks they felt plenty.

"*Yes, Caitlin, I am.*"

She looked at Stasio. "*And him?*" Stasio bowed his head.

"*And Ruric?*"

Ruric reacted in the same polite manner.

"*Is...is that how you became friends?*"

No. But Levka couldn't tell her that. How could he break the news that they had been friends long before this and only when the onset of the bloody plague infected them, did they gain their telepathic abilities? "It's one of the things that keeps us together," he said, skirting around the truth.

She took a deep breath. "I knew you were different. From the first time I saw you, I knew it."

"Are you disappointed?"

She reached for his hand and when he offered it, she used his strength to pull herself up from the bed. Her mouth suddenly gaped. "You're...you're walking."

"I'm almost as good as new." Which was mostly the truth. His rib wasn't quite healed, but everything else felt back to normal.

"I'm so glad." Her words sounded as if the sentiments came from the heart.

"He's too ornery for any injury to keep him down," Ruric joked, trying to pull Levka out of the quicksand.

She gave half a smile, but didn't contradict Ruric.

Levka steered her to the door, wishing she would say his meeting her was the best thing that could have ever happened. Yet, the way he treated her at first wasn't exactly Texas friendly.

"I've only known one other who could talk to me like this," she suddenly said.

Levka's heartbeat quickened. "Who was he?" He couldn't quash the annoyance he felt that he had not been the first. And why he assumed it was a guy, he couldn't fathom.

"He had a name like yours. Russian sounding. He said it was Vlad."

Russian. A vampire? If it was so, knowing another vampire had targeted her and could add to their growing troubles, Levka couldn't look at his friends. "Are you still in touch with him?"

"After the accident, I didn't see him again. But then, I was pretty much out of it for several months. He might have seen me, and I never knew it. Then he gave up on me."

Guardedly relieved, Levka wrapped his arm around her shoulders and guided her into the elevator. "Let's go to one of the lounges."

"Can you help me overcome my fear of water?"

"I can try."

She slipped her arm around his waist, making him realize he was getting in way too deep. "Then take me to one of the lounges with a view of the ocean."

Ruric shook his head. "*Deeper and deeper into the darkest space we go without a single star to light our way,*" he said for Stasio and Levka's benefit.

Levka gave Ruric a scathing glance. "*If the vampire left her to fend for herself in her darkest hour, he has no claim to her.*"

Ruric opened the door to the lounge. "*Didn't I tell you Levka had staked his claim to her for his own?*"

"*Do not use the stake word, but yes, we knew that from the beginning when she reached her hand out to the beast, she had captured his heart,*" Stasio said.

"*I have not claimed her as you put it,*" Levka argued privately with them. "*I will not go there.*"

They both smiled at him, the look they gave him, saying they knew him better.

When Levka escorted Caitlin into the Blue Lounge near the bow of the ship with an ocean view, Arman communicated to them from somewhere else on the ship, "*I haven't located Alicia yet. Is Caitlin all right?*"

"*Under Levka's spell, and he is totally under hers, if you call that all right,*" Ruric answered, his tone amused.

"*Where are you?*"

"*The Blue Lounge, bow of the ship,*" Levka responded.

"*I'll...*"

When Arman didn't finish his telepathic message, Levka asked, "*Arman?*"

"*I'll join you in a few minutes.*"

Levka attempted to seat Caitlin with her back to the ocean in the blue cushiony lounge chairs. Instead, she shifted around so she could see the water.

"Are you going to be all right, Caitlin?" Levka touched her arm above the bruises.

"I used to try and communicate with people telepathically all the time," she said, ignoring his concern and focusing on the waves. "It was just this strange overwhelming desire. I mean, at first, I didn't know that's what it was. Just this compulsion to speak to someone without saying the words. Sometimes, I thought I was a little crazy. I told a girlfriend once. She thought I was nuts. She told her parents, and they wouldn't let her play with me anymore."

Arman walked into the lounge. "*I found Alicia with Dylan and a bunch of his friends, Levka. I couldn't talk to her.*"

"*Thanks, Arman. Get us some drinks, will you?*" Levka asked.

With her back to Arman, Caitlin didn't see him and continued with her story. "After my girlfriend didn't have anything more to do with me, I tried not to reach people telepathically."

Arman brought a tray of sodas to the coffee table, interrupting her.

"I promised I would get your drink the next time," Caitlin said.

He smiled. "A gentleman buys the lady her drinks, not the other way around."

"That's the past," Ruric said. "In the future..."

Levka and Stasio gave him a sharp look.

Ruric smiled. "I'm outvoted. A gentleman always buys the lady's drinks."

Caitlin laughed.

Glad to hear her cheerfulness, some of the tension eased out of Levka's taut muscles. "You were saying about how you knew no one could speak to your mind." He had to know everything he could about Vlad, but he didn't want to come out and say so. What if she thought he was jealous? He wasn't. Well, he was, but he was more concerned the vampire might feel he had an earlier claim to her.

"Yes, well, I couldn't control the urge. I don't know how to describe it. It's like I was a Martian on Earth seeking one of my kind who understood what I was feeling. Anyway, I was at an ice cream shop with some girlfriends, and this guy said, 'Your eyes are like emeralds sparkling in the fluorescent lights. And your full glossy lips look kissable.' But he didn't say this out loud. It was as if his thoughts were projected into my brain." Caitlin took a sip of her drink.

Though Levka normally thought himself patient, he tapped his fingers on the arm of the lounge chair. Ruric cocked a red brow at him.

"Well, you might imagine, it came as quite a shock. When I looked around the ice cream shop to see who had said that, I caught his black eyes watching me. At first, he just stared at me, like he couldn't believe I might have heard him. Then he gave me an odd kind of smile."

Levka fisted his hands. Apparently, Caitlin had drawn this Vlad under her spell just like she'd done with Levka. "And?"

"He became my first boyfriend."

Levka glanced at his friends, knowing what they all suspected, that Vlad would have wanted her, too. Had he tried to get permission with the Orlando league and failed?

"But after the accident," she continued, "I figured he was like my other friends. He didn't want to have anything to do with me as messed up as I was. So, when I got better, and he never tried to get in touch with me, I killed him off." She gave kind of a sad smile. "You know, a friend isn't a friend who won't stick by someone even through their darkest hour. He's dead to me."

"You have us now," Levka said, knowing he was headed down the path of no return.

She gazed at him for several seconds. "*I think you would be a friend always, no matter the circumstances.*"

He would not be her friend, if he took her where his dark heart urged him to take her. He reached out and squeezed her hand.

"*You're different from Vlad. Kind of the same, mysterious, totally intriguing, but there's something different about you. I can't put my finger on it.*" She looked out at the ocean, but he sensed she really wasn't seeing it.

Memories of Vlad? "How long did you know him?" He had to ask, had to know. If they'd been together long...

Levka couldn't imagine anyone wanting her for very long and having the restraint not to make her his.

"A couple of months, but he wasn't around all of the time. He kept saying he had to take care of business. When he returned, he'd seem distant at first, then he'd become his cheerful self. A couple of times guys joined us who called themselves friends of his, but he didn't seem pleased at all. I thought he even acted jealous. But I sensed there was something darker going on. Anyway," she shrugged, "it's all in the past."

Levka hoped it was, because he and his friends didn't need any other complications in their lives right now. She lifted the soda to her lips, and he again noted the bruises.

His blood heated with irritation. Unable to curb how dark his words sounded, he demanded, "What made you go onto the balcony, Caitlin?"

9

Caitlin sensed Levka's concern. He tried to keep his voice calm and unruffled though his tone was slightly hard, but his eyes told a different story, darkening from lighter chocolate to black diamonds. He was not as unconcerned as he tried to show.

Which is why she chose not to tell him what had happened with Dylan. Not that she had any care for him. He didn't deserve anyone's charity. But she did worry what might happen to Levka and his friends. There were way too many of Dylan's buddies on board the ship.

Everyone waited for her to say something, though they drank their sodas as if they didn't have a care in the world.

"I fell," she lied.

"Why?" Levka asked.

"Why?" She didn't follow his questioning. "I guess it was slippery. I was clumsy. The boat rolled and I lost my balance. Why else would someone fall?"

He didn't shift his hard gaze from her. She noticed then that the others watched her with the same dark scrutiny.

"Why," Levka asked, "do you cover for him?" She stared at him, then withdrew her gaze.

"Not once have you wanted to check on Alicia. You wouldn't let her out of your sight before. Why the change?"

"She's nearly eighteen. She can take care of herself." Caitlin rubbed her arms and focused on the ocean, but not really. Her mind shifted to the balcony, to the railing pressing into her stomach, to Dylan's terrorizing her.

"Did he threaten you?" Levka reached for her hand, but she pulled away. "What are you afraid of now, Caitlin? That we will hurt him?"

She looked up at Levka, tears blurring her eyes. "That he and his thugs will hurt you. They outnumber the four of you by ten or so. It's best to just leave it be. Alicia can do what she wants."

Levka pulled out a package of cards. "Do you know how to play Spite and Malice?"

"No."

"Do you want to learn?"

She glanced back at the doorway to the lounge.

"Caitlin? Do you want to learn?"

"To play the card game?"

"What else would I be talking about?"

His hard look hadn't changed, and she didn't think he was talking about cards. She wanted to check on Alicia, because no matter how much she hated Dylan and was afraid to cross him again, she worried more about her foster sister. The creep had too volatile a temper. Would he take his anger out on Alicia, too, if she crossed him?

"I'll just watch you play and learn the rules that way."

For an hour, Caitlin refrained from joining the game. Then she excused herself to go to the bathroom, and the guys all exchanged looks. Though no one said anything, she wondered if they could communicate with each other and not allow her to hear them. How could they do that?

No one offered to come with her, which surprised her a little. On the other hand, she was glad to be alone and stretch her legs without feeling she had to have a bodyguard for her every move. Still, when she left the guys in the lounge, her hands grew clammy. She couldn't stop looking for Dylan, and she hated how he'd made her afraid of something new—him.

When Caitlin walked into the restroom, Lynne opened a bathroom stall door and glanced at her. "What happened to you? I thought you were supposed to be Alicia's shadow. I guess you really do have the hots for the wheelchair guy."

"How's Dylan treating Alicia?"

Lynne washed and dried her hands, then brushed out her tangled blond hair. "One thing I hate about cruise ships is the wind. Every day is a bad hair day." She faced Caitlin. "He's her boyfriend. Right?"

"Let me know if he's...mean to her."

"Well, you know Dylan. He's just..." Lynne shrugged. "Dylan."

"If Dylan gets ugly toward her, let me know, will you?" Caitlin didn't think Lynne would keep her informed, but just letting her know her concern might make Lynne watch him with her foster sister more.

"I take it you're too busy watching her then. What will Thomas and Mildred say?" Lynne gave a smirk, then hurried out of the bathroom.

"She was just talking about you," Lynne said to someone outside of the bathroom.

"Crap." Was Lynne talking to Alicia or Dylan?

"Why don't you talk to Alicia? I want to hear what Caitlin had to say about me," Dylan said, his voice dark and threatening.

Chill bumps coated Caitlin's skin. How she wished he'd tried something with her when she was on shore. He wouldn't come near her if he only knew what she was capable of.

"Is everything all right, Caitlin?" Levka asked telepathically.

She imagined she'd been gone an awfully long time to have just run to the restroom, unless there had been a long line waiting for the stalls.

"Caitlin?"

"Can you...can you come and get me?"

"I'll be right there. Are you at the restroom still?"

"Yes, just let me know when it's all right to come out."

"Wait for me, Caitlin. I'll be right there."

The restroom was near the elevators across the hall from the Blue Lounge so she knew it wouldn't take him long to get there. She prayed Dylan would take one look at Levka and decide not to bother with either her or him. She assumed Levka would bring one of his friends if he thought there might be some real trouble.

"Caitlin? I'm here. Are you all right?"

She opened the door and walked out of the ladies' room. There was no sign of Dylan, thank God.

Levka took her hand. "Are you all okay?"

"Yes, sorry. I didn't mean to worry you."

"Anytime you need me, or any of us, just send out the message. One of us should be able to receive it." He walked her back toward the dining room. "It's lunchtime. Formal dining or buffet-style?"

"I don't want to sit with Dylan."

He studied her for a moment, his eyes dark as the ocean water. "Buffet it is."

"If I communicate silently with you, do all of you hear me?"

Levka squeezed her hand. "Yes. But if you say whoever's name you wish to speak to, the others will try not to listen."

She made a face. "I thought maybe you guys were speaking to each other privately, shielding your communication from me in some way. I hoped I could do that, too." He smiled down at her. Did he think she sounded foolish?

They passed the pool where swimmers were splashing water everywhere. Sunbathers still hogged the loungers and the blue and white-striped swing was again occupied by the same couple who'd earlier laid claim to it.

"Anytime you want to sit in it again with me, just let me know," Levka said.

Thankfully, he didn't ask her why she was afraid to come out of the restroom. If only she had her powers, she wouldn't have to put up with that creep, Dylan.

She wondered if his friends were going to join them since he didn't seem to go very far without them. "It sure is nice to have friends like you have."

"We're your friends, too, now, Caitlin."

They walked into the buffet line where a cook was making hot roast beef sandwiches. Levka handed her a plate and grabbed one for himself.

"Yes, but you'll go back to Texas, and I'll be in Florida. It won't be the same."

"Sour dough, wheat, or rye?" the cook asked.

"Sour dough," Caitlin said.

"Same," Levka added. "And I like my meat the bloodier the better."

Caitlin looked up at Levka. "I'll miss you."

He shook his head. "We haven't even made it to the islands yet, and you're already saying goodbye?" He tsked.

Looking down at her plate, she nodded. "Take one day at a time. That's what my doctor said. I really have a hard time doing that. I keep wanting to plan my whole life ahead."

"One day at a time sounds like a good plan."

When they took their seats at a round table for eight, the place was empty. Before long, Stasio, Arman, and Ruric joined them with three cute girls in tow.

Raising her brows, Caitlin greeted them. She was glad she didn't know any of the girls.

"This is Trish, Amie, and Jaygen from Georgia," Stasio said.

"Caitlin, what had happened at the restroom?" Levka asked her.

She stared at him. Why ask her now? Because she was surrounded by friends? Safe? *"I worried about Alicia,"* she said telepathically. She wished the rest of the guys didn't know what she was saying, but though they seemed to be listening to the girls' conversations, they glanced her way when she began to communicate with Levka. *"Lynne was in the restroom, and I asked if Dylan was being mean to Alicia."*

"Like he was mean to you."

Ignoring his comment, she cut her sandwich in half. She was still afraid he would go after Dylan, and Dylan's friends would take Levka and his friends on. *"I asked Lynne to watch Alicia and Dylan. When she left the restroom, I heard her tell Dylan I'd been talking about him."* At once Caitlin noticed Levka's back stiffen. *"Dylan said he would like to ask me what I'd said. I..."* She tilted her chin up. *"I was afraid to come out of the bathroom."*

Levka seemed totally in control, showing no emotion whatsoever, yet beneath that calm exterior she imagined he was not so easy-going. *"What happened on the balcony, Caitlin?"*

He would not give it up. She squared her shoulders, wishing they were broader and that she was taller. She felt smaller than everyone at the table. Though the girls continued to talk, she noticed then, the guys all remained silent. Waiting for her to spill the truth? *"I fell."*

Taking her hand in his, he studied the bruises. *"Dylan's fingers imprinted on your wrist?"* he asked, looking up at her.

She pulled her hand away. "*Promise me you won't go after him.*"

His mask slipped, and for an instant she saw the feral look in his eyes.

"*Promise me.*"

"*I won't promise not to protect you.*"

She took a deep breath. Figuring he wouldn't quit badgering her about it, and probably would have already guessed, she said, "*I found him and Alicia in the bathroom together.*" Her whole body warmed when she told him about it. "*I told Dylan to get out.*"

A nearly imperceptible smile curved Levka's lips.

She looked at the table. "*He got angry and forced me onto the balcony.*" Glancing at Levka, she felt the darkness again. "*He told me not to say anything to anyone about what had happened between him and Alicia. I imagine he was only referring to my foster parents. He wouldn't care if anyone else knew. But they might forbid her to see him, so...*" She shrugged.

"*What else, Caitlin?*"

"*Nothing else.*"

"*What did he threaten to do?*"

She toyed with her napkin.

"*Caitlin, what did he threaten you with?*" Levka reached for her hand, but she hid it in her lap.

"*I probably can visualize something pretty awful. I have a very good imagination, Caitlin. Why don't you tell me the truth so I won't picture something worse?*"

"He threatened to throw me overboard! He shoved me halfway over the rail and forced me to see the ocean, to see where my family died! He said the fall would kill me so that I didn't have to worry about the sharks. That's what he did, Levka! Are you happy?"

The girls at their table sat with their mouths agape. Caitlin didn't bother to look at Levka's friends to see what horrified expressions they might wear. She jumped up from her chair and stormed out of the dining hall. Despite being upset, she felt better. Just getting the truth out in the open, felt like such a relief. Now Dylan would kill her. Or Levka would kill him. Or Dylan and his thugs would go after Levka and his friends. Whatever! It was out of her hands and not her fault.

But it *was* her fault! She shouldn't have told Dylan to get out of their room. She should have left the proverbial sleeping dogs lie. How she wished she could get him on shore and then she would work her magic on him, and not in a good way.

She bit her lip. Making a disgruntled face, she crossed the deck, then passed the pool. She glared hard at the water. She was *not* afraid of the water. Tonight, when everyone was eating dinner, she would swim. She would prove she could get in the water again.

FOR A MOMENT, no one said a word, then the Georgia girls all began to ask what was going on with poor Caitlin. "I'll see you all later," Levka said, and left his uneaten sandwich behind.

He stalked underneath the covered walkways, looking for Caitlin, but didn't see her. He couldn't have been that far behind her. Where had she gone? He headed down the stairs.

When he reached her room, he listened at the door. He heard nothing. He knocked.

No answer. *"Caitlin, I'm sorry. Let me in, and we'll talk."*

Though he didn't know what he would say. That he wanted to kill Dylan for terrifying her. That he would kill him if he threatened her again. He'd seen enough killing, enough bloodshed that he'd had enough for several lifetimes, but he wouldn't let anyone hurt Caitlin if he could help it.

He knocked more gently this time and leaned up against the door. *"Caitlin, if you're in there, will you talk to me?"* No response.

Taking a ragged breath, he paced. Either she was ignoring him, or she wasn't in there. He fought the urge to appear in her room to find out for sure. If she was, how would he explain his sudden appearance?

Clenching his teeth, he walked away. From one end of the ship to the other, he searched. He checked all the lounges, the restrooms—as much as he could—the dining facilities, the game rooms, the theater. As big as the ship was, she could have been moving from place to place like he was, and he could have just missed her.

Though the idea Dylan might have hurt her again soured his stomach.

When the dinner hour arrived, his friends met up with him near the dining room. Arman shook his head. "I don't know where she is. We searched in a line straight across the ship from deck to deck. But like you said, she could have been moving around on a lower deck, or even visiting with someone in their room."

"Or she could have been in her own room," Ruric said. "You admitted yourself that she could have been sleeping in her stateroom for a couple of hours and didn't even hear your entreaty."

"Or heard it and ignored you," Stasio said. "You did badger her a bit to tell you what had happened with Dylan."

Levka scowled. "Caitlin has not shown up for dinner. Neither have Dylan, Lynne, or Alicia. I don't like this."

Arman shoved his hands into his jeans pockets. "They could have eaten at one of the buffet lines. No one has to eat in the formal dining room."

"Stasio, you sit at our dining table and let me know if she or any of the others arrive. Ruric, you check the buffet line on the deck below us. Arman, you check out the one above us. I'll go to Caitlin's room and see if she's there."

Levka stalked off toward the stairs. How could one small mortal girl turn his world upside down as much as she did? A world traveler, a guy who'd lived for eons, a prince in his world and hers. How could Caitlin McEvin turn him inside out?

10

After taking a nice long nap and going on a tour of the kitchen and the crew's quarters with other passengers—*just like a tourist would on their first cruise*—Caitlin returned to her room. Since it was time for dinner, she slipped into her bathing suit, intending to swim in the pool while most of the passengers were at the evening meal.

She couldn't help harboring a grudge against Levka for forcing the issue about what had happened between her and Dylan. Too late to do anything about it now, she would try to make the most of her trip. Tomorrow, the ship would arrive at the first of the islands, and she had every intention of enjoying a visit to the rum factory and caves. If Dylan or any of his friends bothered her, she would let them have it.

When someone knocked on the door, she grabbed her shirt and threw it over her bathing suit.

"Caitlin? It's me, Levka."

She knew that. Everyone's telepathic voice was like the human voice, distinctive. Just like handwriting, though she hadn't known this about telepathic communication until she'd met Levka and his friends, having only had communicated with Vlad and her parents before that.

"Caitlin, if you're in there, I want you to know I'm sorry for upsetting you. Will you join us for dinner? It won't be the same without you."

She wanted him to go away. She was going to try to swim, but she didn't want anyone watching her.

When he didn't say anything more, she waited another twenty minutes, not trusting that he wouldn't still be standing outside of her door. Finally, she held her breath and opened the door.

She was almost disappointed to see the hallway empty. Yet, she truly wanted to try to overcome her fear of the water alone. With a hurried step, she headed for the stairs before she changed her mind.

When she reached the upper deck, she found the pool still filled with swimmers. Why weren't they all eating? She threw her towel on a chaise lounge, then sat down and took off her flip-flops. She couldn't stand the idea of getting into the turbulent water. The ship's rolling created waves in the pool even on the calmest of seas, but she couldn't handle the kids splashing and acting like wild terrors.

Maybe they would clear out after a while.

She lay down on the chaise lounge. The sun was already setting, leaving a wash of pink sky behind. For a while, she enjoyed the sunset and forgot everything else. Then the day turned to night, and though the lights hanging around the deck should have looked festive or romantic, the atmosphere felt oppressive and dark. Swimmers gave way to a Caribbean dance and food on the deck. She frowned when passengers began to snake around the pool and deck, dancing to the steel drums, guitars, and maracas.

Feeling like a freak still dressed in her bathing suit, lying on a lounge chair, not swimming, and 'sunning' under swinging paper lanterns in the dark, she climbed off the lounger and headed back to her room. When the noise died down from the Caribbean dance, she would try to go swimming again.

As soon as she reached her room, she stuck the key in the door, but then she heard laughing inside. She paused and listened. "*Dylan and Alicia.*" She closed her eyes and shook her head.

If she disturbed them again, Dylan was sure to toss her off the balcony this time.

The air-conditioned hall felt cold. Letting out her breath in exasperation, she left the hallway and found another deck where there was no music, just a great view of—the ocean. She continued to search for a place to stay until she could safely return to her room. Chairs were situated all along the upper deck so passengers could view the ocean. The bow had the most wind and the ship rose into the waves and crashed the hardest here. She couldn't wear a bathing suit in the lounges, and even if she wanted to try and sneak by with it, they were air conditioned and too cold.

Luckily, she hadn't run into Levka or his friends who would probably think she was an idiot, wandering around looking for a safe, quiet place to while away the hours. Her stomach tightened with concern. If Levka found out she couldn't return to her room because Dylan was there... She didn't want to even think of what he might do.

∼

"*Now, where is she?*" Arman asked from the Blue Lounge.

"*Sitting across from a lifeboat.*" Levka watched Caitlin, wondering what she was up to. First, he'd found her lying by the pool. She never went in, and the sun was already setting so she wasn't sunning. She looked beautiful though, a raven-haired, blue-eyed mermaid in a silvery blue bikini.

He thought the pool was too crowded for her, and that she intended to try and swim. But then the band started up, and she left. Thinking she would return to her room and change, he was surprised to see her wandering the decks, back and forth, all around and back again. Just watching her strange antics made him dizzy.

"Why don't you ask her to play cards with us?" Stasio asked.

"She's not properly dressed."

"Fine with me," Ruric said.

"I thought you'd said she returned to her room to change," Arman said.

"Apparently, she changed her mind."

"We have business to take care of a little later," Ruric said, *"but call us if you need our help."*

For now, Levka didn't mind watching her in this way. Not finding her earlier, had been antagonizing and maddening. But knowing she was safe, settled his mind some. Though he still couldn't fathom what she was up to.

In nine hundred years, he still hadn't figured women out one bit.

Well after midnight, Caitlin moved again. She walked around the running track ten times, and following her, Levka felt he'd gotten enough exercise for the night, even if she hadn't. He'd kept his distance at times, drew close when he wanted to feel her warmth and smell her jasmine fragrance, but always remained invisible.

Then she headed down the stairs, and he assumed she was finally returning to her room. Instead, she stalked toward the pool. She couldn't have planned on swimming. The Caribbean band had closed up for the night, the dancers gone. Many of the lights had been extinguished. The place looked dark and eerie like the factory warehouse district where he'd been shot.

Caitlin stood by one of the lounge chairs and jerked off her shirt and shoes, then stepped over to the pool.

It's closed, Levka wanted to tell her. You can't go in. He couldn't help her if she panicked.

He couldn't swim. None of his friends could.

"*I think she's going to try to swim,*" Levka told his friends.

"*Pool's closed at this hour,*" Arman said, always a stickler for the rules.

"*Are you sure that she's going swimming, Levka?*" Stasio asked. "*She doesn't seem like the type to break the rules.*"

"*I think she's trying to prove to herself she can do it without a lot of people around.*"

"*I'm coming,*" Ruric said.

"*Me, too,*" Arman and Stasio said at the same time.

For nearly an hour, Caitlin stood at the edge of the pool, staring down into the rolling waves. Levka wanted to hold her tight, to help her fight the terror she must experience every time she looked into the water. His friends stood with him, silently watching from the shadows.

"*Maybe she won't go in,*" Arman said.

Caitlin shook her head, turned, and jerked her shirt back on. Walking away from the pool, she headed to a water fountain.

Levka sighed with relief. At least during the day if she tried this foolishness, someone could rescue her if she got scared. Again, the feeling of utter uselessness washed over him.

"*Come on,*" Stasio said. "*I had a winning hand. Let's go back to the game. Levka, are you coming?*"

"*In a little while.*"

"*After he tucks her into bed.*" Ruric winked.

Caitlin headed for the door to the elevators and stairs. Lynne, wearing a pink bikini, suddenly walked out. Now Levka could see *her* disobeying the rules. She neared the pool, then dove in.

Caitlin watched her. Did she wish she could swim like that again?

Suddenly, Lynne turned her attention on Caitlin. "What are you doing here? Go away. I'm meeting someone. And he won't like it if you're here, too." She squeezed her manicured brows together. "Do you want him to threaten you, too?"

Caitlin didn't say anything, just sat down on a chaise lounge to watch. Lekva couldn't tell how she felt, but he could have wrung Lynne's neck for saying what she did to Caitlin. He couldn't help being proud of Caitlin for standing her ground. If some other jerk threatened her, there would be less one passenger come morning.

Lynne glowered at her, then she turned around and kicked water in Caitlin's direction. The water fell at Caitlin's feet. She smiled.

For several minutes, Lynne did her best to chase Caitlin away. But suddenly, Lynne shrieked. And went under.

Caitlin jumped up from her chair and stared into the pool. "Lynne! Lynne!"

Lynne broke the surface of the water, gasped for air, then went under again.

Caitlin ran for a round life preserver and tossed it to her. "Grab on!"

The life preserver landed in the water by Lynne, but she didn't grab it.

Caitlin yanked a pole off its hook and stretched it out to Lynne. "Grab the pole, and I'll pull you in."

Lynne grabbed it, but released it and went under again.

"Lynne!" Throwing down the pole, Caitlin jumped into the pool.

"She's in the pool," Levka said, panicked. "*She's trying to save Lynne.*"

Ruric swore. "*Of all the people worth saving, she's not the one.*"

Stasio grabbed Levka's arm just as he was about to jump in. "*We can't swim, Levka.*" It couldn't be that hard. It didn't look that bad.

Arman seized Levka's free arm. "*You would drown.*"

"Caitlin will drown." Levka yanked free and grabbed the pole that Caitlin had tried to use.

Shoving it near her, he stretched it out and shouted, "Caitlin, grab the pole."

"Just a minute!" Caitlin shouted.

Lynne clawed her way on top of Caitlin's head, shoving her under. Caitlin rose to the surface, coughing. Seizing the preserver, she tried to grab Lynne's arm, but the girl pulled her loose from the preserver. They both went under.

Somehow Caitlin managed to free herself and hooked the rope tied to the preserver onto the pole. Then she dove under and grabbed Lynne. When she reached the surface, she captured the preserver again. "Pull, Levka!"

With one arm wrapped around Lynne's neck, she held onto the preserver with the other. Levka hauled them toward the stairs. Lynne dragged Caitlin down again. Both came up coughing. Arman and Stasio leaned over the pool and pulled Lynne, sputtering and gagging, out of the water. Ruric and Levka helped Caitlin out.

She kept coughing, but as soon as she stood on the deck, Levka wrapped his arms around her in a hard embrace. He reminded himself he couldn't have her, but his heart told him otherwise. No matter what the league wanted, he wanted her for all eternity. He wanted her, no matter what she wanted even. The darkness inside him was speaking, and he feared the bloodlust would take over. Even now as he held her against his chest, he listened to her pounding heart, heard the blood rushing through her veins, calling to him to take his fill.

"Hey!" a crewmember shouted from an upper deck. "Pool's closed for the night."

"*Right.*" Levka kissed Caitlin on the forehead. "You got in the water." She hugged him back, but didn't say a word.

A guy came out of the building wearing swim trunks. Lynne's date for the night? "What's going on here?"

"I got a leg cramp," Lynne whined. "And I nearly drowned. Where were you?"

"Maybe you shouldn't have been kicking so much of the water out of the pool," Caitlin said, her voice still gravely from coughing. "It might have killed you."

Lynne glared at her, but Caitlin ignored her and snuggled closer to Levka.

"Can I take you back to your room, Caitlin?" Levka asked, not wanting to let her go.

"Yeah, thanks, I would like that."

"Do you need us?" Ruric asked.

Levka shook his head.

"I'm sorry about what happened earlier today, Caitlin. I wanted to know what had happened, but I didn't mean to upset you."

"I didn't want you or your friends to get hurt, Levka."

She shivered when they reached the air-conditioned hall, and he wrapped his arms tighter around her.

For a moment, she listened at the door.

"*If anyone's in there that shouldn't be, I'll toss him out.*"

She shook her head. "*And make him madder.*"

Levka lifted her chin. "*He wasn't here earlier, was he?*"

She looked away from him.

That's why she hadn't changed her clothes earlier. "*He's not going to keep you out of your own room, Caitlin.*"

She opened the door and stepped inside. She couldn't see anything because of the darkness of the room, but Levka saw Dylan sleeping with Alicia in one of the beds.

"Why don't you take a shower and get warmed up?" Levka asked Caitlin.

"What's wrong?"

How could he tell her he could see people in the dark when mortals couldn't? *"I heard Dylan snoring,"* he lied. *"I'll get him out of here, but I don't want you getting hurt."*

She hesitated.

"Go, Caitlin. Please. I know martial arts."

When she closed the door to the bathroom, Levka said, *"Start the shower. Maybe if they hear it, Dylan will sneak out without my having to make him leave."*

The shower began to run. *"Be careful, Levka."*

Dylan glanced up from the bed when he heard the shower. "She's come back. She can find somewhere else to sleep." He climbed out of bed without a strip of clothes on and headed for the bathroom.

No, she won't, Levka said privately to himself. Instantly, his fangs extended, though in the dark stateroom, Dylan couldn't see the terror he had unleashed.

Levka swooped across the room with vampiric speed and seized Dylan's throat. Dylan cried out in fright.

Alicia stirred. "Dylan?"

"Sleep, Alicia," Levka compelled her.

When she plopped her head back on her pillow, Levka captured Dylan's mind, as the jerk tried to wriggle free, his tongue silent. *"Be still, mortal, and it will hurt less. Or struggle, and you shall feel my centuries-old wrath."*

Dylan stood still like a mannequin while Levka bit into the creep's neck and drank deeply, enough to make the bastard weak for a couple of days. His blood tasted heavily of rum, and

Levka cursed inwardly. Disgusted, he finished feasting and sealed the wounds. In the next instant, he wiped Dylan's memory of having been with Alicia, of knowing her, of knowing Caitlin. Then Levka opened the door to the stateroom and tossed Dylan—more like a rag doll now than a menace to anyone—into the hallway.

Let him explain what he was doing sleeping naked on the floor later that morning.

Levka grabbed up Dylan's clothes, walked onto the balcony, and tossed them over the railing into the ocean. On his way back through the stateroom, he ensured Alicia was still asleep.

"Do you need anything more of me?" he asked Caitlin before he left.

"Is he gone?" Caitlin shut the shower off.

"He's gone and will be no more trouble to you."

"I guess I don't need anything else then. Thanks so much for everything, for helping me save Lynne in the pool, for getting rid of Dylan. Thanks."

"Goodnight, Caitlin."

"Night, Levka."

Assuming she wasn't properly dressed and wouldn't want a goodnight kiss, he finally left. But the compulsion to have her as his mate had not abated.

When Levka returned to his stateroom, Arman was leaning back in bed, reading a medical journal. "You're wearing a path across the zigzag carpeting. If you would at least zigzag when you did it, the wear on the carpet would not be as noticeable."

"Go kiss her. Or better yet, why don't you get it over with and just bite her? You're disturbing my concentration." Ruric flipped another page over in *The Great Galaxy War*.

"Go to sleep, Levka." Stasio tossed a book on the battle strategies of WWII on the bedside table and turned off his light. "You should not disturb the lady in her bed."

"Besides," Arman added, "what if you get caught?"

Levka thought of her dark hair splayed out on the pink pillow, of her long lashes hiding her eyes, of her full pink lips that her old boyfriend "*Vlad*" had wanted to kiss. "I'll be right back."

11

Caitlin slept a fitful sleep. Levka leaned over and kissed her lips. She reached up to touch him like she'd done before, but he moved beyond her reach. It was best she thought she only dreamed of him coming to steal kisses from her...it was best he remain in the shadows of her night.

Later that night, Levka rolled over on his own mattress and saw Ruric was no longer in bed with Stasio. "Stasio, where's Ruric?"

Arman sat up. "What's going on?"

Stasio glanced at the empty space in his bed. "Gone."

Running his hands through his disheveled hair, Levka groaned. "We need to find him."

Arman growled. "You would think after so many years he would outgrow walking in his sleep."

"I'll go," Stasio said, already slipping into his jeans.

Looking at Levka's stern face, Arman let out his breath in exasperation. "We'll all go."

Once they left the stateroom, Levka shouted in his harshest telepathic voice, "*Ruric, where are you?*"

"*Gently,*" Arman warned, going aft while the others went in the opposite direction. "*It's dangerous to wake a sleepwalker suddenly.*"

"I swear I'm going to start tying him to the bed," Levka said.

"I see him." Stasio flew to where Ruric stood staring at the railing. "Come back to bed, Ruric. Time to sleep."

"*He knows he shouldn't stay up too late. It always makes him sleepwalk,*" Arman grumbled.

They all returned to bed, but after an hour had passed, humid air from the sea blew in through the balcony door. Levka stared at the open door, then glanced back at Ruric and Stasio's bed. Ruric was gone again.

"I swear he's a descendent of Eric the Red and he's considering his next navigational course." Stasio walked out onto the balcony and nudged Ruric to return to bed.

This time Levka stood next to the bed holding a pair of socks knotted together. Stasio raised his brows as he guided Ruric into bed.

"I'm sleeping the rest of the night. No more of this nonsense." Levka tied one of Ruric's wrists to the headboard.

Stasio shook his head. "You'd better tell him in the morning that you did it to him for his health."

Returning to bed, Levka punched his pillow into shape. "I did. If he wakes me one more time tonight, I'm liable to push him off into the briny deep."

THE NEXT MORNING the ship docked at the Dutch Caribbean island of Curacao where colorful pastel buildings sat squashed against each other along the waterfront.

Levka hurried to meet Caitlin at her stateroom. She was wearing a baseball cap and carrying a purse. "Are you going ashore?" He wished he'd thought to question her earlier.

"Yes, I'm sorry. I should have mentioned it to you. Thomas paid for excursions for each island. I'm going on a tour of the island, caves, and a rum factory."

"And Alicia?" he asked, as they appeared to be in a footrace to the dining hall.

"She's coming, but she's an awful grouch. Muttering something all morning about Dylan leaving her without saying goodnight."

Levka smiled.

"Are you going ashore?"

"Maybe the next island. We hadn't made any arrangements to get off here."

"Make sure it's the same excursion I'm on."

"If I leave the ship, it will be."

When they reached the dining room, they found Lynne already sitting at the table with Levka's friends. Alicia raced to catch up to them and took her seat.

Lynne wore a perpetual cat-ate-the-mouse smile.

"What's up?" Caitlin asked her. "I don't think I've seen you so 'cheerful' ever."

Giving her a sardonic look, Lynne reached for the strawberry jam for her toast. "Someone created quite a stir on the ship early this morning."

"Where's Dylan?" Alicia grabbed a cup of black coffee.

"That's who created the stir. Seems he was sleeping naked outside of your stateroom." Lynne's blue eyes sparkled with intrigue. "So, what did you do, Alicia? Kick him out without his clothes? Or was it you, Caitlin?"

Alicia faced Caitlin. "Is that what happened? Is that why he left me?"

Caitlin looked over at Levka. "Naked?"

"He intended to throw you out of the stateroom, Caitlin. He was naked when he headed to the bathroom to do it. Do you think

he would have allowed you to dress had he gotten into the bathroom?"

Caitlin's jaw dropped.

"You threw him out?" Alicia asked Levka, her voice and brows raised in unison.

"It was either that, or Dylan forcing Caitlin out of the room. If that had happened, I would have reported it to your parents this time, not Caitlin. So your choice. Your parents know about your behavior? Or Dylan leaves your room?"

"It gets better," Lynne said. "Two old ladies started screaming about a naked guy in the hall, waking him up. He ran to his room but didn't have his key."

Levka smiled.

"What happened to his key?" Caitlin asked Levka.

"Instead of throwing him over the railing, I threw his clothes. I guess his key was in his clothes."

Her brow furrowed, she shook her head.

Lynne sipped some of her soda. "Then more people saw him pounding on his door, trying to get his roommate to open up. But his roommate wasn't in the room because like us, he has to leave early to go to shore. Finally, some of the crew members took a very red-faced and belligerent Dylan into custody. I'm sure his parents are being notified. So are the chaperones who came with our group, though we never see them."

"Couldn't have happened to a nicer guy."

"And now he'll really be out to get me," Caitlin responded, her communication annoyed.

"Well," Lynne said, "if we're going to make our tour bus, we better go. I would say this has already been a memorable day. Maybe, Alicia, you can tell me what you and Dylan were up to before he ended up outside of your room, naked." Lynne grabbed her bag and hurried out of the dining room.

Alicia glowered at Levka, seized her purse, and took off after Lynne.

"I'd better go, too." Caitlin wiped her hands. She tilted her baseball cap back and kissed Levka's cheek, seemingly less disgruntled about what he'd done to Dylan. "Thanks for last night. See you for dinner? We have lunch on the island, then return about two."

"See you when you get back." He wanted to pull her into his arms and give her a kiss that would heat her blood, but she was in too much of a rush. He watched her hurry toward the exit of the room, then glanced at his friends. Everyone wore small smiles.

The girl was a siren. He jumped up from the table and hurried after her. When he caught up to her, she smiled.

"I'll see you off." The passengers were all signing out to get off the ship, but Levka pulled Caitlin aside. "Be good, and don't let Lynne or Alicia bother you. If you have any trouble, communicate with me. I'll come to your rescue."

"You're a true knight." She ran her hand down his chest. "Thanks again for last evening. Maybe because Dylan got into so much trouble, he'll be on his best behavior from now on."

Levka pulled off her hat and leaned down to kiss her. He touched his lips to hers, felt the velvety softness, tasted the sweet tangy blackberry flavor she'd coated her toast with, got lost in her blue eyes sparkling with emotion. Groaning, he released her. "Go, or I'll make you miss your tour bus."

She hesitated. Then she gave another one of her award-winning smiles. "Wow." She stuck her hat back on her head and gave his hand a squeeze. "I've...I've got to go, but...wow." He chuckled.

With a backward glance, she gave him another smile, then headed off the ship.

And took his heart with her.

"Are we going ashore?" Arman asked.

Levka wheeled around. Ruric and Stasio stood nearby, wearing smug smiles.

"We wait here." Levka watched Caitlin's figure diminish in size as she neared one of the tour busses.

"Are you worried about her?" Arman asked.

"No. Dylan is still on the ship and shouldn't be a problem anymore. We need to try to learn something about those who plan some kind of prank on the ship, if they stayed behind."

"Yeah, and whether we can fix the problem concerning the passenger manifest," Arman added.

"Did you send someone else to have dinner with the captain in our place last night, Ruric?" Levka asked.

"Yeah, when we were searching for Caitlin and couldn't find her, I assumed dinner with the captain was out."

They walked back to their stateroom and found a couple of ship's officers standing in front of their door.

"Maybe we should have taken a shore excursion after all," Arman said.

"And miss all the fun?" Ruric grinned at him.

"Can we help you gentlemen with something?" Levka asked.

"There's been some mistake in billeting, I'm afraid," the gray-haired man said. "Somehow two teens assigned to your stateroom were bumped. Now they're staying with teens whose parents paid for single occupancy."

"So, refund them some money," Ruric said. "We've paid for our room, so it appears you've double booked."

"I thought only airlines did that," Stasio said.

"Do you have some kind of receipt to show you've paid for these accommodations?"

Ruric pulled out a confirmation slip. "Right here. It shows the four of us staying in this stateroom. You can't get any more official than this."

The older man looked it over. "Can I make a copy of this?"

"Certainly. Don't tell me you don't already have one though?"

"It seems we've overbooked," the man apologized.

Ruric folded his arms and frowned. "Does that mean you'll put us off on the island, and we'll have to swim home?"

"No...no, somehow we'll accommodate the two teens. It would be a lot more of a problem to move the four of you from the one room."

Ruric smiled. "Good. Oh, and be sure and bring that copy back. It's the only one we have."

"Yes, sir. Right away. We'll take the best of care of it."

"Thank you."

The men hurried off.

"Is it the only copy we have?" Levka unlocked the door, and they walked into their suite.

"No, I always carry a spare." Ruric patted his pocket.

Levka opened the curtains to the balcony. "We could always share someone else's room and have a built-in blood bond."

"Speaking of which," Ruric said, "how was Dylan's blood last night?"

"Polluted," Levka said. "I swear his blood was half rum. If I didn't know better, I would think I had a hangover from his near alcohol-blood poisoning."

"Remember the time when we were stationed in England and those 'old' sergeants talked a green kid into drinking whiskey straight? Darn near killed him. Boy, were those sergeants scared," Stasio said.

"Yeah, well that's how I feel, and that's why I like my blood from the blood bank."

"Didn't help that you were up late trying to get the nerve up to return to Caitlin's room and kiss her," Ruric said.

"I wanted to make sure she was asleep."

"Worse," Arman said. "No wonder people fantasize about vampires being sneaky." They all laughed.

"What are you going to do about her?" Ruric asked, looking out the balcony at the bustling port. "You can't tell her what we are without the league's permission. And they'll only give it if you intend to make her your soul mate, which they have to approve as well. So, what are you going to do?"

"I won't turn her, so I'm not going to do anything."

Stasio sighed. "You said the same about Cassandra."

"And she died before you could obtain the league's permission," Ruric said.

"You don't want history repeating itself," Stasio said.

Arman folded his arms. "I think Levka's right. Leave well enough alone."

"Easy for him to say." A taste of her blood, a kiss from her lips…Levka shook his head. The siren had hooked him good.

CAITLIN WAS glad she'd gotten on a bus that Lynne and Alicia were not on. She could just imagine their discussion about Dylan and what had happened. And how she and Levka were implicated in the great Dylan's downfall. She smiled, although a bit evilly.

Passengers pointed to the rooftops of homes where green-scaled iguanas raced across the red tile. The brown-skinned tour guide laughed. "They roam wild here, and the people catch them and eat them," he said, in a thick Caribbean accent.

"Ooooh," several of the passengers said in a disgusted way, while Caitlin wrinkled her nose.

The tour guide said, "They taste like fishy chicken."

Someone pointed to a Kentucky Fried Chicken. "Guess they have them everywhere."

"Yes, but they do not serve iguana." The tour guide gave a flashy white-toothed grin. "You see the houses here are all painted in bright colors. The governor had ordered the houses painted that way since he suffered from migraines and the white stucco reflecting the bright sun gave him headaches. Later, it was discovered the governor owned the company that produced the paints everyone had to buy."

Everyone laughed.

"Our first stop is the Hato Cave." The guide motioned to a mountainside.

After climbing the narrow path, they finally reached the cave, and Caitlin took a deep breath of the warm wet air. Most caves she'd been to were chilly. Oddly, this one was not. Lights cast eerie shadows on the limestone cut into the coral reef. Stalactites clung to the ceiling and sent their daggers downward. Caitlin reminded herself, stalactites hold tight to the ceiling, which was the only way she could remember the difference in the rock formations. She observed stalagmites nearby, reaching upward like miniature spiral mountains in some futuristic world. In places where the water dripped from the stalactites and deposited limestone on the stalagmite below it, whole twisted columns had formed.

The tour guide pointed to petroglyphs drawn on the walls. "Amerindian Arawaks painted these pictures fifteen-hundred years ago and used these caves for shelter and for burial grounds. A family was found buried together, the male's skull placed in the center. Similar remains have been found on the island of Aruba. Flint tools have been located here also."

The guide pointed to a cave farther back. "A colony of rare long nosed bats lives in there." She guided the group deeper into the cave past dripstone pools.

Their footsteps and the guide's words bounced off the cave

walls. Another group followed behind them, and Caitlin could hear the same talk being given like a distant echo.

"In later years, during the slave trade, escaped slaves hid out for months in here," the tour guide said.

Caitlin envisioned the slaves trying to find food and water and shelter away from their masters and how horrible it must have been.

"Fascinating, eh, Caitlin?" a deep male voice said behind her. Her skin crawled as if the water dripping on the walls of the cave were suddenly slithering down her arms and legs.

Turning, she saw the guy who had captured her heart, swept her off her feet, then given her up for dead after her parents and sister had died. *Vlad.* His hair was black and pulled back in a ponytail like usual, and his eyes glittered in the low light of the cave like glassy, black lava rock. Like Levka, Vlad was not the kind of person she thought she would fall for. A Scottish Highlander tossing logs in the Highland games, strong, muscular, with curly, reddish blond hair--that's what had caught her eye when she was fifteen. So why did she keep falling for these darkhaired, mystifying guys now?

Not comprehending how he could be here, of all places, she stared at him.

"I've been out of the country," he said smoothly, reaching for her hand. "I wasn't aware of your...tragedy."

She tucked her hands in her shorts pockets. For months, after she'd gotten better, all she'd wanted to know was if Vlad still cared for her. When she tried to reach him, and couldn't, she knew there couldn't be anything between them. "What... what are you doing here?"

"Touring the cave, like you are."

"You didn't write or call me."

"I was out of the country... on business."

He was always away on business. He'd said he was an heir to

a glass factory and needed to take care of it from time to time as its CEO. Couldn't he have emailed her a note, or called, or something?

"I've come to be with you."

"You're not on the cruise, too, are you? I've never seen any sign of you."

"I flew in this morning. I'll be on the ship for the rest of the cruise."

"Oh."

"You sound disappointed." Vlad reached out to touch her face, but she turned and hurried after the tour group.

"You haven't already forgotten me? After all we meant to each other?"

He sounded so arrogant. She'd been so wrapped up in him, she hadn't realized how wrong he was for her. And for his information, if anyone had forgotten anyone it was he who had forgotten her. Many a night, she'd lain in her bed wishing he would comfort her. She'd fantasized about him taking her away so she wouldn't have to live with her awful foster sister and attend the high school she hated.

"I tried to get in touch with you," she said.

"Ah, well, at the best of times it is difficult."

She glanced back at him.

He touched the water dripping off the wall.

"You're not supposed to touch the rocks. If everyone does that, it ruins the formations."

"Always by the book, eh, Caitlin?"

"You could have tried to contact me. Email, or call, or something."

"I don't use computers. Don't like them. As for phones, I told you, I don't care for them either."

"Do you know how to write?"

He smiled. "Takes too much time."

"You could have had a secretary or someone send a note."

"It wouldn't have been personal enough." They walked outside of the cave.

"It would have been better than nothing." She gave him her best glower.

He bowed his head, and she wondered if he came from the same country initially as Levka and his friends. She always thought it was a quaint way he had of acknowledging her with a gentlemanly bow of his head, kind of like the Japanese do, except Vlad and the Texans cocked their heads more to the side and not as formally.

A chill shivered down her skin. He was eerily like Levka and the others. Was that why Levka and his friends had caught her attention because they were so much like Vlad?

She still couldn't believe Vlad had followed her here. "How did you know I was going to be here?"

"I called your old home and was transferred to your foster parents' place. They gave me your cruise route. This was the first place I could catch up to you."

"And the cave?"

"I contacted the ship to see if you were planning any excursions. This was the first on your list. If you hadn't left the ship, I would have joined you there. How's your foster sister treating you?"

She didn't know why she felt the need to lie, but she said, "Fine. She's up ahead with another tour group. Their bus just left."

"Why wouldn't she be with you? In fact, you seem to be all alone."

"My friends hadn't made arrangements to come ashore. But we'll be going together on the next shore excursion," she said, defending being by herself. Why? He hadn't tried to be with her any time before the trip. Maybe if he had, she wouldn't have felt so out of place. If he'd still been her boyfriend...

She shook her head.

Levka was the one she wanted to be with now. Yet, he would return to Texas, and she would be left behind in Florida. If Vlad truly intended to continue to be her friend, he was at least living in the same city. Until he had to go away for business. *Constant* business.

Caitlin climbed onto the bus. When she sat beside a girl from her high school, the girl suddenly moved to another seat and Vlad took her place. "So polite. Someone from your new high school?"

"Yes." But the girl had never been friendly, which was probably why she left the seat so quickly.

"Did everyone enjoy the Hato Cave?" the tour guide asked.

Most everyone said yes.

Vlad reached for Caitlin's hand, and this time she let him take it. She wasn't one to hold grudges, though she still didn't trust he wouldn't leave her again without word.

"Next stop will be the rum factory," the tour guide said.

The rum factory was just a big metal building and inside an exhibit room of sorts was used to "explain" the process of producing rum. Photos of the process lined the walls, and small throwaway cups of rum samples were offered to the passengers on a tray. She thought she would actually get to see the rum makers making the rum. A waste of money.

By the time they returned to the ship, Caitlin was dying to get away from Vlad and see Levka again. She hadn't ever felt that Vlad was pushy before, but then she'd changed some, grown up some maybe, since the accident. But now she felt him smothering and oppressive. She couldn't move an inch without him beside her, touching her, as if he were afraid he would lose her again.

She humpfed under her breath. He should have thought of that before he gave her a year of the silent treatment.

Levka stood at the booth where passengers checked back in, a strict security measure to make sure people who didn't belong onboard didn't slip in and that passengers who had left the ship were accounted for.

At once her spirit was uplifted when she saw him, and she smiled.

He wore a broad absence-makes-the-heart-grow-fonder smile, but when he saw Vlad checking in behind her, his look turned dark.

Grabbing her hand, Levka pulled her down the hall and away from the check-in counter.

"Levka, I wanted you to meet—"

"Don't tell me. That's Vlad," Levka said, his voice nearly a growl.

"You know him?"

Levka was silent, and Caitlin looked up at him. "Levka, do you know him?"

12

How could Levka tell Caitlin that the vampire, Vlad, wanted her permanently for his own? How could he warn her when he himself wanted her in the same way?

And no, he didn't personally know the guy. But he was one of Levka's kind. The gold tinge around his black eyes, invisible to the mortal eye, proved beyond a doubt he was one of the ones turned nine-hundred years ago, during the plague that infected some and left others untouched.

The hint of gold was a warning to others, Levka and his kind were ancients and had lived for so many years that others of their kind normally revered them. Except for the ancients who had been older in human years when they'd turned. Most of them still felt the "younger" ones like Levka and his friends were too rebellious.

"Levka," Caitlin said, trying to pull him to a stop. "What's the matter? You're running my legs off."

"I'm sorry." But he was afraid he didn't sound like it at all. Brusque, determined, worried was more like it. He hurried her to his stateroom. He had to let the others know the situation he was in. No way would he let the other vampire have her. Had Vlad gotten permission from his league to make her his?

Levka wouldn't allow it.

The others were gone when Levka walked into his stateroom with Caitlin. "I'm not sure how to tell you about any of this," he said.

"Can I use your bathroom?" she asked.

He raised his brows.

She smiled. "I don't like to use public restrooms."

"Sure, go ahead."

As soon as she walked into the bathroom and closed the door, Ruric entered their stateroom.

"Did you get her?"

Levka waved his hand at the bathroom.

Ruric nodded.

Then Stasio and Arman opened the door to the suite. "You won't believe who's here now," Stasio said, his blue eyes hard, his lips thinned.

"Vlad," Levka said.

"Vlad? Who is he?" Arman asked. "Oh, the guy who was seeing Caitlin?"

"Who were *you* talking about?" Levka asked.

"The tracker or whoever he is. The guy who followed us here from Atlanta," Arman said, sounding exasperated.

Caitlin walked out of the bathroom, and everyone looked at her.

Ruric said privately to his friends, "*What's going on, Levka?*"

"*I have to tell her.*"

"It looks like we're going to a funeral," Caitlin said. "Who died?"

"*She's a live one.*" Ruric sat on the end of one of the beds.

"Have a seat, will you, Caitlin?" Levka motioned to the floral sofa.

"You can't tell her what we are," Arman warned.

Stasio pulled the desk chair around, facing the others, and sat. *"History repeats itself."*

"Maybe this time the future will be better," Ruric said.

Arman sat down on the other bed, but didn't say another word.

"You said you knew we were different, Caitlin," Levka began. "How did you know this?"

She shifted on the sofa to get comfortable. "You have long hair and often wear it in ponytails. All of you. Sure, some guys your age do, but it just kind of struck me as odd. On the other hand, maybe it wasn't so much that, but that I'd known Vlad before this, and he was like you guys."

Everyone exchanged glances.

"It's like that." She waved her hand at them. "You speak to each other without saying a word, like you're one."

"Like the Borg." Ruric leaned forward on the bed. "You know, *Star Trek*. The cyborgs had a collective consciousness."

"In the here and now," Stasio said to Ruric.

"All of you can speak telepathically. All of you can perform hypnosis," Caitlin continued. "You all have Russian-sounding names."

Levka smiled. "You can speak telepathically, and you wear your hair in a ponytail sometimes."

"I'm not explaining myself properly. You're just different. Mystical, intriguing, interesting. I don't know how."

Levka watched the emotion play across her face, the exasperation, the desire to be part of a group, to belong. "Caitlin, you're right, we're different."

She sat very still, waiting to hear the truth.

"You're different, too. You have the ability to telecommunicate when very few people can do that."

"But look at all of you. There must be many more. We just haven't reached them yet."

"You said once there were others with Vlad. That they said they were friends of his, but he didn't like that they'd arrived, and he seemed jealous of you."

Her eyes gazed into his as if she were trying to absorb everything he said. "Yes."

"Sometimes people like us with telepathic abilities have a compulsion to find a mate who has the same kind of gift."

Her mouth parted slightly.

"What I'm saying is he wants you, and he will more than likely try any method he can to get you to agree to be his mate."

"You mean to be his wife?"

"Yes."

She shook her head. "My foster parents wouldn't go along with it. They want me to finish high school first and then my parents left me enough money so that I can enroll in college."

"Caitlin, it's a compulsion. He'll feel compelled to have you."

"Like a stalker?"

Levka looked at his friends who remained deathly quiet. "Something like that."

"He didn't have anything to do with me for a year, so I don't think that's an issue."

"When he learns of me, it will be."

Caitlin opened her mouth to speak, but no words came out.

"Do you understand?" Levka asked.

She shook her head, but he guessed she got an inkling of what he was saying, except she wanted him to spell it out for her.

"What I'm saying is—"

"What he's saying," Ruric interrupted Levka, "is that Levka worships you like you were a goddess."

She folded her arms and smiled. "Right."

"It cannot be helped," Stasio said. "It's as Levka says. When we meet the right girl, we have a devil of a time fighting the urge to make her ours."

"Then why fight it?" she asked, her voice tinged with amusement.

"It's really very complicated." Levka sat down on the couch beside her. "You know we can use hypnotism and telepathic communication. We seek companions that we can't control. You are that for me."

"Why not for Stasio, or Ruric, or Arman?"

"They're special cases," Levka said, with a sardonic smile.

"Alas, it is true." Stasio held his hand over his heart. "Had we been able to steal your heart, we would have tried, but Levka made it clear he desired your company above all others. We would never try to break this friendship."

"But Vlad," Ruric said, "will be furious when he finds Levka is interested in you."

"But I live in Florida and you in Texas." She took Levka's hand. "Long distance relationships never work out."

This was not working as Levka intended, yet he knew he could not tell her the whole truth. "I have no ties to Texas that cannot be broken."

"Us either," Ruric agreed. "Florida is as good a place to live as any other."

"You would move to be near me?"

"Yes, but our moving to Florida will not make Vlad go away," Levka warned.

"You would move to be near me," she repeated under her breath. "But I couldn't ask you to do this for me."

Levka kissed her hand. "I wouldn't want it any other way. The problem is Vlad."

She frowned. "He didn't have anything to do with me for a year. There's no problem there as far as I'm concerned."

"He'll be sweet and polite to all of us, unlike your foster sister and her friends. Vlad will act the perfect gentleman, but he still will want you and will make every attempt to get his way."

"So what do I do?"

"Tell him you've agreed to be mine."

Arman let out his breath.

"Your girlfriend?" she asked Levka.

"My mate." Levka had gone and done it now. Though it wasn't exactly binding because she didn't really know what she was agreeing to. "You say our names sound Russia. They are. In the old country, we call the one we choose to marry our mate. It's just our way. If you said you were my girlfriend, it wouldn't have the same meaning."

"It sounds strange to me," Caitlin said.

"It's just a term, but it will mean something to him."

She shook her head. "Sounds unreal. So, if I do this, he'll leave me alone?"

Levka took a deep breath. "I doubt it."

"Then what good will it do?"

"It will show we've made a commitment to each other, and that you're not alone and available."

"Okay, so I have a question for you."

But could he answer it? "Yes?"

"Arman said there's a tracker following you. What's that all about?"

Levka glanced at his friends, but none seemed willing to help him out. "We're with a telepathic guild in Dallas."

Caitlin's eyes widened. Arman closed his eyes and rubbed his temple. Stasio and Ruric grinned. They would be sure to give him a hard time about being the teller of tall tales from Texas later.

"Only a very select few can be in this guild. We're not

supposed to use our telepathic gift to help mortals...others. But I heard the girls screaming, and I had to help them."

"Why wouldn't the guild want you to help others?"

"If people learned we were different, they would use us as guinea pigs, experiment on us, write us up in their scientific journals. Our life would no longer be our own."

"Sure, sure, I can see that." She tucked a curl behind her ear. "But why have a guild then?"

"It's kind of a watchdog organization to ensure our kind don't give us away."

"Oh. So, you saved the girls and..."

"Got injured. The league warned us not to get involved in things like that, but I couldn't hear the girls' screams and do nothing. Now the league has sent someone to force us to appear before them."

Caitlin sat up taller. "You mean, you came on the cruise because you're on the run from the telepathic police?"

"Sort of like that. They usually cool down after a while and everything's fine." Though he still worried the vampire they sent after them might be an assassin.

"But they've sent a tracker after you. Do you know what he looks like?"

Levka shook his head. "He can sense our telepathic communication though, so we need to try and not use it." He could with his friends, but Caitlin had no way to privately send her messages. If the tracker heard her, who would he assume she was speaking to?

"Can I be a member of the guild?" Caitlin's face brightened. "I'm an honor student in high school. Maybe I would be able to make some more friends like you."

"A member of the telepathic guild," Ruric mused.

"The vampire guild rather," Stasio responded.

"Someday, maybe," Levka said. "For now, we have two problems...Vlad and the tracker."

"And Dylan." Caitlin tugged on Levka's hand. "Come on, mate of mine. I'm hungry. The lunch on the island didn't fill me up."

"Formal dining or buffet?"

"Formal. I don't even care if Dylan's there."

He wouldn't be, Levka could count on that. But he still wasn't sure he could pull off pretending to be Caitlin's intended mate without marking her. And that was another issue.

WHEN THEY TOOK their seats at dinnertime, Levka and his friends suddenly looked toward the entrance to the formal dining room. Caitlin turned to see what had garnered their attention. *Vlad.*

Dressed in a black tux, his narrowed eyes the same color, Vlad considered Levka in a challenging and sinister way as he strolled toward them, his walk confident.

Without invitation, Vlad took Dylan's seat.

Caitlin cleared her throat and introduced everyone at the table. Alicia was even more put out that Dylan hadn't joined them. Vlad seemed to take an immediate dislike to Levka and his friends. She didn't like his attitude one bit. She could see he would never let her have any friends if she had remained his girlfriend, whereas Levka did not seem to feel threatened over her friendship with others. He was protective, but not smothering.

Levka took Caitlin's hand and kissed it so tenderly, her heartbeat quickened. Ruric smiled. Stasio hid a grin and cut into his veal. Arman glanced at Vlad to see his reaction. Vlad's face darkened. Lynne and Alicia talked about Dylan's strange behavior and ignored the rest of them.

"Have you known Caitlin long?" Vlad asked. His voice was controlled, but she heard the bitterness.

Levka opened his mouth to speak, but Caitlin patted his shoulder. "He saved me from the water."

Vlad's black gaze shifted quickly from her to Levka.

"Someone had to do it," Levka said, shrugging.

Caitlin cut into her broccoli. She hadn't lied. He *had* saved her from the pool last night, after all. Did Vlad assume she meant Levka had saved her from the ocean a year ago?

Vlad sipped his water. "You've known her for an awfully long time without making her your mate." His cold voice sent chills down her spine.

"We've been at an impasse. You know how delicate these arrangements can be. But she has agreed to be my mate."

Vlad's eyes widened. "Really."

"Mate?" Alicia asked, bug-eyed. "You mean, like, marriage? Mom and Dad will never agree to it."

Caitlin had thought Alicia and Lynne were too busy discussing Dylan's weird actions to have noticed their conversation.

"Does she know what we are, Levka? Have you told her what becoming your mate will entail? What about your league? Have they approved this?" Vladic asked him privately.

As soon as Vladic began to speak telepathically, Levka knew the tracker would locate them. A dark-haired man with steel gray eyes quickly approached the table. "Good evening. Might I have a word with you gentlemen, *alone*?"

Vlad stared at the man. "Who are you?"

"I'm a member of the Dallas league."

Caitlin choked on her water. "The tracker," she said under her breath.

The man quickly turned to look at her. Her cheeks reddened.

"Do you mind if we finish dinner?" Levka asked, as if he hadn't a care in the world.

"No, go right ahead. I'll meet the four of you in the Blue Lounge."

"I'll keep you company, Caitlin," Vlad said with a smirk.

"I'm going with Levka," she said.

The man said privately to Levka, *"Tell the mortal she cannot come."*

"Sir, the lady is with me."

The man considered Caitlin for a moment more while she lifted her chin under the scrutiny. To Levka, he said, *"You will always be trouble. Very well, meet me following your dinner."* He strode off.

"He's with the Dallas league?" Vlad asked, his eyes and lips smiling. "Did someone get into a bit of trouble?"

13

When they resituated themselves in the Blue Lounge after finishing their dinner, Vlad sat at the bar, but the conversation would be kept private so Levka wasn't sure why he came to watch. Caitlin sat next to Levka, and though he wanted to hold her hand, he resisted the urge under the watchful eyes of the tracker.

"I'm Mr. Petroski," the tracker said first. Then he spoke privately to Levka and his companions. *"You disobeyed the league's ruling on non-interference in mortals' affairs."*

Levka said, *"But—"*

Mr. Petroski motioned for silence.

Caitlin patted Levka's leg. "Are you masking your communication, Levka? I thought you couldn't do that."

Petroski stared at her. *"Can you speak telepathically?"*

"Yes." She smiled broadly. *"And I would like to join a guild, too."*

He looked back at Levka and spoke privately again, *"Do not tell me you want the girl."*

"I do. I want permission from the league to okay our union."

"No."

Levka's face heated. *"The last time—"*

Again, Petroski motioned for silence, then leaned forward in his chair. "*You have disobeyed the league's ruling six times this year already and it's only March.*"

"*That's only twice a month,*" Ruric said.

"*That's six times more than the league allows,*" Petroski said. "*The league could have you eliminated for your constant disobedience.*"

Levka shared looks with his friends, but none of them revealed how they felt.

"*But the league doesn't want to get rid of its claim to having the highest number of royal members—for now. So, you have been given a task.*"

"*With the condition, Caitlin is mine.*" Levka took her hand and squeezed. Even if he didn't make her his in the vampire way, if he had the league's permission, he hoped that would be enough to keep Vlad's hands and teeth off her. Even other leagues would have to honor their commitment.

Petroski glanced at her and shook his head. "*You cannot name conditions, Levka.*"

"*What's the job?*" Stasio asked, giving the tracker a cutting glare.

"*Teen troublemakers make up the most of the league's problems. You'll be required to police them. We'll provide a list, you find them, and report back to us, and we'll bring them in for counseling or punishment as we see fit.*"

"*I'm game,*" Ruric said, shrugging, "*if it gets our names off the list.*"

"*Turning in those who break our vampiric laws sounds good to me,*" Arman said.

Stasio rolled his shoulders. "*Fine with me.*"

Levka turned to Petroski. "*It's a deal if I can have Caitlin.*"

Petroski stood. "*I will get off at Caracas, next stop, and fly home. We'll be in touch.*"

Clenching his teeth, Levka asked, "*What about Caitlin?*"

The tracker considered her, then faced Levka. "*It's hard convincing a mortal she should give up a way of life she's always known. Some love the way of the vampire, others do not. You're drawn to her, I suspect, because she's telepathic, and you cannot control her. Am I right? The truth is, sometimes it's just easier taking a mate you can brainwash.*" Petroski smiled, and the look was purely wicked.

"*Is that what you did?*" Levka asked, unable to hide his irritation.

Petroski's smile faded. "*No. I took a woman who fought me every step of the way. There are advantages and disadvantages to every relationship. None are perfect. Compromise is the key. But when you turn the girl, there is no going back for her, or for you.*"

Petroski paused. "Good day, gentlemen." He gave them a curt nod of his head, then gave Vlad a harsh look and left the lounge.

Vlad moved his drink to where the others were seated.

"How come you can mask your telecommunications, and you wouldn't tell me you could?" Caitlin asked Levka. She definitely had an edge to her voice.

"I don't think everyone can do it, Caitlin."

She pulled her hand away from him. "What did the tracker say?"

Vlad motioned to her with his drink. "*Has Levka not told you what we really are?*"

Caitlin looked at him, sitting slouched on the arm of the sofa. "What?"

"*Abominations. Genetically-mutated monsters. Big mosquitoes, blood suckers. Technically, vampires.*" Vlad gave her a lopsided grin.

"*You're drunk. And you're underage.*" She turned to Levka. "What did the tracker say?"

"We're to track down our kind, who are causing trouble."

"The wolves after the wolves," Vlad said.

"What did Vlad say privately to you, Caitlin?" Levka asked.

"He said you were big mosquitoes." She figured Levka and his friends would laugh, but none of them did. In fact, they looked mortified. "He said you're bloodsuckers, genetically mutated monsters, vampires."

Still, no one laughed or said anything.

"But then again, he's drunk."

Dylan walked into the lounge with two of his friends, but none of them even glanced in the other boys' direction. Following closely behind, Alicia nagged at him. "What do you mean you've never seen me before in your life?" Her makeup was tear-streaked and her voice sounded soggy. "Dylan, quit walking away from me! How can you say you don't know me?"

He snapped his head around. "Quit stalking me! I've never seen you before!" His friends said nothing in response, and Caitlin knew they knew differently. But being his friends, they kept silent.

Standing next to Alicia, Lynne cleared her throat. "Dylan, you've been seeing Alicia for three months now. Really hot and heavy. Heck, you were even found outside of her stateroom naked."

The guys with Dylan chuckled.

His glare silenced them. "I'm sure the whole ship knows about that. But I don't know who she is, and like I told the ships' officers, I don't know how I got locked out of my room like that." He stalked off.

For the first time, Alicia seemed to see Caitlin. "Tell him! Tell him you found us together, and that guy," she said, pointing to Levka, "threw Dylan out of our room."

Caitlin looked at Levka. What had he done to him? She'd never heard of anyone using hypnosis to wipe someone's memories out. And she didn't think Dylan would be embarrassed enough over being found in the hall naked to pretend he didn't know Alicia. He wouldn't have cared after the initial humiliation. Knowing him, he would probably have worn his disgrace like a badge of honor.

"Maybe he's so ashamed about this morning, he wants to keep his distance for a while. The chaperones on this trip probably really chewed him out about it," Caitlin said to her foster sister.

Alicia glared at Caitlin, then tore off after Dylan. "Dylan! Wait up. You even gave me this hickey!"

Caitlin would have laughed, except the implications Levka and his friends could do more than they were saying sent a chill into her bones.

Vlad got off the arm of the couch and stumbled over to Caitlin. He reached down to touch her hair, but Levka moved so quickly from his seat, his actions didn't register until he'd yanked Vlad halfway out of the lounge.

"She is mine," Levka hissed, pulling Vlad out of the lounge. "Don't ever try to touch her again."

"Sorry, Caitlin, but I can't hold my liquor," Vlad communicated to her. *"I'll see you later."* He staggered out of the lounge as Levka helped propel him forward.

"If the league wants you to enforce the guild laws in Dallas, you won't be moving to Florida," Caitlin said to Levka's friends, realizing all of a sudden that Vlad would be free to pressure her.

Ruric ran his hands over the arms of his chair. "You need us, Caitlin, and we need you. So, never fear. We'll work everything out one way or another."

"I wouldn't hold you to anything. I mean, it's important for you to be in good standing with your guild, isn't it?"

"I'll say," Arman said. "Believe me, I didn't want to cause trouble."

"Did you hear the girls screaming?" She couldn't believe as sweet as Arman was he wouldn't want to protect the girls.

Arman looked sheepish. "I warned Levka there would be problems if we interfered."

"I'm glad Levka felt otherwise."

"And you see what it got him? Three bullets and big time trouble with the league."

Her heartbeat quickened, and she faced Ruric. "Three bullets? You said he'd only been shot once."

Ruric gave Arman a disgruntled look. "Levka would not have wished it said he had been so slow to respond that he took three bullets."

Caitlin frowned, wondering how he even survived. It must have taken him more than a few months to heal. "You should have told me." She looked back at the doorway to the lounge. No sign of Levka. "Does Dylan really not remember Alicia? Or is he faking it to be mean or something?"

Ruric raised the palms of his hands heavenward. "Who knows?"

"Levka knows. I'm sure of it." She looked down at the blue carpeted floor, then faced Stasio. "Let me see your teeth."

"Pardon?" His blond brows arched with the pitch of his voice.

"Your teeth. Give me a nice big smile."

Stasio smiled at her, the look pure amusement. "Did I pass inspection?"

"Beautifully." She turned to face Arman. "Let me see yours." He folded his arms, his face unreadable.

"Come on. The next time I see Vlad, I want to be able to tell him I inspected everyone's teeth, and none of them were overly pointed like a vampire's."

Arman opened his mouth to reveal clenched teeth.

"Good, now yours, Ruric."

He gave her a sparkling grin.

"Great. No excessively scary teeth. In fact, you all have beautiful smiles." Ruric waggled his red brows.

But everyone's gaze shifted to Levka when he walked into the lounge and headed for the bar. He did not look pleased. After getting a tray of sodas, he joined them. *"Sorry about Vlad. Apparently he cannot hold his liquor."*

Grabbing one of the glasses, Caitlin said, "He's underage and shouldn't have been drinking in the first place."

Ruric reached for a soda. "Caitlin inspected our teeth and found them all to be satisfactory." Levka didn't say anything, and she wondered if he was still PO'd about Vlad.

"I haven't inspected your teeth," Caitlin teased, hoping to get him in a better mood.

"Someone's planning to pull some prank when we reach one of the islands," Levka said, ignoring her comment.

Why was he communicating telepathically to them? Caitlin wondered. "I heard you talking about this earlier. Do you know who it is?"

"They were male teens," Ruric said. "But I haven't heard their voices since. It's a big ship with twenty-four hundred passengers. It's hard to monitor everyone's conversations. I keep eavesdropping, hoping I'll discover who they are."

Yawning, Caitlin said, "I didn't get enough sleep again last night. I think I'll lie down for a while."

"Escort her to her stateroom, Arman, will you?" Levka asked, his face tense, annoyed.

She couldn't figure out what was wrong with him. Why keep speaking telepathically and why did he send Arman with her?

"Caitlin, whatever you do, do not invite Vlad into your room."

She gave him a perturbed look, as if she would even think of doing such a thing.

"I mean it. He's dangerous. Don't invite him into your room, ever."

"I'll be all right." She hurried off the sofa without bothering to give Levka another look. Was he angry with her for having gotten involved with Vlad? It wasn't her fault the guy was a jerk.

Maybe Levka was irritated with her because he was having to deal with all her problems— Dylan, her fear of the water, now Vlad. She straightened her shoulders. She didn't need anyone to protect her. Glancing to her side, she found Arman shadowing her. He gave her a small smile.

All right. So she would ask Arman what was wrong with Levka. Serve him right.

14

"I take it you want us to look again for whoever plans to cause trouble on the ship, Levka?" Stasio chugged down the rest of his soda.

Levka clenched his teeth, but no matter how much he tried to sheathe his canines, the anger simmering in his blood kept them extended. "*Yes.*"

Ruric grinned. "*Can't get your canines under control? You shouldn't have let Vlad rile you so.*"

"*He's after Caitlin, and you know how much trouble he can cause if he doesn't get his way.*"

"All right, well, I'll go back to searching for the guys who are intending mischief. Are you coming, Stasio?" Ruric tied his curly red hair into a tail and pulled his faux light saber out. Examining it, he said, "There shall be one less Ferengi blood flea after we're through with the vermin."

Stasio shook his head. "Ferengi blood flea?"

"Sure, when flaked, they're a Ferengi's favorite delicacy."

"*Star Trek* or *Star Wars*?"

"*Star Trek*, my friend. I cannot remember any kind of insects in *Star Wars*." The two sauntered out of the lounge.

Levka finished his drink. "*Is Caitlin in her room yet, Arman?*"

"*Yes, I just dropped her off. What now?*"

"*We dock shortly at Caracas. Did Ruric cancel Caitlin's excursion to the city?*"

"*Yes, as you wished.*"

"*Good. The place is not safe for her, and I further fear if Vlad went ashore with her, he would try to spirit her away.*"

"*What are we going to do about the rest of the islands?*"

"*Accompany her.*"

"*Where is Vlad?*"

Levka finished his drink. "*Sleeping it off. Let's join the others in search of the troublemakers.*"

IN HER STATEROOM, Caitlin slipped under her covers to take a nap, still annoyed Arman wouldn't tell her what was wrong with Levka, though she was certain he was angry with her about her involvement with Vlad and the trouble that was causing. Even though Arman tried to cover for Levka, saying he hadn't had enough sleep the night before, she didn't believe it. Well, maybe he hadn't had enough sleep, but that wasn't the reason for his strange behavior with her.

He was mad at her. She would bet the allowance she didn't have that he was.

Just about the time she drifted off to sleep, Vlad spoke to her telepathically. "*Shorry, Caitlin. Forgive me?*"

She tried to ignore him, though she wasn't sure how to block his telepathic abilities. Still, she wasn't going to respond to him, hoping he would go away.

"*We shtop at Venezzzuela next,*" he said slurring the words. "*Venezzzuela. You going ashore?*"

Softly snorting, she tucked her arms under her pillow and

cuddled closer to it, shutting her eyes and listening to the low roar of the ship's droning engines.

"Venezzzuale," Vlad said one last time.

But two hours later, before she was fully awake, she heard Vlad's impatient voice again. "*We are at the port of Venezuela. Invite me in, and we'll go into the town together.*"

Invite me in. She rubbed the sleep from her eyes. Was it one of those odd terms like Levka had used, "mated"? Why not —I'm here to take you to the city? Why—*invite me in*? He had no need to come into her stateroom, and yet vaguely, she recalled Levka pleading with her to invite him in when she sat frozen to the balcony floor. She stretched, yawned, and sat up in bed.

"*Caitlin, invite me in.*" This time Vlad was more insistent, which didn't help her to wake up slowly from her nap. Then she glanced at her watch and realized they must have reached port, and if she didn't hurry, she would miss her bus. She grabbed her hat, purse, and sunglasses, and dashed for the door.

When she jerked it open, she found Levka waiting for her. Looking around him, she asked, "Where's Vlad?"

"He went off to bother someone else for a while."

She smiled. "Are you going to shore with me?"

"Too dangerous."

Raising her brows, she headed in the direction of the ramp where the passengers disembarked for shore excursions. "Vlad said he's going."

"He may be. But your tour has been canceled."

She turned and stared at him. "What?"

"I thought maybe you would like to watch the staff prepare ice sculptures, or—"

"My foster parents paid for my excursion."

"The money has been refunded, credited back to their card."

Her mouth gaped, then she snapped it shut.

Taking her hand, he led her to the ship's railing and pointed to the hillside. "This is how many of the people live."

"You canceled my tour?"

"It's not safe."

Frowning at him, she pulled away. "You had no right to cancel my tour."

He waved his hand at the hillside again. "It is not safe for you here. I couldn't allow any harm to come to you."

Trying to curb her annoyance at his actions—though she couldn't help but like that he was always so concerned for her welfare—she stared at the goat trails winding around the steep hills, hovels built against the earthen terrain. "There are no roads." Studying the land closer, she frowned. "What's glittering all over the hills. It...it looks like crystal."

"Trash. The people dump trash outside of their homes. It remains where it gets tossed. No garbage pickup."

The sound of firecrackers popped in the distance. She glanced in the direction of the noise.

"Fireworks?"

Levka leaned against the railing, but didn't say a word.

"I've read newspaper accounts where people say they've heard what sounds like firecrackers popping, but it's really gunfire," she said.

Taking a deep breath, Levka nodded. "But the ship's crew will tell you the sound you hear is from firecrackers. Did you know the city was founded as Santiago de León de Caracas in 1567 by Diego Losada?"

She leaned against the railing. "You're starting to sound like Stasio. But go on. I find history fascinating. Besides, I missed having a tour guide give me the history, so you'd better do a good job."

A slight smile curved his lips. "English pirates ransacked the place."

"Pirates, beastly characters."

"The city was burned, and earthquakes have ravaged the area." Levka motioned to the slum dwellings. "Recent mud slides have forced inhabitants to build these hovels. The city itself sits in a lush green valley surrounded by mountains. A tropical paradise encircles the city, but like many large cities, it's noisy, filled with millions of inhabitants, has terrible traffic jams, and..." Levka glanced at Caitlin. "...dangerous slums, the stark contrast between those who have, and those who have not."

Caitlin turned her attention back to the hillside. "It's really sad."

"It is. There's a lot of wealth to be had, but most of it is kept in the hands of a few." He ran his hand over hers. "Do you want to get something to eat?"

Facing Levka, she asked, "What happened to Vlad? He was bugging me about inviting him in, and the next thing I knew, you were standing at the door."

Levka gave her a devilish smile and took her hand. "He decided to bother someone else for a bit."

She wondered how Levka and his friends had convinced Vlad to leave her alone, as she was sure they had, but she forgot all about asking him when she saw some of the crew carving ice sculptures. Dragging Levka, she hurried him over to see the one a bearded man was carving of a mermaid.

But just as she was to remark about the beautiful detail the man cut into the mermaid's tail, Levka turned his head as if someone had just startled him.

"Is something wrong?" she asked.

Levka's brown eyes turned nearly black and his jaw tightened. "Stay here and I'll be right back. Don't go anywhere. All right?"

∽

OF ALL THE blasted times for him to hear the troublemakers speaking.

Levka communicated to his friends, "*I hear the ones who are planning some devilment somewhere on the deck below me, mid-ship. But Caitlin's watching the crew carve ice sculptures. I don't want to leave her alone for long.*"

"We're on our way to the location you're speaking of," Ruric said.

Levka concentrated on the voices as he stormed toward the stairs.

"Man, we gotta do it once we leave the last port. Close in, just in case something goes wrong. Don't wanna sink the ship with us on it."

Another teen laughed. "Okay, so we do it after St. Martin."

"Yep. Extend our spring break a bit."

"Cool."

By the time Levka reached the middle of ship the deck below where he had heard the conversation first, a dozen teens heading for some activity flocked toward them. Two of the girls were giggling about something, but no one else was talking so he couldn't pinpoint who might have spoken.

Arman and Ruric joined him.

Levka shook his head and started back for the stairs. "They're planning some disaster so they can extend their spring break."

Ruric snorted. "If I could, I would send them to a Mars penal colony for even thinking about causing trouble."

"Why don't the two of you follow that group and see if you recognize the guys' voices, Ruric."

"I'm on it."

"I'll go with you," Arman said.

"Where's Stasio?" Lekva asked, frowning.

"He hurried to make sure Caitlin was all right while you tried to track down the bad guys," Ruric said.

"And no one's watching him?"

"We can't always keep an eye on him, Levka." Ruric hurried after the teens.

Arman shrugged. "He's right you know." Then he took after Ruric.

Levka did double time up the stairs and stalked back toward the middle of the ship. If he could vanish and reappear without getting caught, he would have. His heart hammered against his ribs as he worried Vlad might make a move against Caitlin. But when he saw her pointing at the ice sculpture of a polar bear while Stasio folded his arms and nodded next to her like a dutiful bodyguard, Levka calmed his breathing. On the deck above, Vlad caught his eye. The vampire gave him a cold, hard stare.

Yeah, if Stasio hadn't been there with Caitlin, the old flame would have tried for her again.

"Thanks, Stasio," Levka communicated.

Stasio glanced back and smiled. *"My pleasure. Vlad's on the upper deck stewing."*

"I see that." Levka looked up, but Vlad had vanished.

THAT EVENING before everyone sat down to dinner at the formal dining table, a crewman dressed like a pirate greeted Caitlin with a charming smile, but instantly, Levka's hand tightened on hers.

Black curly hair touched the pirate's partially bare chest, and a black mustache curled above his smiling lips. A gold hoop earring dangled from his ear, while a red and white striped scarf covered his head, and an authentic-looking sword hung at his waist as he held out his hand to Caitlin. "Take a picture with me, me beauty?" He bowed low as if she were royalty.

Before she could accept, Levka pulled her toward their table. He motioned to Ruric. "If you need a picture taken with a pirate, Ruric is a descendent of the Viking explorer, Eric the Red."

Ruric shook his head. "So, you keep saying, though it is not true, at least as far as I know."

Caitlin considered Ruric's appearance. His wild red curly hair did look pirate like. But then again, Levka and the others with their long hair looked pretty wild at times, too, only none of them had even a hint of facial hair, no matter the time of day or night.

When they reached the table, Alicia gulped down a couple of headache pills, and Lynne grabbed her bottle and helped herself.

"I wish we hadn't gone to the city," Alicia whined, rubbing her temple. "We were in an awful traffic jam in a tunnel forever. No air conditioning on the bus. The windows were open and the gas fumes from all those vehicles nearly asphyxiated us. I have the most horrible headache."

"Oh, oh, and armed guys in uniform were all over the place in the shopping plaza. I just knew someone was going to snatch my purse and one of those guys was going to shoot him and hit me by accident." Lynne gulped another drink of water.

"Guess I'm glad my trip got canceled," Caitlin said, relieved, as they ordered their dinners. She glanced at Levka, wondering if he had been to Caracas before and that's how he knew. Then she turned her attention to Vlad. "Did you go?"

"Without you to accompany me? I think not," Vlad said smoothly.

Alicia rolled her eyes, then she patted Lynne's arm. "I've decided I don't know what I ever saw in that idiot, Dylan. Bobby Drewery asked me if I wanted to see a movie tonight."

Before she could stop herself, Caitlin shook her head. Bobby wasn't any better than Dylan, another spoiled rich kid, both parents' lawyers who had gotten him out of jail on minor shoplifting charges numerous times. Maybe a little tough love, in the form of a little jail time, would cure him of his sticky fingers?

The waiter returned with bread, soups, and salads.

Vlad tapped his fingers on the table, then leaned over closer to Caitlin. "Would you dance with me tonight?"

His black eyes willed her to say yes, but she had every intention of saying no. She buttered her bread. "I..."

Levka put his hand around Caitlin's shoulder and gave her a slight embrace. "Her dance card is full."

Alicia and Lynne stared at him.

Alicia turned to Lynne. "I think I'm going to get majorly sick. Are you finished with your meal?"

"Not interested. I'm feeling really nauseated, too. Sure it has something to do with the company." Lynne shook her head.

The two hurried out of their seats and left the dining room.

Leaning back in his chair, Vlad crossed his arms, his face dark. "She won't be yours."

Caitlin took a spoonful of her vegetable soup.

Levka's lips and eyes smiled. "I don't want Alicia."

Caitlin nearly laughed and sat back in her chair when the waiter brought them their main dishes.

His mouth forming a hard line, Vlad said, "You have your friends to protect you for now, Levka, but what will you do when we reach Fort Lauderdale? You know you'll be outnumbered. Your own league is furious with you, mad enough to send a tracker. There will be no one to watch your backs when you arrive. That isn't your territory. You won't be able to keep her."

Carving up her roast duck, Caitlin said, "Why don't you all eat? Your food will get cold."

"Fort Lauderdale isn't your territory either. But that is

neither here nor there." Levka began to work on his veal. "You have no claim to her."

"Have you taken her blood yet?"

Levka glanced at Vlad.

"I see you have."

"Then as you can see, you have no claim."

"My league backs me," Vlad threw in.

"I don't care anything about this league business." Caitlin finished eating the delicious orange-flavored duck. She folded her arms. "I'm not interested in seeing you anymore, Vlad. I really cared for you at one time, but then I discovered we really didn't mean anything to each other. I can see how controlling you are. You never bothered to see me when I really could have used your kindness. And now..." She hmpfed. "Now, all you can say is you claim me. Why? Because I have a new boyfriend."

"You have a mate," Levka corrected her.

She looked up at him and saw the turmoil in his dark eyes. "Right." She said to Vlad. "I have a mate." Without another word, she glanced at Levka's plate and seeing he was done, she reached for his hand. "Ready to dance, my mate?"

His mouth lifted, and she smiled, then pulled him from his seat to dance in the theater, hoping that Vlad would get the hint and drop dead.

"Do you dance as well as Stasio?" Caitlin asked, as she pulled Levka into the theater where a waltz was playing.

"Better." Levka grinned when she smiled up at him.

"Well, I have to warn you I don't. So you'd better watch your feet."

He walked her up onto the stage and pulled her close. "You will dance like an angel, I have no doubt."

The way he moved her across the floor, she felt like an angel, gliding, effortless, like a slip of fresh air. She'd never danced with a guy who could move so elegantly.

"Yeah," she said sighing, her head resting against his chest. "You're even better."

"You have caught me, and now I can't let you go."

"Good. I could dance with you like this forever."

No matter how much Levka told himself he didn't want her, he knew it was a lie. He wanted her for now and all eternity. Sensing Vlad's presence in the theater, Levka noticed him dancing with Lynne, quickly closing the gap between them.

"When we reach Grenada tomorrow, I've got a sight-seeing trip. Will you come with me?" Caitlin asked.

"If the weather permits. I've heard some of the water excursions have been cancelled."

"I'm afraid I'm not brave enough to try one of those yet."

Vlad and Lynne moved closer to them. Levka tried to pivot away, but Vlad followed him step for step until he was close enough for them to hear.

Vlad's eyes bored into Levka's. "I wish to dance with Caitlin."

Lynne gave an unladylike snort, but everyone ignored her.

Caitlin tightened her grip on Levka, but he gave her a reassuring squeeze and a small, satisfied smile. "Yes, I'm sure you do."

"Let's trade, shall we?"

Glancing at Lynne, Levka noted Vlad had quickly hypnotized her with his vampiric charm. Again, Levka couldn't help smiling. "I don't need to force my mate to dance with me. Why don't you move along?"

Vlad bowed his head slightly, then swept Lynne across the floor. "I can't believe he's being so gentlemanly about it," Caitlin said.

"Believe me, under that cool exterior, he's the devil."

She sighed deeply. "I believe it."

For some time they danced in silence. Levka listened to the beat of her heart, felt the blood pulsing in her wrists, calling to him to take his fill. Already he'd had to clamp down on his teeth to fight the urge to extend them. Only when facing danger, did he have so little control.

"I...I have a question, Levka," Caitlin said.

"Hmm?" He kissed her forehead and smelled the heavenly scent of peach fragrance in her hair, the silk strands tickling his nose.

"It's about Dylan."

He tried not to react, to tense his muscles, but she looked up at him, and he assumed he'd failed to conceal his reaction.

"How come he doesn't know Alicia? It's not a form of hypnotism. It's more like memory loss. You couldn't make him lose his memories, could you?"

He hated to lie to her, but what other choice did he have? Tell her the truth? Vlad was right? They were blood sucking monsters after all? He decided to evade the question.

"Dylan's probably mad that he got into trouble over Alicia. I'm sure he has been told he'll have to fly home at his parents' expense if he causes any more trouble."

She nodded. "Yeah, I didn't think anyone could do that to anybody else."

His own blood raced and his teeth extended. Leaning down, he kissed her neck, felt the blood pumping through her veins, enticing him further.

Moving her head aside, she exposed her neck.

Inwardly, he groaned, but he couldn't control the bloodlust. He grazed his teeth along her skin, careful not to nick her.

"Wonderful dancer," she murmured.

The music, the dancers, the low lights all faded as he concentrated on the angel in his grasp.

"Let's play a game of cards," Ruric said, breaking into Levka's concentration, bumping him abruptly.

Levka bit back a hiss.

Ruric smiled. "You need a break." He added silently, "*Before you bite Caitlin in front of the hundred or so people in here.*"

The dance ended, and Levka led Caitlin off the stage. "*Do you want to play cards, Caitlin?*"

"I'll have a seat and watch."

Levka gave Ruric a heated glare.

Ruric shrugged. "You were ready to go to the moon and back, without a safety net."

"*We are not going to dance anymore?*" Stasio asked, sounding disappointed as he led an older woman back to her seat.

"*Time to rescue lover boy,*" Ruric explained.

Arman hurried to join them. "*What did I miss this time?*"

15

Not long after Levka and Caitlin sat down on a sofa in the Seabrook Lounge where the seawater fish tank divided the room in half, he noticed Vlad taking a seat across the room.

Caitlin glanced his way, then turned her head away from him. "Do you know Vlad's followed us here?"

"Yes."

"I can't believe I ever saw anything in him. And I can't believe after all the time he left me alone, he would be like this now."

Levka didn't say anything and motioned to Arman to play cards.

"Do you want me to get us some drinks? My treat this time?" Caitlin began to rise from the sofa, but Levka captured her wrist and shook his head.

Smiling to put her at ease, he said, "Ruric will be happy to."

Ruric hopped up from his chair, swung his ghostly light saber around and said, "For the lady, I will do anything. Including..." He gave Levka and the others a look of contrition. "...paying for the lady's drink, as it should be." Then he sauntered off.

Caitlin took a deep breath and relaxed on the couch. "I'm so glad I met you guys. I would have had such a miserable time if it hadn't been for you."

But would she feel that way if Levka turned her? Even now, he could barely control the urge to make her his. He couldn't believe how little restraint he'd had on the dance floor with her.

Vlad penetrated Levka's dark thoughts. *"Have you shown her your canines yet? Oh, but you must have because you've tasted her blood. And how did you ever manage that? She is..."* He licked his lips. *"She is resistant to our vampiric charms. I couldn't decide if that appealed to me or not. Then after a year of trying to give her up, I decided it did. After all, one of her kind is very rare. Don't you agree?"*

Levka ignored Vlad as Ruric returned with a tray of drinks.

"Vlad looks like he's wearing lipstick," Caitlin said low to Levka.

He glanced back at Vlad and scowled. *"Wipe your face!"*

Vlad smiled, showing his extended bloodied canines.

Turning to see Caitlin's reaction, Levka was relieved Arman had distracted her.

Arman said, "You see, Caitlin, a pair of the same cards beats a single. And three of a kind..."

"Thanks," Levka said privately to Arman.

Ruric shared, *"The bastard needs to be put out of his misery and shipped off to outer space."*

"By his own league, not us," Levka warned.

"If these were the good old days...," Stasio said.

"But they are not. And unless he attempts to kill one of us, we can do nothing about him." Though if Levka caught him trying to turn Caitlin, he wouldn't be able to control his anger.

"Or if he attempts to reveal what he is to a ship full of passengers," Stasio said.

Levka glanced in Vlad's direction, but he was gone. Relieved, Levka turned to watch Arman giving card game instructions to

Caitlin, but noticed she quickly wiped a tear away. Had Vlad upset her?

Arman stopped speaking and looked at Levka as if he wasn't sure how to proceed.

For a moment, Caitlin attempted a smile, then sipped on her drink and promptly choked. "I'm sorry," she managed to get out between coughs.

"What's wrong, Caitlin?" Levka ran his hand over hers.

She shook her head. "I...I guess it's late enough to call it a night. We have an early morning excursion to Grenada."

"Is it the cards?" Ruric asked Levka and his friends. *"Not once has she joined in on the games. She says she would rather watch, but every time she does, she seems bothered."*

Levka pulled her up from the sofa. *"I think you're right, Ruric. I should have been more observant."* He sighed. *"I wish she'd said something before about this."* The guys all rose from their seats.

"Let me just finish my drink," Caitlin said.

"She has been careful to hide her distress before this," Arman offered.

Her hand trembled, and Levka squeezed it. "I'll take Caitlin to her stateroom."

"And then what?" Ruric asked.

Everyone looked at him as he raised his brows. *"I am her mate, so she has confirmed."*

Arman shook his head and collapsed on the chair.

Ruric bowed. *"I knew you would make her yours."*

"Off to another life-threatening adventure," Stasio said.

"Doesn't anyone want my opinion on the matter?" Arman asked. *"I don't think..."*

"No!" the others said in unison, as Levka guided Caitlin out of the lounge.

Levka was torn as to what to do next. He couldn't take Caitlin for his mate as much as he wanted without alerting the Dallas league. But he couldn't leave her alone in her stateroom to face Vlad who would continue to try and get her alone. Vlad would take her forcibly now that she'd chosen Levka over him if Vlad got the chance. Levka just couldn't let him have the chance.

"I'm sorry about messing up your card game and upsetting Arman," she finally said as she handed her key to Levka.

He unlocked her door, remaining quiet, hoping she would confide in him.

"He's a good teacher, and I don't want him to think he upset me." "But?"

Levka opened her door.

She looked up at him with teary eyes and attempted a smile, but she couldn't hide her grief from him.

He urged her into the room and sat her down on the pink sofa. "What upsets you about playing cards?"

She shook her head. "You'll think I'm a psychological mess. I would rather you didn't."

"No. I won't. You've had a terribly traumatizing experience, and it wasn't all that long ago." He sat beside her and pulled her against his chest. "What upsets you about playing cards?" he repeated. He couldn't help trying to coax it out of her using his vampiric charm. It was as natural for him as taking a breath of air, despite the fact he knew she could resist his abilities no matter how hard he tried.

Was it that she was such a challenge that intrigued him so?

"Sometimes you sound like my psychiatrist," she confided, "coaxing, insistent, caring."

Inwardly, he groaned. A psychiatrist indeed.

She took a deep breath. "A year ago, my foster dad loaned my father his yacht. They had sailed for years together. My father was a good seaman, but the storm came up suddenly. We..." She looked away. "...we didn't stand a chance."

"How long were you in the water?"

"Two days. The nights were hardest. The first night...that was the worst. Lightning struck all around me, lighting up the sky, showing me the wreckage, but no signs of my parents or sister. I was all alone. After the accident, I wasn't right in the head," she said.

"You suffered a terrible tragedy."

"I could hardly sleep, and when I managed to fall asleep, I would have the same night terrors, the black ocean, sharks swimming nearby, bumping me, getting ready to take a bite out of me on the next pass. No water to drink, the sun beating down on me during the day, blistering my face and arms, the return of the wind and cold at night, but worse, my family was gone."

He'd seen enough horror in all his years of living and could imagine the terror she must have felt, adrift at sea after losing her family, all alone.

"I didn't speak for a long time. I was a mess. My friends quit writing to me. They couldn't understand what I had gone through. They didn't know what I needed to get me through the pain. I didn't either." She gave a small laugh. "I felt I would have been better off if I had drowned."

Rubbing her arm, he tried to console her, wishing he could share how much he understood. "They think that after a year you should be perfectly fine."

"Yeah. Like all the horror should be behind you."

"It takes time." A lifetime or several, he should know. He wanted to tell her he would be her friend for all eternity. He wanted her like he'd wanted Cassandra, but he couldn't take her into his dark life. "It'll get better," was all he could say.

Caitlin looked at the door.

"What's wrong?" But Levka knew what was wrong. Vlad was communicating privately with Caitlin. She stiffened in his arms.

"I wish I could block his talking to me," she said softly.

She could, if she became one of them. But even then, it would take some time for her to learn all their ways.

"What does he want?" As if Levka didn't know.

"For me to invite him in."

"And you mustn't."

She shook her head. "You're my mate. You're the only one I would invite in."

Levka kissed her cheek. "He won't give up trying."

"He can try all he wants, but I'm not letting him in my stateroom." Smiling, she leaned over and kissed Levka's lips.

Her mouth felt velvety against his, sweet from the sugary soda she'd sipped. He ran his fingers through her raven curls and luxuriated in the feel of the silky strands. Her jasmine fragrance called to him. Her pulse quickened, sending his hormones into turmoil. Gritting his teeth, he fought extending his canines.

Being here alone with her in her stateroom was *so* not a good idea. Yet what alternative did he have? He couldn't leave her alone. In fact, for the rest of the trip, he couldn't chance having Vlad get her by herself.

Yet her actions, and his, were driving him over the edge.

"Caitlin..." He meant to tell her she needed to go to bed, that he needed to cool his heated blood down, but when she licked his lips, he groaned in defeat instead.

He deepened the kiss as her fingers undid the tie around his hair. She was everything he was not, lightness to his dark, innocence where he no longer had any, trusting when he was not to be trusted. Growling low, he bit back a curse and pulled away.

Her hands dropped away from his shoulders. He'd hurt her feelings when he would rather die than do so, but if he took their relationship any farther, he would make her one of his kind, and that would hurt her more.

"What's wrong?" she asked, the hurt evident in the softness of her voice.

"Nothing." Except he'd lost control of his canines again. He took her hands and kissed them. "You're so beautiful, so precious to me. You have to believe me when I say this."

The bewildered look on her face indicated she didn't believe him at all.

He wanted to kiss her cheek, to assure her in a more chaste way, but he couldn't chance getting too involved again. Already the sweet blood racing through her veins called to him like an aphrodisiac. Already his canines itched to sink into her neck, to take her blood, share his blood with her, and link them together forever.

"I...I was too forward, wasn't I?" She stood.

"No, dear Caitlin. It has nothing to do with you."

"Is there someone else? Someone back in Texas?" Folding her arms, she tried to look like a soldier, straight and strong, but her lip quivered, giving her away.

Feeling like a slug, Levka rose from the couch, but kept the distance between them. If she saw what he was, she would surely have a stroke. And because of her telepathic abilities, he couldn't control her mind or wipe her memories if he had to.

"There is no one else. Although I did lose a girl I loved several years ago."

Her brows rose.

"A couple of years ago," he amended.

"Ruric mentioned her."

"Yes, well I have not felt anything for a girl since. Not until I met you."

"Oh."

She looked so forlorn, he couldn't endure not giving her a quick embrace, just to reassure her, he told himself.

Closing the distance between them, he gathered her in his

arms, and she returned the embrace. Soft, warm, cuddly, and needy. What was he do to with her? He couldn't let Vlad have her, and he couldn't take her for his own without the Dallas league's permission. Until he and his friends proved their worth, he feared the league wouldn't go along with his taking her for a mate.

"You don't think I'm a clinging vine, do you? Too many troubles? Too insecure?"

He kissed her head and tightened his hold. *"You're perfect."* For me, he wanted to add.

She ran her fingers over his back. "I...I was playing cards with my eleven-year-old sister, Tanya, when the storm began. Dad told me to stay with her and keep her from getting scared. I...I wanted to help my father. Mother went up to aid him as the yacht slammed into the pitch-black waves. I knew the boat would soon break in two. I knew it like I knew I could never win at chess against my little sister. Tanya was a much better actress than me. She talked away about what we would do when we got home, about how she had a new friend at school who wanted to start an online newsletter club with her. She was the one who tried to calm me.

"I made her put on a lifejacket when I could no longer hear my mother and father's voices shouted above the wind. The lights went out on the yacht, and when the boat rolled on its side I grabbed my sister's hand. Somehow...somehow, we made it out of the sinking boat, but I lost hold of her hand."

Tears streaked down Caitlin's cheeks. "I lost hold of her. I was supposed to take care of her." She looked up at Levka and sobbed. "My brave little sister was lost, and me...oh, Levka, why did they have to die?"

And why not herself? He knew that's what she failed to say, knew in her heart that's what hurt her the most. Why did she live when her family had to die?

"You are not so different from me," Levka said, kissing her cheek. "I felt the same way concerning the death of my family."

"You said your father died in the war? Was it the Persian Gulf War?"

"An earlier one in a foreign land. Many battles fought overseas are not even mentioned in the States." Which was the truth. The Marcher Baron battles along the border of Wales were not in the history books taught in the States. Or at least the classes he took. His extended canines began to recede.

"You said your mother and sister were killed, too."

"Yes, by an army that slaughtered the innocents along with those of us who fought them."

"You, you fought these men?"

"Not then, not until I was older." And then to his horror, he'd come down with the plague. Some had died, and others... He shook his head. Others like him and his friends became a new race. Improved in some ways, cursed in others.

"Levka, do you need us to relieve you sometime during the night?" Arman asked.

"Thanks, Arman, but I'll manage."

Levka kissed Caitlin's lips one more time and hugged her to his chest. "You will be my undoing, siren."

She smiled sweetly, but the look was too sexy to be that.

"I'll come for you in the morning. But remember, don't invite—"

"Vlad in. Yes. I have that down. Thanks for listening to all my woes and still being a friend."

"That's what friends are for."

The door opened and Alicia glared at them. "*Out*, Levka. If you can throw Dylan out of here..."

"He's not a creep like Dylan is," Caitlin said.

Pleased she would defend him, Levka squeezed her hand. "See you in the morning."

"Goodnight, honey," Caitlin said to Levka, then gave Alicia a smug look.

Alicia's look couldn't have been any more fired up. When Levka shut the door behind him, Alicia said to Caitlin, "Honey? Mate? When my parents hear of *your* behavior, they'll ground you until you graduate from high school. And here you've always pretended to be Miss Goody Goody."

Caitlin didn't say a word.

Levka paced in the hallway outside their stateroom. He had every intention of returning to the room, but should he wait until the girls had gone to bed?

He couldn't risk it. Invisibly, he returned to the room.

Caitlin was gone. He assumed from the sound of the shower, she was taking one. Alicia was already wearing a long T-shirt and pajama bottoms, pea soup green, sitting on the farthest bed from the sofa, closest to the bathroom, painting her toenails.

Levka retired to the sofa. A little too short for his long legs, but it would have to do. At least while he was in the room, Vlad couldn't get to the girls.

He yawned. But when Caitlin walked out of the bathroom wearing only a towel, he quickly closed his eyes.

"Bathroom's free."

Even though she spoke with annoyance, her voice was like the mermaid's sweet melody. He fought opening his eyes, gentleman that he was. After nine-hundred years you would think he could be a bit of a rogue when it came to women.

He couldn't help himself. She would be his mate, and he wasn't a eunuch after all. He opened one eye.

16

To Levka's disappointment and relief, Caitlin had already slipped under her covers. He watched her until she fell asleep, then got a little more comfortable on the sofa. It would be a long night.

Early the next morning, still invisible, Levka napped a bit while the girls got ready to go on their island excursion. Finally, Alicia shoved her purse on her shoulder and headed for the stateroom door, her face as stormy as the weather. "I can't believe they would cancel the beach trips just because of a few clouds."

Levka sighed and returned to his stateroom to shower and change with every intention of chaperoning his minx the rest of the day, but he couldn't help worry that Vlad might try to grab her and whisk her away.

~

BACK AT CAITLIN'S STATEROOM, Alicia slammed the door open and rushed off.

Caitlin hurried after her. "Maybe the cruise director is afraid the water's too rough. You're just lucky the Concord Falls tour isn't already booked, and you can still go."

"Lucky?" Alicia glowered at her. "Seeing a bunch of waterfalls isn't what I would call lucky."

"Why didn't you just go shopping then?"

"What? And buy another stupid T-shirt? Shell necklace? Spice necklace?" Alicia made a sour face. "When we get to St. Martin, that's where I'm spending my money. Gold jewelry and tons of it." Alicia stalked after Lynne who was headed for the off ramp, too. "Did you get booked for the waterfall excursion?"

"Are you kidding? Some of us are..." Lynne gave Caitlin a look like it was private business.

"Why don't you go on?" Alicia said to Caitlin, her tone of voice suddenly saccharine. "I'll catch up later."

Caitlin smiled when she saw Levka and his friends headed for her.

"Sorry we couldn't come to your stateroom this morning," Levka said, showing his I.D. to a crewmember.

Caitlin showed hers, then they walked down the gangplank. "Alicia was coming, but some of the kids from my school are up to something." She couldn't disguise the worry in her voice.

Levka looked back at Ruric, who gave a small bow, then turned back.

Caitlin frowned. "I can't understand how you can communicate privately with him. What did you tell him to do?"

"I asked him to see if he could find out what the kids planned to do."

"Oh. Will he make sure Alicia doesn't get hurt?"

"Certainly."

When they boarded the bus, Arman and Stasio took seats near the back while Levka and Caitlin sat near the front. She kept watching for Alicia, hoping her foster sister would get smart and come on the waterfall excursion. But knowing Alicia and the way anyone could easily influence her, Caitlin didn't figure she would come with them.

The bus door closed. *No Alicia.*

Caitlin slumped back in her seat.

Patting her hand, Levka said, "Ruric will put a stop to whatever they are planning. Never fear."

"Thanks, Levka, for everything." She glanced out the window as the bus took off. "Looks like Vlad's not coming."

Levka didn't say anything, and Caitlin glanced at him. "I'm glad, aren't you?"

"I want you to stick close to me or to Arman or Stasio at all times."

"He can't do anything to me. Vlad, I mean." Levka's face was so dark, Caitlin frowned. "Well, what do you think he intends to do?"

"Spirit you away from one of the islands. I'm afraid he might try to take you to an airport and leave."

Caitlin shook her head. "I would have to agree, and I wouldn't." When Levka didn't respond, but continued to stare straight ahead, she squeezed his hand. "He couldn't force me to go with him."

"We can't risk it, Caitlin," Levka finally said, his words icy. "We always have to be on our guard."

She twisted her mouth and looked out the window as the bus traveled through the capital of St. George, then up to a lookout. The view of the town nestled amongst the hills, its white and redbrick buildings topped with green and red roofs, the busy harbor, and the island's south coast edged in sugar white sand surrounded by aqua water looked just like the advertisements she'd seen for island paradises. For the first time, she was really glad she'd come.

Traveling through the rainforest canopy, Caitlin pointed at a monkey with a yellow beard, black mask, and yawning mouth, sitting in a mahogany tree. Suddenly, he swung to another. "Isn't he cute?"

"A mona monkey. They live in the forests of Africa, but British sailors introduced them to Grenada."

"How do you know so much? You're an encyclopedia of information."

"Believe me, I know a lot about nothing," Levka said, smiling. "You know, lots of trivia, but when it comes to something important, nah."

"I bet."

Beneath the trees, lacy ferns crouched at their feet and yellow-billed cuckoos and purple throated carib fluttered in the lush greenery along the hairpin curves of the one-lane road. Houses hugged the tree-covered mountainsides. Surrounded by tropical flowers and ferns, the first of the falls suddenly appeared.

After leaving the busses, they headed for an aqua pool at the base of the fall, inviting swimmers to cool off.

Caitlin stared at crystal-clear pool, wanting more than anything to get in, just once, just to prove she could do it. And not this time because she was forced to.

Levka looked down at her and raised his brows.

Realizing she was squeezing his hand to death, she relaxed her grip.

He smiled. "Do you want to wade in?"

"I want to swim."

"Can you?"

She shifted her gaze from his hypnotizing chocolate eyes to the inviting water. "I want to."

"I can't swim, or I'd take you in myself," Levka said.

She looked up at him. "I wish I could teach you."

"Someday I would like that."

Taking a deep breath, she nodded. "Okay, I'm going to do it."

She sat down and pulled off her sneakers, then peeled out of her T-shirt and shorts.

She smiled when Levka's eyes focused on her shimmering blue bikini. "Do you want to wade with me?"

He pulled her up from the ground. "Lead the way."

Stepping into the water, she shivered. "Woooh, it's really cold. Oh, look, shrimp clinging to the moss-covered rocks and..." She drew closer to another. "...snails." Watching swimmers sitting under the falls, she pointed to them. "I want to do that."

"It's twenty-feet deep out there."

She sighed. "Yeah."

"Are you going to be all right?"

She walked into the deeper part. "Yeah, I think so. It's clear, not like the ocean. There are no sharks. Nothing to get me." She spoke her fears out loud, trying to reassure herself this was not anything like her experience in the ocean. She could do it.

"I'm going to get in and swim a little way out to see how I feel." Yet she couldn't let go of Levka's hand. Though the surface was clear, maybe down to about seven feet, the rest was dark, and she couldn't help fear something was down in the blackness just waiting to get her. But the water wasn't rough like the ocean. "I...I can do this!"

With a deep breath, she let go of Levka and jumped into the water.

Levka's heart nearly stopped when he saw Caitlin go under. He swore he would learn to swim if it killed him. Before now, neither he nor any of his friends had had any desire to learn.

When she resurfaced, she looked horrified. Then she quickly swam out of the water, her lips blue, but her eyes smiling. "Man, is the water cold!"

Without hesitation, Levka yanked off his shirt and covered her with it. Rubbing her arms vigorously, he warmed the siren...*his* siren up.

She smiled. "I did it! I..." Her teeth clattered. "I got in, and I wasn't afraid. If it hadn't been so cold, I really would have swum to the waterfall."

"You nearly gave me a heart attack when you went under." He kissed her cold, wet cheek.

"I'm sorry, Levka. I promise when I get better about the water, I'll teach you how to swim. Though a warmer place would be better."

"I would like that."

She looked around. "Where are Arman and Stasio?"

"They hiked up to the second waterfall."

"Oh, let me get dressed! I want to go, too."

"It's a forty-five-minute hike."

"I'm game. Only..." Losing her balance, she grabbed Levka's arm. "...do you feel kind of funny? Like we're still on board the ship rolling back and forth in the ocean?"

"Yeah. We still have our sea legs."

As soon as she was dressed, they began the hike up toward the second fall through a nutmeg plantation that smelled heavenly of sweet and spicy nutmeg. Blood red soil dotted the mountainsides where vegetation had been cleared.

Levka picked a small red fruit off a tree that looked like a miniature apple. "Taste."

Caitlin bit into the fruit and smiled. "It has the texture and taste like a pear. What is it?"

"A French cashew."

Caitlin laughed. "If you had told me that to begin with I would have thought it was a really strange-looking nut."

A few feet away, Levka pulled cocoa off a yellow tree growth. He opened one, revealing a gooey white substance surrounding about twenty cocoa beans. "Rip off a bean and suck on it."

Caitlin hesitated, then smiled. "Okay, I'll trust you just this once." She took the bean covered in the white sticky stuff and touched her tongue to it. "Hmm, really sweet."

"And to think you didn't trust me."

"You've got to admit, it looks kind of yucky."

He pointed to a spring. "You can drink from the natural spring water, too." She sipped from the cold water, then they continued their trek.

Surrounded by tropical vegetation on the narrow trail, they were halfway to the second waterfall when Vlad suddenly appeared from behind a teakwood tree. He smiled, but the look was menacing enough for Levka to tighten his hold on Caitlin's hand.

"Vlad's here," Levka communicated to Arman and Stasio.

"We're on our way," Arman said.

"Alone at last, I see." Vlad stalked toward them.

Levka pulled Caitlin behind him.

"Why don't you go find another one like her? You don't really care for her like I do," Vlad said.

Caitlin attempted to move around Levka, but expecting the worst, he blocked her view of Vlad.

"You didn't even try to see me for a year, Vlad!" she shouted.

"Willing to fight for her?" Vlad showed his fangs and lunged forward, but Arman appeared and pounced on him from behind.

Levka continued to shield Caitlin's view of them as Stasio got into the brawl.

"Let me see him! I can help," Caitlin said, sounding highly annoyed and extremely frustrated.

Levka shook his head as he thought how one sweet human girl could fight a vampire with a dark-hearted lust for her, and kept her behind him so she couldn't witness what was happening.

Monkeys and birds chattered in the forest, making a raucous melody, hopefully masking Vlad's hisses.

Before either Stasio or Arman could do much damage to Vlad, he vanished.

"Stop this, Vlad!" Caitlin said, still trying to get around Levka.

"We'll get cleaned up and meet you at the second fall," Arman said, his and Stasio's mouths bloodied from the fight.

They both disappeared.

"Vlad's gone," Levka announced, allowing Caitlin to see for herself.

Caitlin stared at the trail where there was no sign of anyone. "Where did he go?"

"He must have worried someone might come. Let's go to the second waterfall. Then it'll be time to return to the ship."

"But I thought he was going to fight you."

"I did, too, but he just took off without another word." He took hold of her hand, noting the way she kept looking for signs of Vlad.

By the time they made the forty-five minute hike to the taller fall, an overheated Caitlin, her cheeks flushed, hurried to strip out of her clothes. Spying Arman and Stasio nearby, she waved, then dove into the pool.

Breaking the surface of the water, she said, "Cold, cold."

Stasio and Arman joined Levka at the water's edge and though Levka tried to tell himself she was okay, there were fewer people here to rescue her if she had a panic attack.

"I got a good bite into Vlad's neck," Arman said.

"As did I," Stasio added. *"He won't be bothering the two of you for the rest of the day."*

"He's going to continue to be a problem." Lekva folded his arms while he watched his mermaid swim in the glass-like water.

"*Vlad couldn't make up his mind about Caitlin before, but now it seems no amount of dissuading him—*"

"Short of killing him will stop him," Arman finished Levka's communication.

Levka nodded. "*But I can't kill him in front of Caitlin. We have to be alone.*"

Stasio shoved his hands in his pockets. "*No deal. Too risky. For nine hundred years we've been a team. You're not facing Vlad alone. This isn't Medieval times. You've decided you want Caitlin, and she doesn't want Vlad. That's as far as it needs to go.*"

Levka looked at Arman.

He shrugged. "*It's as Stasio says. We've been watching each other's backs for far too long to stand on the sidelines now. One for all, and all for one. It has always been our way, and no sense changing it now.*"

Caitlin climbed out of the water. Chill bumps dotted every inch of her bluish skin. "Brrrrr," she bit out between chattering teeth.

Levka helped her into her clothes. "The hike down will help warm you up." He rubbed her back as they headed down the path.

"I wasn't afraid. Did you see?"

"We sure did. You did great, Caitlin."

Arman nodded. "You'll have to teach us how to swim, too."

Her lips still blue, she smiled. "Very invigorating, but way too cold. If we can find a nice warm swimming pool somewhere, I would go for it. But not on the ship. It reminds me too much of the ocean."

"Do you want to talk more about it?" Levka asked.

Caitlin shook her head.

Levka couldn't help feeling disappointed that she didn't feel comfortable enough to open up more with him. He reminded himself patience wasn't one of his greatest virtues, and he would have to give her more time.

When their bus arrived at the ship, his attention shifted to Alicia arguing with one of the parents who came along to chaperone as they stood on the gangplank.

Ruric watched from nearby and gave an elusive smile when he saw Levka.

"What news?" Levka asked.

"Alicia and her buddies planned to take a boat of their own out. But word got to their chaperones somehow."

Levka nodded. *"A vampire told them, no doubt."*

Ruric bowed his head slightly. *"What happened to Vlad? I heard him cursing telepathically all the way through the ship. Though he moved invisibly, I followed his trail of blood to a stateroom. Have some trouble?"*

"Arman and Stasio took care of it."

"Levka's thinking of fighting him alone," Stasio said.

"No way," Ruric said. *"Together. Always, we stick together."*

"I need to change into something dry so we can eat dinner." Caitlin headed for her stateroom.

"We'll meet you at the dining room shortly," Levka told his friends.

When they reached Caitlin's room, she turned to Levka. "I know you only mean to protect me, but the more I try to discern what had happened, the more it seems I heard growling and hissing or something, and then Vlad disappeared on the jungle path. What really happened?"

CAITLIN KNEW Levka wasn't telling her the whole story about why Vlad had suddenly left. But no matter what, he wasn't saying, so when they sat down to dinner in the main dining hall, she was still annoyed.

She greeted Arman, Stasio, and Ruric but ignored Levka. If she was to be his "mate," he shouldn't leave her in the dark.

Vlad was noticeably absent from their table.

Lynne and Alicia's high pitched voices headed their way, grating on her. But most of all, Caitlin was perturbed with Levka's silence.

Alicia plopped down in her chair. "I can't believe someone told one of the chaperones what we'd planned to do."

Caitlin looked over at Ruric. He gave her a devilish smile. "*Thanks, Ruric.*"

He bowed his head.

The waiter arrived and Caitlin ordered chicken on a bed of steamed rice. "You should have come on the excursion, Alicia, since your mom and dad already paid for it."

Stasio ordered a steak, rare. "Ocean water was too rough to swim in, but you could have swum in the pools fed by the waterfalls like Caitlin did."

Alicia gave them a dirty look and when she began to butter her roll, she slapped her knife on it so hard, the soft butter flipped onto her lap.

Caitlin screened her smile.

"Where's the Vlad guy?" Lynne asked. "I thought he was stuck to the rest of you guys like peanut butter."

"He wanted something lighter to eat," Levka said. "He might be downstairs at the pizza bar."

Just then, Dylan walked by the table, and Alicia looked as if she wanted to jump out of her seat and tackle him. He glanced her way, but hurried on past.

Alicia sank in her seat.

"I thought you had a thing going with Bobby, now," Lynne said.

"He's not Dylan."

"You talked to Vlad about his dinner plans, Levka?" Caitlin asked, finally realizing that Levka and Vlad probably weren't having a polite conversation.

Levka remained silent.

"When did you talk to him?"

Ruric raised his glass and his brows.

"He passed by your stateroom while I was waiting for you, probably hoping to see you again. I asked if he would join us at dinner. He said no, he felt like eating light. I don't think—"

Vlad suddenly appeared and stalked toward the table, his neck covered in bloody bandages, his dark eyes angry. "*Sorry, old chap. But you're not keeping me away from Caitlin.*" Vlad gave them an arrogant smile.

"Jeez, what happened to you?" Lynne asked. "You look like someone got the best of you."

Alicia made a face. "Really gross. Do you have to sit here and eat? Levka said you were getting a pizza."

"I would rather dine with my favorite companions." Vlad scooted into Dylan's old seat. "Did you enjoy the falls, Caitlin?"

She quickly shifted her gaze from the bloodied bandages on his neck to Levka. "*What happened to Vlad?*"

Vlad smiled, and again she wished she could privately communicate with Levka.

"*Arman and Stasio attacked me without provocation,*" Vlad said.

What did Vlad think? She was an idiot? "They were at the second waterfall, not anywhere near where we were."

"*Vampires, my dear, can move invisibly to other locations. They can move at a speed faster than the mortal eye can see.*"

"So you're saying Arman and Stasio bit you?" she asked.

Arman sipped his water and didn't react. Stasio almost hid a smile.

"Oh come on," Alicia said. "What? They're werewolves?"

"That's good, Alicia," Lynne said. "Yeah, the guys turned into wolves and bit Vlad. They do have long hair."

Vlad's mouth curved up, and his eyes remained focused on Caitlin. She felt the gentle tugging at her mind and knew he was trying to control her like he had tried a hundred times in the past, but he couldn't. Was that what intrigued him most about her?

"So they're vampires and you are too," Caitlin said. *"Why didn't you fight back?"*

"Three against one? Seems hardly fair."

"Let me see your teeth."

"You are the one for me." Vlad grinned.

"Your teeth look perfectly normal to me."

"Thank you."

The waiter served their salads and Caitlin speared a tomato. *"So you can't be a vampire."*

"The canines extend when we have need of them."

She glanced at the others. Though Levka and his friends poked at their salads, she was quite sure they listened to her telepathic communication. Were Vlad's responses to her private? She couldn't be sure. If they were for her hearing only, she was certain the others were deciphering what was being said anyway.

Alicia and Lynne were still talking to each other about werewolves and not paying any attention to the rest of them.

"You extend them when?" she asked Vlad.

"In anger or in lust." Again, Vlad grinned.

"Lust?

"Bloodlust. It's when we have to feed. But it also occurs when we desire to make our chosen mate ours permanently. It takes a great deal of control not to make the girl our own before getting our league's permission."

Vlad suddenly glanced at Levka, and Caitlin had the feeling

Levka had spoken to him telepathically. Shifting his attention back to her, Vlad smiled but didn't say anything.

Turning to Levka, she frowned. "What did you say to Vlad?"

"To let you eat your lunch in peace."

"Do you know what he tells me?"

"Of course. That we are big mosquitoes."

"I want to know what really happened to Vlad."

"Hasn't he already told you?"

"Sure. Arman and Stasio bit him. But I want the truth."

Levka pushed his empty salad plate aside. *"The truth is who knows with Vlad? I'm beginning to think he's crazy. Self-inflicted wounds maybe?"*

Now that, she could believe. Vlad was crazy. Obsessive over her. She could see him making up wild stories. Sure, maybe even hurting himself to back them up.

She took a roll from the bread basket and buttered it. "Next time you extend your teeth, be sure and show them to me, will you, Vlad?"

His smile and the menacing gleam in his eyes were wicked. *"Rest assured, my love, I will show them to you the first chance I get."*

17

After dinner that night, Levka, his friends, and Caitlin watched a movie. But halfway through the show, Levka's head drifted to her shoulder, and she found him sound asleep.

"Rough night," Arman explained.

"Trouble sleeping?" Caitlin asked.

Arman nodded. "Ruric sleepwalks when he's overly tired, and Levka went looking for him for a couple of hours last night."

"Oh. Poor thing. Levka should have gone to bed and not stayed up for the movie."

"He should have, but when I suggested it, he nixed the idea. Seems being with you was too much of a draw."

She sighed. "Well, you should have told me, and I would have gone to bed earlier so he could get some sleep." She took Levka's hand and held it, wishing he already lived in Orlando and went to her high school, that he could take her to the dances, to movies, to just hang out and talk. Why did he have to be from Texas, so far away? She couldn't ask him to pull up roots just to move near her, especially not when his league had a job for him to do.

Trying to take her mind off the return trip home and the realization they would soon part ways, she attempted to concentrate on the movie as the jewel thieves tried to make their big museum heist, but she soon saw Vlad watching her from several rows away. Chill bumps coated her arms.

Why didn't *he* live in Texas *instead*?

∽

LATER THAT NIGHT, Arman and Levka escorted Caitlin to her room, though Levka was still pretty groggy.

"*Are you sure you don't want me to relieve you sometime tonight?*" Arman asked.

"*I'll be all right.*"

"*You fell asleep during the movie. Caitlin asked you twice about your trip to Martinique tomorrow, and you never answered her.*"

"*Check on me about three in the morning.*"

Arman nodded.

"*And make sure Ruric doesn't sleepwalk again. The sock trick does wonders, except wait until he's asleep before you tie him or you're liable to suffer a black eye.*"

Arman laughed. "*Later.*"

As tired as Levka was, he knew he should have Arman watch over the girls. But some primitive part of him didn't want Caitlin spending the night with another vampire, even if he was his good friend. He'd only felt the same primal possessiveness over one other girl, Cassandra, and he knew beyond a doubt Caitlin was meant to be his. Yet he knew it couldn't be.

By the time he settled onto the couch, the girls had already gone to bed. With the injuries Vlad had sustained at Arman and Stasio's teeth, he wouldn't be fully healed until tomorrow.

Even so, it was best to be vigilant, Levka reminded himself.

In the middle of the night, he woke to hear Caitlin speaking telepathically, *"Go away, Vlad. I'm not inviting you in, so quit asking. It must be what? Two in the morning?"*

Levka held his breath, wishing that he could hear Vlad's telepathic communication. Then to his surprise, Vlad granted him his wish.

"Did you know Levka's watching over you right this very minute? Ever on the alert, not wishing to lose you to me?"

"You're certifiable, you know?" Caitlin responded.

"He will not be as much of a gentleman as me. So take care when you get up in the morning. He will be watching every move you make."

Not *every* move, Levka thought. But keeping his eyes off Caitlin proved a challenge. Still, Levka couldn't help berating himself for falling asleep sometime during the night. What if Caitlin's telepathic communication hadn't woken him? What if in a moment of weakness, she had let Vlad in?

"Go away!" Caitlin said to Vlad.

"Goodnight, dearest Caitlin."

The telepathic communication ceased for a time, then Vlad said, *"Goodnight, Levka. You won't be able to watch her always."*

Levka sensed Vlad moved away from the door. He called to Arman, *"Are you awake enough to relieve me?"*

"I'll be there as soon as I dress."

Within a few minutes, Arman was standing before the sofa. *"Get your rest. I'll see you in the morning."*

"I'll return at six."

Arman smiled, all knowing.

Yeah, no way would Levka let any other vampire watch his siren when she got up in the morning, even if her usual routine was to dress in the bathroom. What if she changed her habit this morning?

∼

CAITLIN TOSSED in her bed for the umpteenth time. She couldn't get Vlad's words out of her head. *Levka was watching her every move in the stateroom. Right.* Vlad was nuts. Yet despite knowing this, she couldn't get to sleep, waiting to hear more of his insane communication.

Before she had truly slept much at all, her alarm rang. Bleary-eyed, she stared at the clock.

Hadn't she just gone to bed?

She slapped off the alarm and headed to the bathroom before Sleeping Beauty beat her to it.

After rushing to get ready and missing breakfast, she and Levka and his friends arrived at Martinique's Balata Botanical Gardens, nestled at the foot of towering mountains. Razor-backed ridges surrounded the volcanic mountain, Mt. Pelee, shrouded in dense clouds.

"Stick close to me, like before," Levka warned her at Les Ombrages, the path leading through a mini-rain forest.

"Hmpf. After Stasio and Arman bit Vlad I can't imagine he would try to bother us in the gardens today," she teased.

Levka frowned at her. She smiled.

"I'm serious." He tightened his hand around hers.

Caitlin breathed in the sweet floral fragrance from the thousands of varieties of flowers and tugged him down another path, until she noticed Arman watching them from an intersecting walkway.

"Besides, this time even Ruric is with us," she said to Levka.

"Yes, he was disappointed he didn't get to see my mermaid swimming in the pool at Concord Falls yesterday."

"Hmm, well, there are lots of ornamental lakes here, if the park caretakers didn't mind me swimming." Slowing her pace, she observed the blood red hibiscus, purple begonias, and orchids in a rainbow of colors. She looked up at Levka. "I wish I could swim in the ocean's aqua surf, just once before we return home."

"We still have St. Martin tomorrow, if you want to go to the beach."

"Maybe..." She pulled him along. "Maybe we could go to one for a little while. I could try and wade out a little ways."

"We can certainly give it a try."

Caitlin caught a glimpse of someone watching them near the Creole mansion in the center of the gardens. She swore it looked like the tracker, Petroski, but then he faded away down another path.

"Would the tracker still be keeping an eye on you and your friends?"

"Why would you ask that?"

"I thought I just saw him over there." Caitlin pointed in the direction he had taken.

"No. He told us he would be returning to Dallas. He knows where we are and would have no reason to monitor our movements after we said we would return and do the league's bidding."

Maybe so, but she swore it was Petroski, and he *was* watching them. "Will you tell your friends?"

Levka smiled at her.

"Well? Even if you don't believe he's here, I bet you've told the others to keep an eye out for him."

"You're right. I've told them what you think you've seen, and they're keeping a lookout for him as well as for Vlad, though they feel as I do, that Petroski is not here."

"You are absolutely sure?" She raised her brows with the question.

He wrapped his arm around her shoulder. "No. That's why I told the others to watch for him."

"If he's here, then what?"

He didn't answer.

"Levka?"

He directed her down another path. "Seems Stasio and Arman's biting Vlad was not enough."

"You're kidding. He's here?"

"In the flesh."

Suddenly, Vlad converged on their path, but tourists strolled down virtually every walkway, and she didn't believe he would create a scene here. She stared at his neck. The bandages were gone, and there wasn't a mark of any kind on the skin.

"Vampires heal fast, Caitlin," Vlad said, as if he'd read her mind.

Now she realized the wounds weren't even self-inflicted. He must have gotten blood from meat in the ship's kitchen.

"I'm here with Levka."

"And his friends. What's one more? Even that pesky Dallas tracker is wandering around here somewhere."

"You saw him?" Caitlin asked.

"Back that way." Vlad motioned with his arm. "So, what kind of trouble are you in now?" Vlad asked Levka with a devilish gleam to his eye.

Levka moved Caitlin around to his other side, isolating her from Vlad.

She couldn't help being amused by his protective possessiveness. "If you're all vampires, how come you can be out in the sun? Aren't you supposed to burn up in the sun's rays?"

Vlad humpfed. "A myth perpetuated by fiction writers."

"Ah. So, then what about your aversion to crosses?"

"What we are has nothing to do with religious persuasion."

Glancing up at Levka, she observed his solemn expression, then she asked Vlad, "Do you have a reflection in mirrors?"

"Again, this has nothing to do with what we are. We have a need to replenish our blood. That is all."

"And you heal quickly."

"Yes."

And you can't go into someone's room unless invited, she thought to herself as she recalled Levka's insistence she not invite Vlad in. "What about earth?"

"What about it?" Vlad asked.

"Don't you have to sleep on your native soil?"

Vlad laughed. "Sure, stuffed in my pillow, though housekeeping has a fit about it. And I keep it in my shoes during the day so that I can move around."

"I see. What about you, Levka?"

"If I have dirt in my shoes, it's by accident."

Loving his sense of humor, she wrapped her arm around his waist and gave him a warm embrace. When Levka leaned over and kissed her head, his lips turned up just a hair.

"We've seen, Petroski," Ruric warned. *"I don't like it. Since he's here, it means he's not satisfied."*

∽

AFTER THE TOUR of the botanical gardens, they returned to the ship, but everyone seemed to be ill at ease. Levka's friends didn't even join them for lunch.

For the third time, Caitlin asked Levka, "Why are your friends not joining us?" Though she enjoyed spending time alone with Levka, she worried his friends' absence was an omen of ill tidings. She lifted another slice of pizza to her lips.

Levka gave her a polite smile, but his dark eyes seemed worried. "I've told you twice they were tired and would grab a bite to eat later. Are you sleepy?"

"Exhausted. I'm going to lie down after we eat." But she didn't believe Levka for a moment.

"Were they worried the tracker would get on the ship?"

When he reached over and patted her hand, she pulled it away to show she didn't like it one bit. She was not going to be pacified.

"Nothing to worry about," Levka assured her.

"Right," she said, sarcastically. "Just like Vlad is no one to worry about, right?"

He didn't answer her, and she knew then he really was concerned about Mr. Petroski.

After lunch, she was a little curt with Levka when she retired to her stateroom. She couldn't help it. Why did he keep leaving her in the dark when she was supposed to be his "mate"?

She gave a haughty laugh and started to climb into bed when she saw Alicia was fast asleep.

Caitlin realized she hadn't worried about what was going on with Alicia for some time now. Where did she go for the day?

Caitlin pulled the cover to her chin. She wasn't her foster sister's babysitter, she had to remind herself, which didn't stop her from stressing about her.

ALL THE REST of the day and into the evening, Levka and his friends tried to determine if the tracker was on board the ship. Though they couldn't locate him, Levka couldn't quash the sinking feeling the tracker wasn't through with them yet.

Ruric took Levka aside and said, "I've heard more whisperings about the plot against the passengers, but nothing sure about what is going to be done or when."

Levka shook his head. "It's the tracker I'm most concerned about."

"I think he doesn't want you to have Caitlin."

Leaning against the ship's railing, Levka looked out to sea and watched as the pale cold moon turned pink, then pumpkin orange and then eerily blood red in its entirety. *Blood moon... hunter's moon, so named when the hunters tracked and killed their prey in the moonlight.*

"Vlad won't have any say in it."

"Do we kill him, then?" Stasio asked.

Letting out his breath in exasperation, Levka said, "We'll deal with this matter if it becomes more of an issue."

Arman shook his head. "No good will come of this."

Ruric touched Levka's shoulder. "Caitlin just walked into the building that houses the dining room."

Levka glanced at his watch. "She's early and didn't wait for me to get her."

"She doesn't appear to be happy."

Clearing his throat, Levka said, "She's angry because I won't explain what worries me about Petroski."

"So, then she is most likely assuming the worst," Stasio said.

"Well, I can't explain what might be the worse-case scenario, can I?" Levka headed for the dining hall, assuming unless he explained more, Caitlin was bound to give him an icy reception. And if he did clarify what he thought the tracker was up to? Ensuring he stayed away from Caitlin?

She wouldn't understand.

SEVERAL HOURS LATER, Levka watched over Caitlin in her stateroom. He wasn't sure now what to do. Return home and do what the league wanted, but leave Caitlin to fend for herself against Vlad? No, he would never do that. Maybe Petroski knew that.

Then what? Move to Orlando and guard over Caitlin there? He would have to be ever vigilant, and he didn't think he could manage watching over her constantly even just on the cruise, let alone day in, day out wherever she lived, forever.

Which meant his only option was to turn her.

And that meant the death sentence for both of them.

He unbound his hair and ran his fingers through it as he reclined on the couch. As much as he wanted her and desired more than anything else in world to keep her safe, he couldn't see any way out of their dilemma.

18

The next day when they arrived at St. Martin in the U.S. Virgin Islands, Caitlin couldn't curb the nervous jitters skittering around in her stomach as she dressed in her stateroom.

Alicia gave her a snide look as she pulled her shorts on over her swimsuit. "So, you're going to swim in the great, big, scary ocean. Well, don't go where I am because I don't want you to embarrass me by screaming bloody murder if you have one of your panic attacks." Hurrying out of the room, Alicia slammed the door behind her.

Taking a deep breath that didn't settle her nerves, Caitlin soon joined Levka and his friends who all acted as her moral support for her swimming excursion. Or at least attempt at swimming.

She still wanted to know what was going on concerning Petroski, but today she wanted to put that concern aside as she tried to suppress the way her skin pebbled up in tiny goose bumps all down her arms and legs.

The white sand was warm and silky between her toes as

ivory-shelled crabs ducked into holes that disappeared immediately afterwards.

The rolling aqua waves beckoned her to come and play. Having loved the ocean since she was very small, she hated how afraid she was of it now.

She waded out to her knees, then turned back and motioned to Levka. "Come in. Water's nice and warm." She wanted him nearby. Something about him gave her an inner strength when she couldn't seem to conjure it up herself, and she could definitely use some of it now.

The only thing that helped her slightly was the fact she could see through the crystal-clear water all the way to the sandy white bottom. No sharks. Just pretty blue and yellow fish swimming in schools around her legs, some attempting to nibble on her.

After Levka surrendered his T-shirt, he walked in up to his knees in his denim shorts.

She smiled. "Sorry. I didn't think about you wearing shorts, not swim trunks."

"They'll dry." He took her hand and strolled in the water along the beach for a little way.

Then she pulled him to a stop. "Okay. I'm going to get in. It's shallow up to our chest a way out. Do you want to come with me?"

"As long as you promise to rescue me if I get in over my head."

"Absolutely." She tried to tamp down the edginess that threatened to unravel her resolve.

Wading deeper, she watched for any signs of fins.

When she was waist deep, she stopped, trying to bolster her waning courage.

"Did you want to go any farther?" Levka asked.

She nodded and headed farther out.

When she was up to her neck in the warm water, the tide reached Levka's chest, and he pulled her close. She wanted to pretend the ocean didn't terrify her, that she could manage this all on her own, but the longer she stood there unable to see what was all around her, the more her fear got the best of her.

Tamping down her panic, she tried to reason with herself, but Levka's next words made her realize she just couldn't push her recovery any faster.

"You're trembling. Are you cold?"

"I'm ready to go back in," she said, disappointed in herself. Did Levka realize she wasn't cold? She hoped not, the water and air were warm.

She cried out when she saw a silvery fish with a torpedo-shaped body and dagger-like teeth. "A tiger of the sea!"

"What?"

"Barracuda and their jagged teeth can rip your skin to shreds." She grabbed Levka's hand and tried to rush into shore, but the wall of warm, salty water she pressed against slowed her retreat. She glanced back to see the barracuda following them.

The water tugged at their legs, and the sand sifted beneath their feet, impeding their movement. Small waves pushed them toward the shore, then the tide pulled them back out, as Caitlin's heart picked up its pace.

But Levka suddenly lifted her out of the water and seemed to move so quickly it was a blur. Squinting her eyes, she wondered if she'd had too much sun. She cleared her throat, tasting of fishy seawater. "Here I was mad at you about Petroski. You're such a hero in my eyes. Did you know?" she said softly.

He smiled down at her, his dark eyes sexy and intriguing. "You're the only one for me."

When they reached the beach, he still held her tightly.

She smiled. "I can walk now, and thanks."

He set her down and they looked back at the water, but there was no sign of the barracuda.

She shook the sand from her shorts and pulled them on. "And here I thought I was about ready to go back in the ocean."

When they returned to the ship, it was time to depart and Caitlin and Levka headed back to their rooms to change into something dry. Afterward, they planned on having lunch. But for now, Caitlin stared at the tons of gift bags sitting on Alicia's bed.

Caitlin looked in one. A gold necklace. In another, a pair of gold earrings. A gold watch, gold bracelets, and a gold nose ring filled the other sacks. What did Alicia do? Buy out the store? Examining the receipts, she found Alicia had spent over a thousand dollars.

Shaking her head, Caitlin hurried to get a shower before the gold princess returned and took over the bathroom.

AFTER RURIC CALLED to Levka with some concern, he met him on the upper deck.

"Levka, I've heard more from the teens who intend to cause trouble aboard ship. They repeated they want to delay its return somehow so their spring break is extended."

"But you don't know how they intend to do this?"

"No. I believe they're still in a quandary as to how to accomplish their plan."

"We must find them before they try anything."

Just as the words were out of his mouth, two explosions rocked the ship's stern, the blast deafening. Plumes of black smoke billowed out the back end.

"This is the captain speaking. All passengers and crew to the lifeboats! Abandon ship! The ship is on fire!" boomed a voice over the public-address system.

Confusion and panic immediately seized the passengers. Some headed for their lifeboat stations, donning lifejackets. Others hurried to the lifeboat stations without their lifejackets.

Meanwhile, crew members tried to maintain calm.

"The pranksters," Ruric warned Levka. "It's the same voice I heard speaking before."

"Maybe so, but the ship *is* on fire." Levka headed toward Caitlin's stateroom. "Find the others and meet us at our lifeboat station. We'll make plans from there."

"Right." Ruric stalked off toward the ship's bow.

A girl screamed near the boat's stern and Levka whipped around to see, Amie, one of the Georgia girls they'd dined with, wearing her lifejacket. Her broom skirt had caught fire as the wind whipped the flames over the deck. Her face was white with terror as she screamed again. Before he could reach her, she climbed over the railing and jumped.

Without thinking, Levka vanished, reappearing beneath her over the ocean and caught her before she impacted with the water. Dropping into the ocean to douse the flames, the realization he couldn't swim came too late. Amie flailed her arms in the water, sobbing and screaming, but her lifejacket kept them afloat.

"Are you burned?" he asked, trying to calm her. She was too hysterical to respond coherently, and her flailing threatened to drown them both. "*Amie, look at me,*" he said. "*You're floating in a pool, enjoying a lazy day on your spring vacation. Relax and enjoy.*"

Levka wished he could allay his fears as well. Amie grew still in his arms and floated in the slight swells of the water.

"*Turn the ship around!*" Levka commanded his friends. "*Two of us are in the water. Amie, one of the girls from Georgia, is burned, but*

I can't learn the extent of her injuries. And someone make sure Caitlin gets to a lifeboat."

"At once, Levka. Can you manage?" Ruric asked. Levka held tight to the girl. *"Amie is wearing a lifejacket."*

"I'll go for Caitlin," Arman said.

"Ruric and I will get the captain to turn the ship around," Stasio said.

~

"Levka, where are you?" Caitlin asked, grabbing her own lifejacket and Alicia's, her heart racing. She couldn't believe the announcement the ship was on fire and they had to abandon it, but the blast had to be the cause. *"I'm getting my lifejacket, but I don't know where Alicia is."*

"I'm coming for you," Arman assured her.

"Where's Levka?" she asked, grabbing her purse.

"Helping a girl in need, as usual," Arman said, his voice dark.

"Good. Do you want me to wait for you here or..." Someone knocked on the door, and she rushed to get it.

"Caitlin?" Arman asked.

She yanked the door open, expecting to see Arman. Vlad gave her a wicked grin, shoved her into the room, and slammed the door. *"Going somewhere?"*

"The captain said go to our lifeboat stations. I've got to find Alicia. Why don't you have your lifejacket on?"

The menacing look in Vlad's fathomless ebony eyes exuded pure evil. He walked toward her. She backed away from him, until she bumped into the balcony door.

"Open it."

She glared at him. "We have to go! The ship's on fire. Didn't you hear?"

He grabbed the doorknob behind her, twisted, and pushed her onto the patio.

"*Déjà vu.*"

"Listen, Vlad, for a year I didn't hear from you. I've got other friends now who are a heck of a lot more loyal than you ever were. The only reason I think you're even interested in me is because Levka is. So give it up, will you?"

Vlad jerked the lifejackets from her hands and dropped them onto the patio floor.

"Vlad, listen to me. We have to leave!"

Tilting his head to the side, Vlad listened. "They're turning the ship around. Probably to return to port. But you will be mine before then." He grabbed her shoulders and pressed her against the railing.

"Quit it, Vlad!"

He gave her a small smile. "I told you we're vampires. Levka wants you, but he can't have you. My league has already approved my having you. Levka's league hasn't. You know the old saying, 'the early bird gets the worm.'" Then his smile broadened, and he showed her a pair of wickedly white canines.

"They're...they're fake," she said, hoping to God Arman would hurry and get to her. Vlad was certifiable.

"*Of course they are, love, if it makes you feel more comfortable.*" And then he sank the fake teeth into her neck.

She screamed out when the sharp fangs penetrated her skin and sank into her vein. His hands pressed against her shoulders, attempting to hold her still.

"*Don't struggle, Caitlin. It will only hurt if you fight me.*"

She tried to kick him and to hit him with her fists, but her strength was dwindling as she felt him sucking the blood from her neck, draining her of energy.

"*That's right. Nice and quiet, Caitlin. I'm nearly finished.*"

She didn't want to obey him, but she couldn't thrash about

anymore, her muscles were so unresponsive. Then out of the corner of her eye, she saw Arman and vaguely wondered how he got into her stateroom without a key. He didn't rescue her, didn't shove Vlad aside, but instead grabbed up the lifejackets.

He wouldn't lift a hand to save a mortal, she thought as her mind drifted into a dark haze.

∽

LEVKA COULDN'T BELIEVE it when he saw Arman flying above the ocean with Caitlin in his arms, limp and unresponsive. He was supposed to get her to a lifeboat, not put her life in further peril!

"*What is going on, Arman?*" Levka asked, still clinging to Amie, held afloat by her lifejacket.

"*I had no choice, Levka. Vlad got to her.*"

Levka's heart nearly stilled. "*What's happened?*"

"*He has taken too much of her blood. I had to save her from him. It was either bring her to you, or let him have her.*"

Arman dropped into the water beside Levka with Caitlin still secure in his arms and shoved one of the lifejackets to him.

"If I take her without their permission, the league will kill both of us," Levka said.

"Very possibly, but what a noble way to die, eh?" Arman wrinkled his nose. "Did I ever tell you how much I fear the water?"

Levka put on the lifejacket, then took Caitlin in his arms while Arman held onto Amie. "I won't tell the others you're afraid of the water." Levka bit into his own arm and offered his blood to Caitlin's lips. "*Drink, sweet angel,*" he coaxed her.

Caitlin's eyelids fluttered, but she didn't react any more than that.

Arman turned his head. "The ship's returning."

"Thank God for small miracles." Levka tried again. "*Caitlin, drink my blood, and stay with me.*" Levka looked up at Arman. "Does she realize what we are now?"

"Vlad told her what we all are and showed her his teeth right before he sank them into her neck. She didn't have a chance."

"I'll kill him," Levka hissed.

"His league will sign his death warrant for taking her by force as soon as we report him."

Arman touched Caitlin's wrist. "She's slipping away."

"I know it. I can't control her mind to make her drink."

"Maybe it's like Petroski said. It's better to take a mate we can control."

"Caitlin, you know what we are. If you choose not to be one of us, so be it. I lost a girl I loved dearly a very long time ago. If you die, I will sink to the bottom of the ocean and die with you."

"Subtle, Levka. No pressure. Let her decide for herself?" Arman gritted his teeth. "There's a shark headed our way. Your arm is dripping blood into the water."

"If...if...we...were..."—Caitlin's words were so soft, he could barely hear them—"...on...on land...I could..." She swallowed hard. "I...could...help." She wasn't making any sense. Had to be the blood loss.

Levka's blood chilled as the gray dorsal fin headed in their direction. "Make him think we're dolphins ready to kick his butt."

"Give me all the tough jobs, will you?"

"It'll keep your mind off being in the water."

Caitlin licked some of the blood dripping from Levka's wound onto her lips. He shifted his attention to her. "*Caitlin, will you be mine?*"

Her eyelids fluttered open this time. "*Vlad...*" Her eyes shut again, and his heart sank.

"*Drink my blood, and you will be safe from Vlad.*" Levka tried to drip the blood into her mouth, but managed to get more of it in the water.

Arman shook his head. "Can you keep the blood out of the water, Levka?"

Caitlin's hand touched Levka's waist. He tried to encourage her to drink from his arm again, but she turned her head away.

"She doesn't want our way of life, Levka. Give it up." Arman shifted his concentration back to the shark. "He has gone under."

"Is what Arman says is true? You want no part of our life?" Levka asked her, praying it wasn't so. He would do anything to make her his, yet he couldn't force her even if he wanted to. "Where... where...are...we?"

As weak as she was, he could hear her heartbeat quicken, felt the panic in her blood. He hesitated to say, afraid she would be paralyzed with fear if she learned she was in the ocean again. With a shark somewhere nearby.

"In the Atlantic," Arman said. "But we're with you this time, and you have nothing to fear."

"Thanks, Arman. Why don't you tell her about the shark again while you're at it? She doesn't seem totally aware of her surroundings. As weak as she is, it would be ideal if she doesn't have to worry about little niceties like that."

"Kiss...," she said, then swallowed hard.

"I think she means you, Levka," Arman said. "The shark's circling."

"Who isn't being subtle, Arman?" Levka said privately to his friend. *"Could you quit mentioning the bloody shark?"*

"Sorry, but he's really got my attention. I mean, I really don't like water, but I like it even worse when a ten-foot-long shark's swimming in it. I know I'll heal if he takes a big chunk out of me, but the idea of the pain and suffering, the blood loss, the time it takes to heal, and keeping the whole thing quiet—"

"Kiss me...," Caitlin said, her telepathic voice weak but more urgent.

"You are making this harder for me," Levka responded and kissed her cold lips, certain that's all she wanted, nothing more. He licked her dry lips and pressed his mouth against hers, wishing she would want to join him, hoping he wasn't making a mistake if she did want to be his.

Her tongue touched his lips, and he closed his eyes and kissed her harder.

"It's coming in for a bite," Arman warned.

"If you can't keep it from biting, let it get your leg. You will heal at least. But keep it away from Amie and Caitlin."

Levka leaned over to kiss Caitlin again, to give her what she wanted before he lost her forever. Though his dark heart wanted to force her to accept him. He didn't want to lose her.

Her lips parted slightly. "You...you...don't...know...what..." She paused. "...I...am."

"My angel."

She shook her head slightly. "A...witch."

Arman suddenly splashed frantically at the water.

Caitlin bit Levka's lip hard. Searing pain went through his mouth. His first instinct was to pull away, but her hands grasped his arms, locking him in place. She moved her mouth toward his, her eyes bright and determined. Her tongue flicked at his bloodied lip.

Arman kicked in the water again. "I hit it in the nose, but it's circling again, not giving up."

Levka spoke to Ruric this time. *"Ruric, make the ship go faster!"*

The shark's dorsal fin skimmed the top of the water near Levka and Caitlin.

"Remember to let it bite you and not the girls," Arman said, sarcastically, "as you will heal from the wound just fine."

Caitlin reached up and pulled Levka's face to hers, and sucked hard on his lip.

"Oh boy, are you in trouble with the league now," Arman said.

He wrapped his arms around Caitlin in a fierce embrace. *"You are mine."*

Arman coughed and sputtered after swallowing a mouthful of saltwater. "The shark's coming in for another attempt at a bite."

Levka felt the turbulence in the water, and the way Caitlin stiffened in his arms. But he offered her his wrist so she could have a greater dose of his blood. Trying to ignore the shark, he concentrated on the siren drinking her fill, the one who would be his for all eternity. If the league let them both live.

After several seconds, he pulled her away from his arm, then licked the wound, sealing it.

Her heartbeat was stronger, her pulse still slow though. She clung to him weakly.

"What have we done?" she whispered, her eyes misty.

"Levka will be your teacher and your protector," Arman said, kicking at the shark's short blunt snout. The shark twisted away. "You're now a fledgling, and it'll take some time to learn our ways. But then again, you have forever."

Caitlin's grasp on Levka grew clingier. "What...what are we doing in the ocean?"

He sensed her horror. "I went overboard to save a girl who'd jumped ship because her skirt was on fire. Do you remember Amie from lunch the other day?"

Caitlin looked over at Amie, her long dark hair floating in the water. "Is...is she okay?"

"Sleeping, but I don't know how badly burned she is." Levka gave Arman an annoyed look. "I hadn't expected Arman to bring you out here to me."

Caitlin caught sight of the shark making another pass and closed her eyes tight. "Just hold onto me and never let go. I can endure anything if you're with me."

Levka let out his breath. If he could get permission from the league to make her his *after the fact*, maybe all would be well. If they could first avoid the shark.

The predator's beady eyes sat forward on its broad nose, giving it a sinister appearance, but suddenly the jaws opened, revealing jagged, and serrated teeth close to Arman.

"Bite it, Arman," Levka shouted.

"You bite it, Levka!" Arman yelled back at him.

"Grab onto him and drain his blood!"

"He could...crap!" The shark bit into Arman's lifejacket.

Beating the shark's nose with both fists, Arman yelled ancient curses. Levka reached over and grabbed one of the ties to Amie's lifejacket before she drifted away. When Levka moved, Caitlin tightened her grip on him.

"I'm not letting go of you," he tried to reassure her.

Caitlin clenched her teeth, her eyes still shut tight. "Vlad, he said he was a vampire. That you all were, and that I would be his. He said his league approved it, not yours. Then he bared his sharp pointed fangs at me and sank his teeth into my neck." She shuddered. "I tried to break free. He telepathically communicated to me that it would hurt more if I struggled. I couldn't quit fighting him. After that, I don't remember what happened."

The shark released Arman's lifejacket and disappeared underneath the black waters.

"I came to your rescue," Arman said, his voice strained, part of his lifejacket shredded. "I appeared in your stateroom when I sensed your distress and found Vlad at your throat. I did the only thing I could think of. I grabbed the lifejackets, pulled you free from Vlad, and flew out here to where Levka and the girl floundered. I knew Vlad wouldn't try to fight me for you over the ocean."

"You saved me when you don't believe in helping...mortals?"

Arman shrugged. "I'm afraid Levka's a bad influence on me."

"You said you can fly? Why can't you take us out of here?"

"We're not..." Arman moved in closer to Amie again. "...not capable of flying when we're in water. I guess it's like a bird that isn't a waterfowl, getting its feathers too wet. Anyway, we don't have the capability to fly long distances over water either. Like over the ocean. Rivers, small lakes, ponds are all right. We have to use ships just like..." A dorsal fin appeared near Levka.

"We're on our way!" Ruric communicated. *"The captain's lowered a lifeboat. How in the world did Caitlin and Arman end up in the water with you?"*

They noticed then the cruise ship sat nearby, idling in the water. Passengers crowded the decks to get a look at the passengers in the water. Hands pointed in their direction. Probably at the shark that kept circling.

"Hurry the boat up! We have a bull shark ready to make us its next meal," Levka responded.

The lifeboat's engine roared in their ears. Smoke billowed out the stern of the cruise ship, and Levka realized the ship itself might still be in danger.

The shark bumped Levka, and his heart jumped. Releasing Caitlin, he turned around and socked the shark in the nose as hard as he could manage. On land, his strength was such he probably could have put his fist through the cartilage. But in the water, he was barely more than a mortal except for his mental abilities.

"Grab hold!" a crewman shouted and tossed a rope.

Caitlin treaded water with no lifejacket, her eyes wide with fright. Levka swam to her, wrapped his arm around her, and grabbed the rope when Arman wouldn't take it.

As quickly as they could, they pulled Caitlin into the lifeboat. Levka helped Arman lift Amie in next. "Her clothes caught fire," Arman said, his voice grave.

Arman and Levka scrambled to get aboard as the bull shark slid by, brushing against the boat.

One of the crewmen cursed out loud when he saw how big the shark was.

Turning the craft around, another crewman taxied back to the cruise ship.

"How bad is the fire?" Levka asked, pulling Caitlin into his arms. Someone had wrapped a blanket around her. She looked exhausted from the ordeal, not to mention the blood loss.

"As soon as we get you folks on board, we've got to head back to the Virgin Islands. We'll put into port and make arrangements for passengers to fly home."

"That bad?" Levka asked.

"We should make it into port," the man said, with a heavy Greek accent.

Caitlin closed her eyes and nestled her head against Levka's chest. He looked over at Amie, but the crewman shook his head.

Arman said privately to Levka, "*I didn't want to say anything in front of Caitlin or while we were still in the water, but Amie's burns must have been too severe. She died peacefully sometime after I first took hold of her.*"

As soon as they boarded the cruise ship, Amie was carried away on a stretcher, and Levka turned to see Vlad watching Caitlin and him, his look as deadly as the shark's. Levka tightened his arm around her shoulders still wrapped in the blanket.

Caitlin slipped her arm around Levka's waist. "I don't really believe in vampires, but if I did, what's about to happen now?"

19

Ruric and Stasio hurried to join Caitlin, Levka, and Arman.

"How Arman and Caitlin ended up in the water is what I want to know," Ruric said, his face covered in soot. "The cooks are preparing a makeshift meal on one of the upper decks. Most everyone has been fed. But we need to make sure Caitlin—"

"Caitlin's already eaten, though she might need some water," Levka said. "What happened to you?"

"Trying to put out the fire, but we didn't have much luck." Ruric studied Caitlin for a moment, then raised his red brows. "You can't mean to say you've made her yours, Levka. What will the league say?"

"They'll agree to it under the circumstances." Levka's voice was resolute, but even so he seemed unsure of his words, which made Caitlin's skin feel twitchy.

Vlad moved closer, and for the first time, Caitlin noticed how Levka, his friends, and Vlad moved panther-like, not like typical male teens. And, and now she noticed the oddest thing. Each of them had a halo of pale gold around their eyes.

"We didn't have a chance to finish business, love," Vlad said, bowing his head. "But you're still mine."

"This is not the Dark Age, Vlad, and for your information, I chose *Levka* to be my champion." Figuring that sounded like the right words to say, she gripped Levka's waist tighter, afraid Vlad still had some kind of bizarre claim to her. She didn't feel any different though, so she couldn't believe vampires truly existed, or that she had somehow been transformed into one.

Though she cared a great deal for Levka, thinking she could become immortal had quieted her fear of the water and of the shark, and that's why she finally drank a drop or two of his blood. The notion it would turn her into a blood-sucking monster was too absurd to believe. She hadn't seen any evidence of anyone flying anywhere either. Though she couldn't reconcile the fact Arman had appeared in her stateroom without a key. Maybe he got it from Alicia.

"Alicia, is she okay?" she quickly asked, furious with herself that she hadn't been more concerned about her foster sister.

Stasio folded his arms. "She has been sunbathing all this time, while you fended off the sharks."

Her mouth dropped open. "Sharks, as in plural?"

"There were two."

She shuddered all the way to the marrow of her bones.

Rubbing her arm, Levka leaned down and kissed her forehead.

Vlad's mouth twisted wryly. "You'll have to excuse me for my abruptness, but I'll leave you to contemplate your fate. I wish to remind you that the Orlando league already approved my having you. And Levka's Dallas league did not. In lieu of this, you are mine. But under the circumstances, I'll permit you to stay in Levka's company until we return home. Then, you'll obey me. Ancient rules, you know. You are a fledgling, my dear. My very own fledgling." He gave another bow and stalked off.

"I don't know what I ever saw in that arrogant creep!" Then she looked up at Levka. "If he's so powerful why doesn't he just claim me now?"

"There are four of us, Caitlin. He figures when we return to Fort Lauderdale he can call in some more of his muscle and even up the odds, or even call on more to outnumber us."

"He's not really right, is he? About the ancient/fledgling stuff?"

"We do have a pecking order," Levka said. "Can we return to our stateroom?" he asked Ruric.

"The fire is still burning in the stern, but our room is far enough away it should be okay," Ruric said.

Levka explained to Caitlin as the five of them walked to the stateroom. "It's like having elder statesmen. The ones who have lived the longest, have been in charge the longest, make most of the decisions."

Caitlin gave a ladylike snort. "Like parents with a child."

Levka smiled. "Not exactly. The thing of it is, many of the elders in our organization treat us as teenagers—"

She raised her brows.

"When we are much older, turned at the same time they were."

"Don't tell me. You're thousands of years old."

He looked at his friends. "Do I look that old?"

She chuckled. "No. You look like you're about my age, but you act a lot older sometimes."

"Good, you had me worried."

"I don't believe any of this, you know," Caitlin said, as she watched Ruric unlock the door.

Stasio bowed his head and vanished in thin air before her eyes.

Her mouth dropped open.

Arman disappeared next.

She grabbed Levka's arm. "Don't you dare do that to me, too."

Ruric opened the door.

Their faces solemn, Arman and Stasio stood inside the room.

"I...I can't do that, can I?"

"No, not right away." Levka guided her into the room.

She collapsed on the couch. "Did you wipe Dylan's mind of knowing Alicia and me?"

Levka inclined his head. "He was too dangerous to both of you. It was best he didn't remember you, as if you didn't exist. Everyone else who knows differently, thinks he's playing a con game. Alicia gave up on him, which was the best thing that could happen."

"Besides," Stasio said, "Ruric discovered two of the boys who started the fire, and Dylan was the one who instigated the whole thing."

"Have they arrested them?" Levka asked.

"They're in custody," Ruric said.

"Poor Amie." Caitlin collapsed on the sofa. "They ought to get life for hurting her the way they did. So, what are we going to do about arriving in Fort Lauderdale?"

"I haven't come up with a plan yet," Levka said.

"What about this job of yours? You'll have to return to Dallas, and..." Caitlin glanced out the window. "What will happen to me?"

"I've been trying to figure out what to do, Caitlin." Levka crouched before her. "You have to come with us. I can't leave you behind. Now that you're a fledgling, you need an ancient's protection. My protection, though all four of us will always be at your beck and call."

"What about what Vlad said concerning the Orlando league approving I could be his, and the Dallas league not granting approval?" She rolled her eyes. "I feel like a piece of property."

Levka smiled. "It's just our way. We take a mate and protect her until she's strong enough to protect herself."

"Great. You didn't tell me I would be in danger from other... other, well, if I believed in them...vampires."

Taking a deep breath, Levka reached for hand and held it. "Caitlin, you were already in danger from the others. We are drawn to those we can't control. If others had known about you—"

"What about the others who came to see Vlad that time? Were they like him?"

"More than likely. And that's why he was perturbed. He probably didn't want them to know about you."

"If he wanted me so badly, why did he abandon me for a year?"

Levka shrugged. "Maybe he was having trouble getting approval from his league. Or maybe he was having doubts about turning a prospective mate who could fight him. I truly believe he intended to have you even before he learned I wanted you though."

"But what about the league business?"

"I will take you to the ends of the earth and live in sin with you if they don't approve our mating." Levka grinned.

"Oh, that's just great."

"We'll go with you," Stasio said.

Arman grunted. "Just when I thought we would get back in the league's good graces."

Caitlin leaned back on the couch. "What if I don't want to be like you?"

"You don't have any choice, Caitlin." Levka's face wore a slightly worried frown. "Vlad drained too much of your blood. You were near death. I offered my blood to you freely, and without coercion you accepted."

"If you don't count saying you would sink to the bottom of the ocean and join Caitlin in death not coercion," Arman said.

Levka gave him a scalding look, then faced Caitlin again. "Even if the league doesn't officially approve, we're blood-bonded. Forever, we're tied to each other."

"What if we don't get along?"

"We'll have our ups and downs. I'm certain of it."

Caitlin looked at the zig-zag carpeting. "My foster parents will kill me."

"We'll have to wipe their minds of you. You'll start over again."

"In Dallas? If you have to work there, and Vlad will be bugging me still in Orlando, shouldn't I move to Dallas?"

"She should," Arman said, "if we're ever to make it right with the league."

"They have to approve of her being turned or we're back to the beginning," Ruric said.

Caitlin squeezed Levka's hand. "Prove you're a...a vampire. What special abilities do you have?"

Levka pointed to the wall behind the beds. "Listen. What do you hear?"

Closing her eyes, Caitlin listened.

A man was arguing with someone in the stateroom next door. "I told you we should have taken a flight to Hawaii. Rotten kids. They ought to string them up."

Caitlin opened her eyes wide. "He must have raised his voice."

"No. Our hearing and sense of smell is much greater than mortals'."

"And you can vanish and reappear places."

"Only places we've been before. We can't enter a private dwelling unless we're invited in."

Caitlin slapped her legs. "Vlad! How did he come into my

stateroom? I never invited him in. He shoved his way into the room, but he couldn't have if he hadn't been invited in, right?"

"He probably convinced Alicia to let him into your room earlier. As long as someone is easily brainwashed, the vampire can gain entrance. Which reminds me, unless it's one of us or someone we say is all right, don't invite them into the place, whatever happens."

"I...I have to tell you something, too. I told you already, but I...I don't think you were listening. Or believed me."

Levka didn't look concerned. But she was.

"I'm a witch."

Levka and the others smiled.

She frowned. "Really. I am."

Suddenly the P.A. system came to life. "We have docked at the port and evacuation of the ship is mandatory. Secure all of your belongings before you depart. No one will be returning to the ship."

Levka helped Caitlin up from the sofa. "Don't leave my side, whatever you do."

"Because of Vlad?"

"He has had a taste of you. He'll want to finish the process and claim you for his own. So stick close to me. The others will keep an eye out for us, too."

She was certain they meant well, but she couldn't shake the fear Vlad would get around Levka and his friends somehow and get to her. But once she was on land, she could use her magic again. Although, her parents had always taught her to keep it secret from others.

She glanced at the mirror before they departed the stateroom. "How come you have gold around your eyes and I don't?" She turned to look at Levka. "Are you sure I'm really one of you?"

"A plague changed us many years ago," Levka said, hurrying

her out of the room. "*We're ancients, but those who have been changed by a vampire's bite do not exhibit this same condition. Only vampires can see this. Therefore, you are vampiric.*"

"Most vampires revere us for being ancients," Ruric said.

Caitlin glanced at his superior smile and shook her head.

Arman chuckled.

"Arrangements for airline transportation need to be made once you depart here," a crewmember announced on the P.A. system. "Busses will take you to the airport, and accommodations will be made for those who can't get flights out by this evening."

A light rain was falling over the port when Caitlin and her friends walked down the gangplank. "What about Alicia?"

"Her school chaperones will ensure she gets home all right. We'll have to return to your foster parents' place to wipe their minds that you exist." Levka glanced down at Caitlin, tightening his hold on her hand. "How do you feel?"

"Normal."

He gave her a small smile.

"Not that *you* aren't normal," she quickly said, as she felt the blush rise to her face.

Vlad looked in their direction, then boarded a nearly full bus. The doors shut, and the bus drove off.

"You would think he would stick closer to us," Caitlin said.

"I'm betting he wants to get to the airport soonest to get a seat, contact who he can back home, and prepare for our arrival." Levka steered Caitlin to the last bus. But when Vlad's bus vanished from view, Levka guided Caitlin and his friends in the opposite direction and headed down the pier.

"What are we doing?" Caitlin asked.

"Going on another cruise." Levka pointed at one of the cruise ships among the three others. "It's getting ready to leave, and we're going to be on it."

"This is a cruise for the newlywed or the nearly dead," a crewman said to another privately, though Caitlin could hear their words clearly as she boarded the ship.

Levka smiled at her when she furrowed her brow at the men. "Eavesdropping?"

She shook her head. "Not trying to."

"Yeah," the other crewman said. "How many do you think will keel over this time?"

"By the end of the cruise, five. The two we dropped off in St Martin are part of the count though."

Ruric patted Levka on the shoulder. "Got our rooms."

"Were they already available?" Levka asked.

"One of them was. We needed two more to accommodate us this time. Two single beds in each room. For them, I had to wrangle some moves."

"What?" Caitlin asked, her eyes wide. "Did you do the same on the other ship? Dylan was furious he got stuck with snoring Michael."

Levka raised his brows. "You wouldn't object, would you?"

"Not for him. But who did we move on this ship?"

Arman puffed up his chest. "Just what I like. Someone with a conscience."

"A widow and a widower are now sharing a stateroom. They seem very content with the arrangement." Ruric flashed a toothy grin. "Everyone should be a couple on long voyages, just like in deep space."

"That gives us one room. Who else?"

"We have to have rooms, Caitlin," Levka said, taking her hand.

"Two kids had separate accommodations from their parents. The parents needed more family time." Ruric folded his arms, as if waiting for her agreement.

"All right."

"Good." Levka pulled her toward the ship's theater as the ship moved away from port. "If all goes as Vlad plans, he will arrive at Fort Lauderdale and wait for us to appear at the airport."

"But instead?"

Stasio cleared his throat. "The ship will dock at port."

"If people die on these cruises, where do they put the bodies?" Caitlin asked, suddenly wondering how they could keep the bodies for so long.

"In cold storage," someone behind them said. They turned to see a crewman wink. "We have a storeroom to keep the ice for the ice sculptures and flowers in refrigeration. That's where we keep the bodies. But we already removed the two we had."

"So there's room for more?" Arman asked.

"Yep."

"What about their traveling companions?" Caitlin asked. "It must be horrible for them."

"One was with a tour group. She just went face down in her potato soup. The rest of the guests finished their meal while we took her away. She was widowed. The other was a man. His wife sent him home at St. Martin, but she'd paid for the cruise, and she intended to finish it."

"I guess it's not such a bad way to go, if you like cruises," Caitlin said.

Levka rubbed her arm. "I didn't even ask if it was okay to take the ship back, Caitlin. I'm sorry. I should have asked."

She shook her head. "I'm going to get used to the water, one way or another."

When they reached the theater, music was playing and couples dancing. Older men serving as dance chaperones were seeking single ladies to dance with.

"Dance with me," Levka said, offering Caitlin his arm.

"You know I'm not very good."

"For me, you are perfect."

To the dance escorts' surprise, Stasio, Arman, and Ruric spread out and escorted ladies up to the stage to waltz. Flattered at the attentions of younger men, the older women didn't hesitate.

But an hour into the evening, Caitlin leaned against Levka, the strength she had dwindled.

"What's wrong, Caitlin?" he asked.

"I...I feel really tired."

"She needs new blood," Arman said as he danced nearby. *"That's the problem with a fledgling. They need frequent small feedings."*

"I don't want her feeding off mortals for now. She's too newly turned."

"We can't get to a blood bank source right now, and you shouldn't give her anymore of your blood for another day or so," Arman warned.

Ruric smiled. *"She can feed off me."*

She started to pull away from Levka.

"Not now," Levka said.

She hissed, and he clamped his hand over her mouth.

20

Stasio chuckled at Caitlin as they moved toward the entrance of the ballroom. *"It has been a while since I've seen a fledgling's actions. This should be interesting."*

"Ruric, get a couple of people to give blood. Arman, go with him and take the blood, then bring it back to me to Caitlin's stateroom. Stasio, you come with me."

"It would be so much simpler if she just fed off one of us," Ruric said, then headed out of the ballroom with Arman following behind.

"She is not feeding off anyone this early on." Levka returned her to her stateroom with Stasio in tow.

"Quit calling me a fledgling," Caitlin snapped, then collapsed on the bed.

Stasio grinned. *"Maybe Petroski was right. A mortal who was more controllable..."*

Caitlin glowered at him.

Stasio chuckled. "Except for Levka's getting us involved in rescuing mortals from time to time, life has been rather dull. I can see now, that will change. Well, actually, it changed the instant the two of you saw each other. I'm surprised Arman isn't raising more of a fit about all of this."

Levka placed his hands on his hips and studied Caitlin's mutinous expression. If she wasn't so exhausted, he assumed she would be giving him more of a fight. It didn't matter. What was done was done and could never be undone. She was his to protect for all eternity, and someday when she was strong enough, she could even protect him, if need be.

Like the trials of training a puppy, accidents would occur, no doubt, and he would have to call on every shred of patience he possessed and deal with it.

Half an hour later, Ruric and Arman arrived at the room, blood vials in hand.

Levka offered the blood to Caitlin, but she turned her head away.

Arman sat on the desk chair. "She is worse than a new fledgling because we can't control her actions."

She speared Arman with a dagger of a look.

Arman simply smiled.

"Caitlin, drink and you'll feel better." Levka reached for her chin, but she bared her teeth at him.

Ruric laughed. She turned her animosity on him. A smile plastered to his lips, he bowed. "She is a live one, Levka. I want one like her, too."

"Not me," Arman said. "If I ever get desperate enough, *first*, I will get league approval, and second, I will find a girl who is completely brain-washable. I don't like conflict."

"Hmm, for me," Stasio said, "the girl has to have a love of history. If she doesn't, it will be a no go."

Levka sighed. "Maybe we need privacy."

"We'll see what's going on in the rest of the ship," Stasio said, then vanished.

"Stay with him," Levka ordered.

"We're on it," Ruric said and disappeared.

"If you need our assistance, just holler." Arman bowed to Caitlin. "We're truly glad you're part of our family. If you ever need anything from any of us, we'll come to your aid." He left with the others.

"Caitlin, honey, drink," Levka coaxed, sitting beside her on the bed.

"I...I can't. When I did it before, it was because I was terrified of the shark. I told myself that I was doing this because it was going to make me immortal, though deep down I truly didn't believe it. I thought Vlad was wearing false teeth. I thought it was all a lie, made up in his sick mind. But I wanted to live, and somehow felt if I did as you asked, I would be okay."

"I care for you more than life itself, dear Caitlin. I would let no harm come to you ever. You must believe me. But you need to drink."

She sighed, and her eyes shifted from the vials of blood to his lips.

He leaned over and kissed her, wanting to control her just this once, make her drink the blood so she could see how much she needed it.

Wrapping her arms around him, she pulled him close and kissed him back. He dropped the vials on the bed and ran his fingers through her windswept curls. "My nymph from the sea." She licked his lips, then extended her teeth.

He grinned and grabbed up a vial of blood. "Not from me, love." Opening the vial, he offered it to her.

For a moment, she stared at the blood. "Your blood mixed with the seawater drew the shark."

"Yes, I tried not to drip it in the water, but you wouldn't drink from me."

Her eyes shifted to his. "I'm...I'm a pill, aren't I?"

"No. All of this will take some getting used to."

She lay back on the bed. "I'm just tired. I'll sleep and feel better."

Shaking his head, he pulled the stopper out of the blood vial. Then he touched the blood to her lips. "You need to sleep after all that has happened. But you need blood, too."

She licked her lips and frowned at him, then rolled onto her side. "I'll drink it later."

Touching her lips with more of the blood, he tried again to encourage her to drink. She took in a deep breath, smelling the blood. Closing her eyes, she sighed deeply. Then she swept her tongue over her lips again. Groaning, she reached for the vial.

He offered it to her. "Drink slowly."

Caitlin tasted the sweet, coppery taste, but it wasn't the same as Levka's. "I like yours better." After handing him the half-finished bottle, she lay back down.

"I'll leave the rest here for now." He set the two vials on the bedside table. "You'll sleep."

Touching her temple, she stared at him. Levka's face seemed to blur. "The stuff is doing funny thingsss to my eyesss."

"Sleep, Caitlin. I'll be back in a while." Levka kissed her cheek, and then he watched over her.

She tried to focus on him, but the longer she watched him, the more he faded from her sight until she saw no more of him.

For some time, she drifted in and out of sleep. But even when she was partly aware, she was unaware, too.

"Invite me in," someone coaxed. The telepathic voice sounded a million miles away.

"Come in," she said, her mind still fuzzy. How long had she been asleep?

Petroski's gray eyes studied her. *"They drugged you."*

She stared at him, her mind not at all clear. Who drugged her?

Reaching down, he turned Caitlin's head to the side. "Levka's turned you after all. Know this, fledgling. I'm not just a tracker as Levka and his friends assumed. I'm an assassin. If you persist in staying with Levka, I will kill you both. You don't have the Dallas league's permission to be his."

"Vlad's..." She sighed heavily, wondering why the blood hadn't given her strength like Levka said it would. "Vlad's the one who forcibly took my blood and left me near death!" She meant to sound as mad as she felt, but her words came out no louder than a whisper.

Petroski's brows rose. "So, Vlad has claimed you."

"No." She closed her eyes against the swimming sensation in her skull. "Levka saved my life."

Petroski shook his head. "The league doesn't want to lose the princes. They fear the four will stick together in this travesty. But you can't be Levka's."

Her eyes popped open, but she felt she needed toothpicks to keep them that way. "You...you will kill him?"

"Easily. Would you wish that on your conscience before you die, too?"

She stared at the bed. "What am I supposed to do?"

"You wouldn't be able to fly invisibly this early after the change. Levka will have to take you to the airport in Fort Lauderdale if he's to take you anywhere. Make excuses to go to the restroom. Leave a note telling him you wish no part of him now. That you wish to explore your newfound freedom on your own. You will be able to turn invisible and leave. But you can't do this and fly. Leave the airport and you can go anywhere you please."

"What...what about Vlad?"

Petroski shrugged. "Don't return to Orlando. You'll be able to tell who is vampire and who is not. Stay away from them. In time, you will gain your own powers."

She closed her eyes against the pounding in her head. Nothing in life was ever easy. Why couldn't it be like before when her family was alive? "How will I survive?"

"We have a natural instinct for survival, Caitlin. Take what you want, go where you want, just stay away from Levka and his friends."

She opened her eyes, but Petroski was gone. The nightmare wasn't about to go away. With tears in her eyes, she hugged the death out of her pillow. Levka had saved her life.

Now it was her turn to do the same for him. She had her witch's powers. Sure. But a fledgling vampire, on her own?

TWO DAYS LATER, they were at the Fort Lauderdale airport, just as Petroski had predicted. Would Vlad and his buddies be here, too? But what about Petroski? Was he watching Caitlin's every move? She'd had a devil of a time pretending to be cheerful toward Levka and his friends, pretending that she planned to stay with them forever. She knew they sensed something was wrong with her, though she'd overheard Arman say he thought it was because she'd been newly turned. They hadn't been around a fledgling in a hundred years they'd said, so they couldn't remember how it would be for one exactly.

She couldn't help the way her stomach did horrible flip-flops when she headed for the airport ladies' room. Just turn invisible, Petroski had said. Leave a note for Levka.

With tears in her eyes, she rested the folded note on the bathroom counter.

Could she truly survive on her own? With no money, a craving for human blood. She shuddered. She had to because there was no way she was going to put Levka and his friends at further risk for her sake.

When a woman pushed the door aside, Caitlin concentrated on becoming invisible and slipped out with her.

She stifled a sniffle as she saw Levka leaning against the wall, his hands in his pockets, waiting for her to exit the restroom. *I love you,* she said silently to herself, and hurried toward the exit, leaving Levka, her love, and her new friends behind.

FROWNING, Levka sniffed the air, certain the jasmine perfume Caitlin wore had grown closer, then faded away.

Suddenly, he grew concerned about Caitlin. She'd acted strangely distance all morning, though he'd assured her the best way to get to her foster parents' house and wipe their memories was to fly out of the airport in Fort Lauderdale. He thought it was because she worried Vlad might still be waiting for her. It was all a risk.

Vlad might very well be waiting for her at her home.

When a woman headed for the restroom, Levka said, "Excuse me, miss, can you check to see if my mate…girlfriend is in there? Her name is Caitlin."

"Sure."

Minutes later, the middle-aged woman came back out. "There's no one in there. Are you Levka? Here's a note left next to one of the sinks."

"Yes, thank you." His heart thundering, Levka reached for the envelope and ripped it open.

Dear Levka,

I thank you from the bottom of my heart for giving me a chance at life when I was so near death. I will always treasure our friendship, but I must become my own person. Please understand and let me go. Your friend always, Caitlin.

Arman looked over his shoulder and communicated the letter to Ruric and Stasio.

"Find her. She can't have gone far," Levka ordered.

The four headed in the direction of her perfume, but Ruric took off at a run. Of the four, he was the best tracker of the bunch.

"Caitlin, talk to me," Levka called to her telepathically.

Silence.

"I think she's headed for the taxi stand," Ruric said to Levka and the others.

"Tell me what the matter is, Caitlin. If you need time to adjust, I have no trouble with this. But you're not safe on your own. Not as a fledgling."

"She's at the taxi stand, but indecisive. Should I attempt to grab her?" Ruric asked.

"She'll probably cry out if you touch her. I'm on my way there, but if she gets into a taxi before I reach you, go with her."

"I think she's pacing. Her perfume seems to be moving from place to place."

"I'm nearly there." Then Levka said for everyone to hear, *"I love you, Caitlin. From the moment I laid eyes on you, you stole my heart. If I have not made that clear to you before..."*

"She's crying."

"Invisibly?"

"Yes. Should I grab her? Five airline passengers are staring in the direction of her sobs."

"Caitlin, please don't leave me."

"I can't go with you, Levka. I'll be the death of you and your friends."

Levka's heart stilled.

"Someone's gotten to her," Arman warned.

"Who says this, Caitlin?" Levka asked.

Silence.

"Caitlin, who says this?" Levka asked gently, standing next to her. He felt the connection to her at once, heard the blood pumping rapidly through her heart, smelled her sweet fragrance, felt her slight body's warmth. *"Tell me."*

"Petroski." She sobbed louder and two of the people waiting for taxis backed away.

Another two headed inside the building.

"He's an assassin," she said.

"He's a tracker, nothing more."

"He came to me and told me he's an assassin." She sniffled.

"Did he tell you that you would be safe, a fledgling among our people?" Silence. *"Caitlin?"*

"Yes. I can't let you and your friends be sacrificed. He said he would kill us both and your friends would be next."

Levka wrapped his arms around her, and she cried out.

One elderly lady fainted, and another ran back inside the building screaming.

"We are one. You are mine with or without the league's permission. I have already said so. Together, we will fight this. But not today."

Arman grunted. *"What now, Levka? We give up our "guild" and become hunted vampires?"*

"We have thirty-six-hundred and eighteen years between us. Surely four ancients and one sweet fledgling can come up with a plan." To Caitlin, Levka said privately, *"Agreed, love?"*

She wrapped her arms around him and held him close. "I don't want any harm to come to you."

"Communicate telepathically. People will think the taxi stand is haunted." He leaned down and kissed her lips.

She kissed him back, her fingers clinging to his waist with a death grip.

"*Don't look now, but I see Vlad,*" Ruric warned, "*and some of his muscle.*"

Levka hurried the group in the opposite direction, his heart hammering against his ribs.

"*There are seven of them,*" Stasio said. "*Odds are in our favor just like when we fought the Marcher Barons. Should we stand and fight? I mean, away from where the mortals can see us, but—*"

"*No, it's too risky. Anything can go wrong.*" Most of all, Levka feared losing Caitlin. Somewhere, they would go and live in peace. They had to, because this time Levka would not exist without his mate.

Levka held onto Caitlin's hand tightly, but when a passenger walked in front of her, he couldn't pull Caitlin out of the woman's path quickly enough. Suddenly, Caitlin became visible, and the woman let out a squeak. But everyone was in such a hurry to get to flights no one else seemed to have noticed that Caitlin wasn't there, then was.

Pulling Caitlin around the woman who still held her heart and gasped for air, Levka warned Caitlin, "*Fledglings can't go through solid objects when they're invisible. You'll have to avoid them. It's like playing chicken. Your mind tells you that you can't walk through the object. It takes years before you can retrain your thinking.*"

"Jeez, Levka, I wasn't trying to walk through that woman. She just suddenly stepped in front of me, and I didn't have time to dodge her."

"*Vlad's seen Caitlin,*" Ruric warned.

"*Shouldn't we make a stand?*" Stasio asked again.

"*Quickly, Caitlin, turn invisible,*" Levka ordered, dragging her away from Vlad and his goons.

"In front of..."

"*Do it! And don't communicate with us or he can track you.*"

"But I can use magic!"

When she vanished, Levka gathered her into his arms and said to the others, "*It's time to go home.*"

"*But the Dallas league...oh, you mean home,*" Arman said.

Levka glanced back to see Vlad and his blood hounds heading straight for them.

Then he heard a strange rumbling behind him, thought it had to do with the planes, and hurried on his way.

"*Everyone use your vampire speed and find the first flight out of here that's now boarding passengers.*" Levka ground his teeth when he saw Petroski watching the gate where the plane was bound for Orlando.

No one said a word, though as long as their communication was kept privately between them, Petroski wouldn't hear them. Even so, Caitlin's heartbeat quickened, but he heard her mumbling some pretty strange words. A foreign language? Cursing?

"*He can't see us, can't hear us,*" Levka reassured her. "*Just don't speak.*"

But Petroski did look in their direction. Had he smelled Caitlin's fragrance? With their heightened sense of smell and the fact Petroski was a trained tracker would be to their disadvantage. He didn't move from where he stood though. He looked as though he wanted to, as if he tried to, but he stood frozen, his face contorting in anger.

Vlad and his buddies remained visible, still in hot pursuit, but suddenly, he spied Petroski and stopped at the Orlando terminal. Vlad began talking to Petroski.

"*They must assume we're going to see Caitlin's family,*" Ruric said.

"*My foster parents will worry...*"

"*Shhh, Caitlin. We'll take care of them when we can.*"

Stasio bumped into Levka. "*Petroski heard Caitlin. He's after us again. Well, Vlad and his minions are, too.*"

"I can use my magic again," Caitlin said. Once more, she began speaking in some foreign tongue.

"Here's a flight leaving. Just slip among the passengers. Ruric, get us some boarding passes," Levka communicated, trying not to sound as panicked as he felt, ignoring Caitlin's comment.

"I'm on it."

Stasio said, *"Petroski and the others seem to be having some kind of problem."*

"How's that?" Levka asked, looking back over his shoulder.

Petroski was wiping at his eyes, not moving an inch, two of Vlad's henchmen were headed in the wrong direction, and Vlad collided with another of his guys and showed his fangs. What was going on?

Levka reached the passageway leading to the plane until he sensed Ruric nearby. *"Did you get the boarding passes?"*

"First Class for all five of us."

They hurried onto the plane, then each took turns going into the airplane's restrooms, changing into their visible forms, and took their seats in First Class.

"I slowed them down," Caitlin said, squeezing Levka's hand. "But my foster parents will have the police looking for me. They'll be worried and—"

"We'll take—"

Suddenly, a red-faced, chunky guy in a three-piece suit stopped in front of Ruric's seat and scowled at him. The businessman held up his boarding pass. "You're in my seat."

Ruric showed him a boarding pass for the same seat. "Airline must have overbooked."

"I have to take this flight home."

Ruric smiled. "Me, too. It's a matter of life and death."

The man stalked off toward the airline hostess. "Miss! Miss!"

As soon as he moved away, another gray-suited guy waved a

boarding pass in Arman's face. "I think you have the wrong seat."

"Nope. Afraid not." Arman showed him his boarding pass, then pulled out his medical journal, flipped it open, and ignored the man.

"*Where is this flight bound for?*" Stasio asked. "*Did anyone notice?*"

The airline hostess asked to see Arman and Ruric's boarding passes, then left.

Caitlin rubbed her arms. "I wish we would just take off."

A few minutes later, the stewardess offered free airline tickets to two passengers who would give up their seats to the businessmen.

A young couple got off.

The hostess announced, "We have a slight delay, but we will be taking off for Dallas in just a few minutes."

Ruric, Arman, and Stasio looked at Levka.

Caitlin groaned.

Levka shrugged. "They will not expect us to return there." Grabbing a blanket and pillow for Caitlin, he handed them to her and pulled her close. "So we'll go to Dallas first, then from there, make our way to Wales."

The airplane taxied down the runway, and Levka swore he saw Petroski staring out the observation window. But then again, the way the sun reflected off the expansive glass, maybe not.

"*You should have taken the Dallas league's offer, Levka,*" Petroski communicated for all of them to hear.

From a greater distance, Vlad shouted, "*She's mine, Levka. You can't always watch your back. She'll be mine, soon.*"

Stasio leaned his seat back. "*This reminds me of the time we were in England during the war and the league was pissed off at us for wanting to fight the Germans—leave the battles for world domination to the mortals. Stick with your own kind—did we?*"

"Nah," Ruric said. "What's life worth living if you don't find some adventure? What we need is a spaceship outfitted with hyperspeed that can travel the galaxy. Just set it on cruise control, jump through a few wormholes, and we're on our way."

"We should have taken the league's offer to find the vampire rabble who are causing troubles," Arman said, his voice resigned.

Everyone was silent for a moment, then Levka grinned. "We are trouble, my friends. Would we want it any other way?"

"I love you, Levka," Caitlin said.

Levka squeezed her against his chest and kissed her lips. "I will have to teach you to speak privately to me."

But for now, he had to figure a way to get around the Dallas/Fort Worth airport without getting caught, find a way to take care of the mess with Caitlin's foster parents, and then... they would have it made.

Arman folded his arms. "Do you think the Welsh league will have forgiven us by now for the trouble we caused the last time we were there?"

Caitlin's brows rose.

Levka kissed the top of her head. "I'm certain between the five of us, somehow, we'll manage. Don't we always?"

"And maybe you can use my magic." Caitlin smiled at the four vampires, who for the first time looked at her as though they took her seriously, or maybe were just a bit curious as to what she had to say. "I can command the earth, but I have no power over water. Rivers and tidal waves and waterfalls can carve the earth up or carry it away. But I can command the earth and the plants growing in it. Use herbs in potions. And can conjure up some nice little spells."

Still no one said a word. She thought they didn't believe her. She nestled against Levka. "You've shown me some of what you can do as vampires. When we're on the ground again, somewhere that I can use my talents out of sight of others, I'll show you what I can do. And I'm not a fledging at it at all."

"What happened to Vlad and the others back there?" Levka asked.

"I froze Petroski while he was still in my range. Dust on the floor, the furniture, the walls suddenly gathered together and clouded their visions. The earth trembled under their feet, making them stumble. I slowed them down, at least."

"*I told you that you should make her yours,*" Arman said, with a glint of malice in his eyes.

Ruric shook his head. "*She might be more dangerous than we can handle.*" But she could tell he was teasing when he gave her a smile and a wink.

Stasio frowned. "*This reminds me of the witch hunts in England. And here I thought that witches were declared as such because villagers were superstitious or someone needed to serve as a scapegoat.*" He smiled. "You are definitely a welcome addition to our little group."

Levka didn't say anything for a while, then Caitlin looked up at him and said, "Well?"

He kissed her forehead. "*A witch, eh? I like a woman who can command the earth, who already has command of my heart. I should have known there was something even more special about you.*" He said to his friends, "*We will be a force to be reckoned with, if anyone should give us further grief.*"

Gladdened that they still accepted her for what she was, she thought about Alicia and how her foster parents had said she would have to chaperone her on her vacation this summer in Hawaii. At least she didn't have to deal with her and Alicia's friends ever again.

Although she wasn't sure what to expect with her new vampiric condition and that might even be worse.

Her stomach grumbled in protest. She glanced up at Levka and frowned. "I'm hungry."

"Again?" Levka and the others said in unison, looking surprised and a little worried.

Despite the problem with having a fledging among them, the others vowed to keep Caitlin safe—and well fed. Now, if she could only keep her fangs sheathed as she listened to Levka's delicious heartbeat until they could figure out a way to safely feed her again before their next big adventure.

ABOUT THE AUTHOR

USA Today bestselling and award-winning author **Terry Spear** has written over a hundred paranormal romance novels and four medieval Highland historical romances. Her first werewolf romance, *Heart of the Wolf,* was named a 2008 *Publishers Weekly*'s Best Book of the Year, and her subsequent titles have garnered high praise and hit the *USA Today* bestseller list. A retired officer of the U.S. Army Reserves, Terry lives in Spring, Texas, where she is working on her next werewolf romance, shapeshifting jaguars, cougar shifters, vampires, hot Highlanders, and having fun with her young adult novels and playing with her grandchildren and Havanese dogs. For more information, please visit www.terryspear.com, or follow her on Twitter, @TerrySpear. She is also on Facebook at https://www.facebook.com/TerrySpear-ParanormalRomantics. And on Wordpress at: Terry Spear's Shifters http://terryspear.wordpress.com/

And her Wilde & Woolley Bears, award-winning teddy bears, that have found homes all over the world: **www.celticbears.com**

ALSO BY TERRY SPEAR

Heart of the Cougar Series:
Cougar's Mate, Book 1
Call of the Cougar, Book 2
Taming the Wild Cougar, Book 3
Covert Cougar Christmas (Novella)
Double Cougar Trouble, Book 4
Cougar Undercover, Book 5
Cougar Magic, Book 6
Cougar Halloween Mischief (Novella)
Falling for the Cougar, Book 7
Catch the Cougar (A Halloween Novella)
Cougar Christmas Calamity Book 8
You Had Me at Cougar, Book 9
Saving the White Cougar, Book 10
Big Cat Magic, Book 11

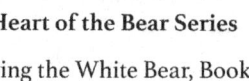

Heart of the Bear Series
Loving the White Bear, Book 1
Claiming the White Bear, Book 2

***

Heart of the Grizzly Bear Series

Bear in Mind

The Highlanders Series:

Novella Prequels:

His Wild Highland #1, Vexing the Highlander #2

Winning the Highlander's Heart, The Accidental Highland Hero, Highland Rake, Taming the Wild Highlander, The Highlander, Her Highland Hero, The Viking's Highland Lass, My Highlander

Other historical romances: Lady Caroline & the Egotistical Earl, A Ghost of a Chance at Love

Heart of the Wolf Series: Heart of the Wolf, Destiny of the Wolf, To Tempt the Wolf, Legend of the White Wolf, Seduced by the Wolf, Wolf Fever, Heart of the Highland Wolf, Dreaming of the Wolf, A SEAL in Wolf's Clothing, A Howl for a Highlander, A Highland Werewolf Wedding, A SEAL Wolf Christmas, Silence of the Wolf, Hero of a Highland Wolf, A Highland Wolf Christmas, A SEAL Wolf Hunting; A Silver Wolf Christmas, A SEAL Wolf in Too Deep, Alpha Wolf Need Not Apply, Billionaire in Wolf's Clothing, Between a Rock and a Hard Place, SEAL Wolf Undercover, Dreaming of a White Wolf Christmas, Flight of the White Wolf, All's Fair in Love and Wolf, A Billionaire Wolf for Christmas, SEAL Wolf Surrender (2019), Silver Town Wolf: Home for the Holidays (2019), Wolff Brothers: You Had Me at Wolf, Night of the Billionaire Wolf, Joy to the Wolves (Red Wolf), The Wolf Wore Plaid, Jingle Bell Wolf, Best of Both Wolves, While the Wolf's Away, Christmas Wolf Surprise, Wolf Takes the Lead, Wolf on the Wild Side, Her Wolf for the Holidays (Highland Wolf, 2023)

SEAL Wolves: To Tempt the Wolf, A SEAL in Wolf's Clothing, A SEAL Wolf Christmas, A SEAL Wolf Hunting, A SEAL Wolf in Too Deep,

SEAL Wolf Undercover, SEAL Wolf Surrender (2019)

Silver Bros Wolves: Destiny of the Wolf, Wolf Fever, Dreaming of the Wolf, Silence of the Wolf, A Silver Wolf Christmas, Alpha Wolf Need Not Apply, Between a Rock and a Hard Place, All's Fair in Love and Wolf, Silver Town Wolf: Home for the Holidays

Wolff Brothers of Silver Town Wolff Brothers: You Had Me at Wolf, Jingle Bell Wolf, Wolf on the Wild Side

Arctic Wolves: Legend of the White Wolf, Dreaming of a White Wolf Christmas, Flight of the White Wolf, While the Wolf's Away

Billionaire Wolves: Billionaire in Wolf's Clothing, A Billionaire Wolf for Christmas, Night of the Billionaire Wolf, Wolf Takes the Lead

Highland Wolves: Heart of the Highland Wolf, A Howl for a Highlander, A Highland Werewolf Wedding, Hero of a Highland Wolf, A Highland Wolf Christmas, The Wolf Wore Plaid,

Red Wolf Series: Seduced by the Wolf, Joy to the Wolves (Red Wolf) Best of Both Wolves, Christmas Wolf Surprise,

Novellas: A United Shifter Force Christmas

Highland Wolves of Old: Wolf Pack (Book 1)

Heart of the Jaguar Series: Savage Hunger, Jaguar Fever, Jaguar Hunt, Jaguar Pride, A Very Jaguar Christmas, You Had Me at Jaguar

Novella: The Witch and the Jaguar

Dawn of the Jaguar

Romantic Suspense: Deadly Fortunes, In the Dead of the Night, Relative Danger, Bound by Danger

Vampire romances: Killing the Bloodlust, Deadly Liaisons, Huntress for Hire, Forbidden Love, Vampire Redemption, Primal Desire

Vampire Novellas: Vampiric Calling, The Siren's Lure, Seducing the Huntress

∼

Other Romance: Exchanging Grooms, Marriage, Las Vegas Style

∼

Science Fiction Romance: Galaxy Warrior

Teen/Young Adult/Fantasy Books

The World of Fae:

The Dark Fae, Book 1

The Deadly Fae, Book 2

The Winged Fae, Book 3

The Ancient Fae, Book 4

Dragon Fae, Book 5

Hawk Fae, Book 6

Phantom Fae, Book 7

Golden Fae, Book 8

Falcon Fae, Book 9

Woodland Fae, Book 10

Angel Fae, Book 11

The World of Elves:

The Shadow Elf

Darkland Elf

Warrior Elf

Blood Moon Series:

Kiss of the Vampire, Book 1

Bite of the Vampire, Book 2

The Vampire…In My Dreams

Demon Guardian Series:

The Trouble with Demons

Demon Trouble, Too

Demon Hunter

Non-Series for Now:

Ghostly Liaisons

The Beast Within

Courtly Masquerade

Deidre's Secret

The Magic of Inherian:

The Scepter of Salvation

The Mage of Monrovia

Emerald Isle of Mists

Made in the USA
Monee, IL
06 July 2024